XENA WA~~RRIOR PRINCESS~~
GO QUES~~T, YOUNG MAN~~

**Join Xe~~na and Gabrielle~~
as they jo~~urney~~ for justice,
battle serpents and seas,
and fight the forces of evil!**

"Gabrielle!" Xena shouted. Draco came halfway around, completely dropping his guard, and three of the King's men leapt at him.

"Gabrielle?" He spun to gaze where the warrior's eyes went, and smiled, oblivious to everything but the pale-haired woman with the fighting staff and her companion. He scowled suddenly, and spun around again, his hands pale-knuckled fists. "Xena!" he bellowed. "You lied to me again, damn you!"

"Draco—look out!" Gabrielle cried, but the warlord brought up both fists and slammed them back into two unhelmeted men. A dozen more, heavily armed, sprinted into the chamber.

"Gabrielle!" Xena called. "Get—out—of—here! There isn't enough room for all of us!"

Gabrielle snapped her staff at a soldier. "Gotcha!" she yelled, and slammed it onto the nearest bare head. Four of the men she'd fought earlier followed. *Easy pickings,* she thought cheerfully. "Hey, come on," she said as two of the soldiers eyed each other warily. "You gonna let Xena flatten all of you, or can the rest of us play, too?"

Look for BOOK TWO in the exciting trilogy coming from Ace in November of 1999!

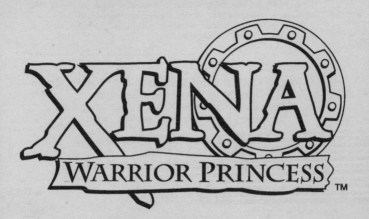

GO QUEST, YOUNG MAN

Ru Emerson
Based on the Universal
television series created by
John Schulian and Rob Tapert

ACE BOOKS, NEW YORK

XENA: WARRIOR PRINCESS: GO QUEST, YOUNG MAN
A novel by Ru Emerson. Based on the
Universal television series XENA: WARRIOR PRINCESS,
created by John Schulian and Rob Tapert.

An Ace Book / published by arrangement with
Universal Studios Publishing Rights,
a division of Universal Studios Licensing, Inc.

PRINTING HISTORY
Ace edition / August 1999

The Penguin Putnam Inc. World Wide Web site address is
http://www.penguinputnam.com

Check out the ACE Science Fiction & Fantasy newsletter
and much more on the Internet at Club PPI!

ISBN: 0-441-00637-X

To Doug

To Roberta

To Ginjer with thanks always

and to Rob Field, who asked for it

Acknowledgment

Once again, I would like to thank the fans of *Xena: Warrior Princess*: I've never met such a highly eclectic and generally nice bunch of people, and you've made my on-line experience very enjoyable. And, of course, the creators of the show, and the actors: It's been a pleasure and often a challenge to try to create on paper what I see on the screen.

If you would like to drop me a line, or if you would like to arrange to get your books signed, or get a signed label for them, I can be reached at the following e-mail address:

XenaBard@aol.com

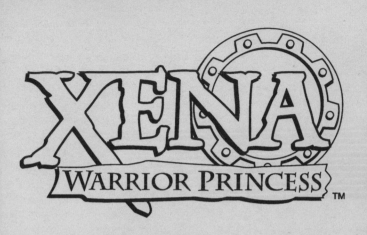

1

Gabrielle settled back on her heels, slowly flattened grubby and aching hands on her knees, and scowled down at the firepit: nothing but acrid, eye-burning smoke, and even that was dying. *Prometheus himself couldn't start a fire under these conditions,* she thought gloomily. Four days of cold, wintery rain had left everything soaked; even the pine and fir needles in normally sheltered spots were soggy. The bark she'd collected all along the trail wasn't any better, and the neat pyramid of twigs practically oozed liquid. A last thin curl of smoke went straight up her nose; by the time she'd finished coughing and wiped her eyes, the fire was dead again.

And Joxer hadn't shut up yet.

''You know, Gabrielle, if you'd just picked up some of the branches that must have been inside that cave we passed, like *I* suggested—'' She fixed him with a look almost the equal of Xena's; Joxer tittered nervously and was silent. But not for long. ''You've got to know the

1

tricks, Gabrielle. My mother used to pour a dab of olive oil on the wood when it wouldn't—"

"... nine minotaurs, ten minotaurs ..." Gabrielle's voice topped his easily. "Joxer, do you mind, I just happen to be *busy* here? And the last thing I need is your *help!* All right?" She pulled the soggy little stack apart, yelped as her fingers brushed the one twig that smoldered a sullen red, and fixed him with another look. "One word, just one! And I swear—!" she warned him.

"I mean, it's not like we really *need* a fire, Gabrielle. It's warmed up, haven't you noticed?" Gabrielle glared. Joxer's lips twisted; he cast up his eyes and dropped back onto his log with a heavy thump, yelping as he missed the smooth section someone had fashioned into a seat, and came down on one of the broken-off branch ends. Gabrielle did her best to ignore both the flailing limbs and his ongoing dialog; mumbling under her breath, she carefully reassembled her tinder.

"No, we *don't* need it for heat. But unless you like your meat raw, Joxer ... ?" Joxer fussed with his armor, making a show of ignoring her. "I don't like raw meat," Gabrielle finished shortly, and bared her teeth at him.

She bent down to blow cautiously on the single tongue of flame, but he cleared his throat as she began poking twigs and broken bits of inner bark into the pyramid of sticks. "You know, I don't understand why you're always *mad* at me," he complained, his voice at that reedy pitch that annoyed her most. "I mean, we've been together for a long time, and if it wasn't for me, you and Xena wouldn't ... you wouldn't ..." Apparently, examples failed him. Gabrielle felt anger flush her cheekbones.

"*Wouldn't what*, Joxer? Oh, wait, let me guess! We wouldn't have had all that extra—ah—excitement? Ad-

2

venture? The first time I met up with Callisto?'' Her smile fell short of stormy eyes. ''When you kidnapped me, in case you've forgotten how I wound up in her clutches and hanging by my *wrists* over a nasty drop to a hot fire?''

''Well, how was I to know she was that bad?'' Joxer snarled—or tried to. It still came out as a whine. ''And you weren't exactly Princess Diana herself, you know! Do you have any idea how many bruises I had after that little set-to we had in the market—?''

I'm gonna mangle him, this time! ''Set-to? Oh, of course! I see! I should have just—just let you haul me off to Callisto, is that it? Of course, I'd be long dead, but I'd die a lady, is that it?''

''Yes—*no!* Of course not—I mean . . . Gabrielle, why do you always argue with me?'' Joxer demanded. She snorted, gathered up a handful of almost-dry fir needles and concentrated on dribbling them onto the struggling little fire. Joxer grumbled under his breath, drew one of his daggers, and found a stone to sharpen it with. Gabrielle's eyes bored into his, and she leveled a blackened finger at his nose.

''Don't start, Joxer! Don't even think about it. Last thing I want to hear besides you whining is you honing those crummy blades of yours, got it?'' He hesitated, eyed her warily, then tossed the stone aside, resheathed the dagger with a flourish, and folded his arms across his chest. A corner of his mouth twitched.

''Oh, I see,'' he replied loftily. ''Just who died and made *you* Aphrodite?'' She looked up, puzzled; Joxer rolled his eyes. ''I mean, really, Gabrielle! Have you ever noticed that when we're together, you make the rules, and I either follow them, or put up with your hissy fits. When do *I*—?''

"Hissy fits?" she inquired in a reasonable voice, but her eyes were furious. "Hissy fits? Joxer, *I* do not have hissy fits! I happen to be busy here, doing something important and I—oh, Hades, Joxer, why am I arguing with you?" she yelled, and plopped down cross-legged to blow on the tiny flame, finally licking its way skyward.

"Because you—I mean, because I just happen, for your information, Gabrielle—I mean, because . . ." Joxer sat back in a furious clatter of metal plates, creaking leather, and cheap used-market weaponry. "Why am *I* arguing with *you*?" he demanded, and exasperation edged his voice. Gabrielle eyed him levelly and silently over her shaky little fire. Joxer pursed his lips, rolled his eyes. She waited, visibly holding on to her temper. The silence stretched; Gabrielle cast up her eyes and went back to her fire; Joxer sighed heavily. "All right, Gabrielle. I can't think why I should even *bother* to tell you this, but for your information, I have just been extended an invitation to take part in a very important heroic quest. To lead the quest, as a matter of fact." Silence; she glanced at him sidelong and clearly disbelieving before returning to her fire. "Quest—you know," Joxer went on. "Like Hercules and the Hydra? Like Jason and the Golden Fleece? Like Cecrops and the Minotaur?" He smirked complacently. "Of course, I have a lot of demands on my time, so I may not be able to find the time to go sailing off just like that. But, then again, if my *current* companions are going to treat me like dirt . . ." He paused encouragingly.

"The Minotaur was Theseus, not Cecrops," Gabrielle corrected him absently; she was alternately blowing the flame to life and breaking up more skinny sticks. For some reason, this remark seemed to annoy Joxer more

4

than anything she'd said thus far. He jumped to his feet, and she looked up, ducking in alarm at the wild clatter. He flailed, just managing to right himself.

"Fine," he snapped. "When I return from perils dire and . . . and . . . and?"

"Durance vile?" Gabrielle suggested; she was having a hard time not laughing. Joxer scowled down at her—majestically, no doubt. At least to *his* thinking.

"You scorn me," he said grandly. "But when I return with the Sacred Ewer of Persephone which holds three golden pomegranate seeds in its hidden compartment—one for each season except winter, when she gets to hang out with Mom, get it?" he added in his own voice, then shifted into declamatory stance once more. "Once I do—despite perils and durances and . . . and . . . uhhhh?"

"You did that part," Gabrielle put in helpfully; despite her best efforts, a snicker escaped her lips.

Joxer sneered, clicked his heels together and bowed deeply. "Sure, laugh and scorn me. Well, in that case, too bad, and good-bye, Gabrielle. Just remember, if you'd been nice to me, you could've come along—you and Xena, even. Maybe. Remember you had the opportunity to be my sidekick—and rudely declined the honor." He turned and strode away.

Amazing, Gabrielle thought with some awe. Down that trail with all its litter and twists and he didn't trip once; he must really be peeved. Well . . . "Fine, Joxer," she grumbled. "Go quest. You'll remember how hard life really is out there, without me and Xena to haul you out of trouble!" Serves him right for all the times he'd driven her half mad. "All this time and I never *did* strangle him," she reminded herself, then turned back to the fire, now crackling merrily. She carefully fed it increasingly thicker sticks and finally a pair of forearm-sized branches. "Now, if that will only dry out the bigger stuff . . . I don't believe it, Joxer on a quest for some holy gods-blessed vessel." She laughed aloud. "As if! He made it up!" He had to have. "Who'd be dumb enough to choose *him*? And a *holy* quest, yet! That calls for skill, intelligence, purity—hey, wait a second," she mumbled to the bright flames and got to her feet to gaze down the now-deserted path. "Joxer couldn't come up with a story like that off the top of his head! So—gods, you don't suppose someone really *did* pick him to retrieve the—a—what did he call it, the Sacred Ewer of Persephone?"

She considered this very briefly, then got to her feet to gaze down the path. Something was very wrong here. Off in the distance, she could still hear the occasional clank of Joxer's so-called armor.

"Ewer of Persephone?" Another point to consider. Joxer didn't make up something like that: So someone else did. "There is no Sacred Ewer of Persephone. I'd've heard. There'd be bardic history, if nothing else." Odd. Why would anyone bother making up a quest for something that didn't exist? In order to get *Joxer* to join in the quest for it? Something was *really* wrong here. She caught up her staff: Amazon made, her first chosen weapon—and still her best.

She gazed all around the campsite, testing the air, listening as she held her breath. No immediate physical threat. But this with Joxer . . . "Someone might—no, that's ridiculous," she decided. "No one would lure Joxer into a trap so Xena would come rescue him. Would they? I mean, why would she?" Gabrielle leaned the staff against the log Joxer'd just quit, where she could catch it up at a moment's notice, and tried to gauge the hour from the sky—no easy task with such a

6

heavy layer of cloud between her and the sun. "Joxer— augh! He's driving me crazy! Xena's in town getting food and trying to track down that stupid blind Cyclops and her old friend Mannius, we've got *important* stuff to do—and . . ." Her voice died away. Xena wouldn't be back for some time, by the sun; Gabrielle's decision, whatever it was.

Automatically, she checked the fire, fed it more sticks and broke a few branches over her knee. "Wet outside, dry in the middle—well, that's something."

Maybe she wasn't dealing with a ludicrously baited trap. But it still made no sense that anyone would choose Joxer for anything but a funny costume contest. His weapons skills were improving—and even she had to admit his heart was in the right place—but he was still a stumbling, clattering collection of spare parts. His skills with people were—well, if he lived long enough, if she didn't strangle him any time soon . . .

If she got the chance to strangle him. It suddenly occurred to her Joxer might have meant exactly what he said. *Not that I'd miss him, or anything,* she told herself flatly. But if he was hoping to do something heroic and had somehow stumbled into a trap . . . If he'd taken on the quest to impress her and Xena . . . Gabrielle sighed heavily and jumped to her feet. "Joxer!" Her voice echoed, and she had a sudden uncomfortable sense the woods didn't like so much noise. *Deal with it,* she thought flatly, glaring at the nearest trees, then stood very still, scarcely breathing, listening hard.

To her surprise, Joxer yelled back—his voice faint and snotty: "Just forget it, Gabrielle! You had your chance! I might even have let you be my sidekick on this quest, but no, you had to make smart cracks and hurt my feelings! Well, *some* people realize there's more

7

to me than what *you* think!'' A clatter of stones, a distant splash and a startled yelp. ''Owww!'' Then silence once more.

Gabrielle stared in the direction of the sounds and the voice, then with a low oath, started after him. ''Joxer! Wait a minute, we gotta talk, okay?'' No reply. She drew a deep breath and pitched her best carrying bard's bellow. ''Joxer! You come back here *right now* and tell me exactly what's going on, you got that?'' No answer—except another faint yelp of pain; it sounded as if he might have turned to hear what she was saying and walked into a tree. Silence, broken only by the faint patter of a few raindrops. Gabrielle tipped her head back to glare at the dark gray sky and leveled a finger at the clouds. ''Don't you dare—don't *start* with me! You got that?'' she snapped. The rain lessened, stopped. ''Right.'' Gabrielle cast one anxious glance at her now merrily burning fire, shoved two rotted chunks of log into opposite sides, then snatched up her staff and set out down the trail after Joxer.

Not far down the main path, a narrow, rutted track led through tall stones, winding steadily downhill. Gabrielle hesitated there for a long moment, but there was no sign of footprints in the muddy ground of the main path—no new ones that might be Joxer going away, at least—and she could clearly make out where stones had recently broken away from the granite slab of the side path. Just beyond the rocky debris, she could make out a long scrabbly rift in the mossy surface that could have been where Joxer'd hit.

It was hot, sultry, and still here, and suddenly she could smell water: a green, stagnant pond somewhere off to her right. Moments later, she fought her way into the open, but through underbrush that looked very recently disturbed. Thick bushes lined the narrow track on her left, making an impassible barrier, but to the right, open ground sloped down to a small lake. New rains had swollen the banks, and water in midlake rippled in the faint breeze, but the shoreline closest to her was choked with slimy green weed and thick with cattails.

Trails broke off, going around both sides of the water, while the main branch headed toward a skinny log bridge perhaps her height above the choked outflow of the lake. On the far side of the lake, the trail headed straight across open meadow for a goodly distance beyond the skinny bridge, then vanished into the woods.

A brief glint of sun flickered on something just inside the trees: Joxer's helmet? ''Joxer, will you just listen to me?'' she shouted. No response. She started cautiously across the narrow, makeshift bridge, staff up and out as a counterbalance. It didn't help: The log was slick with rain and blackened, slimy moss. And if it had once been snugged into the banks, it had come loose somehow.

For one awful moment, the young woman teetered back and forth, fighting for her balance, then with a loud splash, went into the swampy muck.

She emerged moments later, coughing, swearing, and gasping for air, streaming greenish water and scummy weeds, looking more like a gone-to-seed Nereid than a human. Gabrielle spat repeatedly, scrubbed both hands vigorously over eyes, nose and mouth, then transferred her staff from right to left so she could pull disgustingly slimed hair and weeds out of her eyes. ''Joxer, I swear when I get my hands on you,'' she shouted toward the trees as she clambered up the far bank and regained the trail.

''Ya gonna *what*?'' a reedy male voice jeered. Gabrielle froze but only momentarily: Her hands shifted the staff automatically into attack position as she tossed her head to flip hair, weed, and water off her forehead.

Three reasonably neat-looking soldiers stood on the far bank, two clad alike in the sort of well-made hardened leather short armor that only a rich warlord or a king could afford for his men. Black leather and bronze helms with exaggerated cheek-protecting wings covered their heads, though one guard now removed his, revealing a middle-aged, hard face, short hair, and a neatly trimmed beard. *Someone can not only afford to dress his boys but insist they keep dress code,* she thought sardonically. *And someone else is in charge, because they've kept their pretty toys shiny.* The bronze parts of the armor shone; the leather was polished; the one sword she could see was beautifully edged, its hilt well cared for.

The third man briefly held her eye: He was older, and gray hair and beard straggled from beneath a boar's tusk cap that tied under his chin. A knee-length, loose corselet of brass plates dangled heavily to his bronze-clad shins. He wore old-fashioned open-toed sandals and held a fat-shafted javelin, its cutting end covered in a leather pouch—judging from the dull eyes and slack mouth, Gabrielle decided the protective cover must be to keep him from tripping over his own feet and impaling himself. Servant to the leader, possibly. Certainly no officer.

Still, even he was a cut above the riffraff she and Xena usually encountered on trails this near to prosperous villages.

The man in the lead had a horsehair crest standing upright on his helm—to her mind, it resembled nothing so much as a terrible haircut, but by the way he kept smoothing the thing, he was obviously proud of it.

Gabrielle smiled. "Excuse me, I'm looking for a

10

friend of mine. He's tall, skinny—not a fashion votive like you three—and he seems to have passed this way, so I'm assuming you saw him?'' Silence. ''Funny hat.'' Silence. The three eyed each other. ''Funnier than yours,'' Gabrielle added with a wry smile, her eyes fixed on that stiff comb of horsehair bobbing above the bronze helm.

''Was that meant to be a jest, little girl?'' the leader replied in a hoarse, whispery voice that was probably intended to be menacing. He'd blacked the skin all around his eyes, something Gabrielle knew a lot of professional warriors-for-hire did to keep the sun from blinding them. *Right. Xena's a warrior, and does she black her eyes?* She stifled a sigh. *Do they all follow the same lousy bards who tell the same tough-boy stories?*

''Joxer,'' she said firmly. ''The guy I'm looking for, okay? Someone's supposedly sent this Joxer on a hero's quest . . .''

''Supposedly?'' the second male held a pike, long skinny staff, curiously cut head with plenty of nasty points and sharp edges. He was obviously trying to copy his leader's style of speech and having a hard time getting his voice that low.

Gabrielle nodded. ''Supposedly. Because anyone who talked to Joxer for long enough to swallow half a cup of cheap mead would realize he's not exactly Jason. Or Hercules.'' On impulse, she smiled: all teeth, no eyes. ''Or Xena.'' Silence. ''Oh, come on, now! Surely you've heard of Xena?''

''Xena,'' the older man hissed; the horse-crested leader elbowed him in the ribs and the graybeard staggered back, fighting for air.

''Xena,'' Horse-Crest growled. ''You know, I thought you looked familiar. You're that yakky little girl who

11

follows her around and makes up all those stories about the heroic stuff she *supposedly* does, aren't you? Except, I thought your hair was red?''

Swell. They all learn to talk from the same school, too. Gabrielle smiled sweetly, shoved reeking and greened hair off her face once more as the wind shifted, and braced the end of her staff against the ground, planting her squelchy boots on the path. ''Red, gold—green— things can always change, right?'' she asked. It got her the blank look she'd expected. ''But, there's no *supposedly* involved between me and Xena—and, you know? She actually lets me walk next to her on occasion. Sometimes, gosh! I even get to lead.'' Silence. The three eyed each other. Gabrielle smiled again. ''Now, I'm gonna pretend you haven't been working at being deliberately rude and forget you ignored my question, provided you move out of my way, all right? I have someone to catch.''

''Why should we?'' The pikeholder's voice was high and reedy; he cleared his throat and tried again, but the leader brushed him aside and croaked, ''Who says you're going anywhere, little girl? Someone *we* know might like to talk to *you*.''

''Fine,'' Gabrielle said evenly. The smile was still in place; her blue-green eyes were cold. ''Later, if you don't mind.'' She took a step forward. The pikeman brought his weapon across the path, and the older man stepped off to his left, hauled the leather bag off the javelin.

She sighed heavily. ''Look, you don't want to fight with me. Xena's taught me everything she knows, okay?'' The leader eyed her through narrowed eyes that from her perspective were all charcoal; he wasn't buying it. His companions exchanged wary glances and began

12

to ease away from him, but he hissed something and they moved back into place. "Your choice," she warned. "You all move now; I won't have to kill you, right?" Silence. "Messily, I'm afraid," she added with an apologetic smile, and twirled the staff. "Xena did try, but you know? I'm a lousy student that way. Came this far short of failing because I spilled way too much blood, you know?" She held up thumb and forefinger, a handspan apart. "Xena gets *really* peeved when she's gotta scrub blood off all that leather she wears. Me? Hey, I don't care!" She spun the staff again and set her feet shoulders-width apart.

The two underlings were buying every word of it, she decided with satisfaction. Unfortunately, their horse-crested leader wasn't. He held a nasty curved sword in one hand, and now hauled a short net from his belt, snapping it so it pooled to his left. She glanced at the two flanking him: The old man's javelin was something new to her. Its tip hooked, twisted, pointed and edged in a pattern that made her stomach drop alarmingly. If that went inside her anywhere, she didn't want to think what it would bring back out.

"Drop the stick and step away from it," the leader barked sharply. "Now!" he added as she shifted her heels sideways to solidify her base of strength. He raised the sword and shifted his own weight so that she could see his first move would be to halve the staff—and her. *Messy*, she decided, but he was assuming she'd be there to receive the swing. Gabrielle shrugged and smiled as nervously as she could manage.

"Ah—OK, sure, whatever you say." Before the words were out, she'd spun around and slammed the hardened tip into the old serving man's exposed feet, swung back to catch him with a broad swing against his belly and another across the back of his neck as he went down howling. A quick jab to his exposed temple silenced him. Pivoting away from him, two long steps taking her out of his reach in case he started moving again anytime soon, she leaped at the startled pikeman, slammed one end of the staff and then the other across two sets of exposed knuckles. The pike clattered to the ground; Gabrielle spun away from him and slammed a foot into his face, came back around to crack the staff down across his shins, swept his legs from under him and smacked him across the nosepiece of his helmet; he rolled into a ball, howling and clutching his bleeding nose.

She spun around to face the horse-crested leader, shoving his second's loose pike as far behind her as she could, then bounced back, fast; the leader snapped his net at her, trying to snare the staff or her feet.

A moan from her left; she glanced that way quickly, battered the oldster into unconsciousness again with another slam to his temple—he was dazed, if nothing else, unable to play for a while. Long enough to dispose of their captain. She hoped.

He was casting the net—he was too far away to catch her, but he might be counting on the weapon to unnerve her. "Give up now, and I won't hurt you, little girl," he snarled.

For answer, Gabrielle planted the end of the staff midpath and launched herself straight at his face, smashing both heels into the exposed parts of his face as hard as she could, then bringing the side of one foot up hard under his chin. His head snapped back and he cursed with pain, but he was still in control of himself and his weapons: He flung the net toward the head of her staff, slashed at her legs with the sword. Gabrielle shoved off

14

his chest with both feet, replanted herself and snagged the net with the staff, spinning into him in a maneuver he clearly didn't expect; the free end of the staff cracked down on his helm, momentarily dazing him, and before he could react, she'd spun back and cracked the staff across the knuckles of his right hand, twice, as hard as she could. The net fell; the staff caught it and flung it well behind her and before he could recover enough to swing the sword, she'd jabbed the staff into his throat. He staggered, choking, and dropped to his knees; the staff came back around and clanged into the back of his head.

She stepped back, eyeing his companions and then him—but no one seemed ready to fight. Gabrielle took two careful steps back and held the staff at ready, hooking the curved sword aside with her foot, then retreated far enough to watch all of them for threat.

All at once, she was aware of herself again: Sweat and the impelling reek of sour campfire smoke that had permeated hair and clothing, had covered her skin, was barely overwhelmed by the reek of the green swampy water that plastered her hair to her neck and filled her boots; her hands were so slicked with the green mess she wondered how she'd held on to that staff, and something small, multilegged, and normally aquatic was moving under her skirt, seeking a way out. She shifted her grasp on the staff, shook the hem of the skirt vigorously.

It was still too warm, windless and humid: She angrily shoved reeking hair aside. ''All right!'' she snapped and nudged the pikeholder with one hard foot. ''I tried being nice and look where it got me! Now, I want some answers, and you'd better deliver because if you don't, I just might actually *hurt* you, you got that?''

A faint groan escaped the older man; the pikeman was

too involved with his bloody nose to pay attention, seemingly, and the leader was out cold. At least he didn't move when she nudged him vigorously with the tip of her staff. She considered the situation uncertainly.

The sound of applause brought her around, staff at the ready. Xena, a sardonic smile on her face, stepped from the brushy shadows next to the path.

"Not bad," the warrior said dryly.

Gabrielle shrugged and spun the staff. "Just did what I had to—hey, how long were you watching?" she demanded.

"I wasn't that far behind you when you went into the water," Xena admitted. The smile broadened.

"You—what, these three weren't enough to get your creative juices flowing?" Gabrielle demanded sarcastically. Xena laughed.

"It wasn't that. You didn't need my help, that's all."

"Well—no, I didn't." The younger woman smiled and planted the end of her staff in the trail with a loud thunk. "They didn't take me seriously, even after I warned them."

"Their mistake." Her eyes moved beyond her companion, and Gabrielle whirled around, staff at the ready, only to see the captain and his pike-bearing fellow disappearing into the trees.

"Hey!" Gabrielle shouted, then half-spun to plant hardened wood against the throat of the third man. "Don't *you* try to go anywhere just yet, you got it?" He swallowed noisily, moved his head in careful assent. "Now," Gabrielle went on, "you want to tell me what that was all about, or should I give you another headache?" She glanced behind her. "Or maybe you'd like Xena to ask you a few questions?" She smiled unpleasantly; he closed his eyes, shook his head feebly.

16

"Somehow, I don't think that'll be necessary, Gabrielle." Xena squatted next to the fallen man and tapped his shoulder, hard. He winced, squinched his eyes closed even tighter. "Because we know each other, don't we, Botricas?" Silence. Xena tapped him again, harder this time. "What, you liked the last pinch so much you want another? Talk to us, Botricas. Tell us what Menelaus's picked guard was doing up here in Thessalonika?"

"Menelaus!" Gabrielle caught her breath. "*That's* why he looked familiar—that captain, I saw him in Troy, didn't I?"

"Denos. Leader of the men who hid inside the horse," Xena said tersely. "Just now, when I was in town, there were four Spartans sitting in a dark corner of the tavern and talking to some of the locals—mostly the restless young men who're looking for something to do besides harvest grapes. Place like this, there's plenty to choose from, but no one wanted to talk to me about why Denos was recruiting."

"Maybe King Menelaus is planning another war," Gabrielle offered.

Xena shook her head. "He's got an army; he doesn't need green boys. Or Joxer." She glanced up. "I saw Denos talking to him, decided the best thing to do was follow him back here, find out what was going on. Ran into a few of Denos's men just into the woods—seems Denos didn't want me talking to Joxer."

"Yeah," Gabrielle said. "Me, too, I guess."

"Well, by the time I got past them, Joxer was on the trail heading south, and you were climbing out of the lake." She sniffed gingerly. "New fragrance, Gabrielle?" she asked dryly.

Gabrielle wrinkled her nose. ''Can't we do this back at camp? After I wash up?''

''No, because Botricas is gonna tell me what's going on. *Right. Now.*'' Steel edged the last words. Botricas eyed her nervously through tiny slits and nodded cautiously.

''Don't let her hit me again, please?'' he whispered.

''Only if you quit stalling,'' Gabrielle snarled.

''Sure, whatever you say.'' Botricas licked his lips. ''Denos had orders from the king—supposedly from the king, he and Klomes were talking a couple nights ago when they thought I was asleep, Klomes was convinced that priest was behind all this, and Denos was starting to listen, he's awful stubborn, Denos—''

''Never *mind* that,'' Gabrielle broke in sharply. ''What's all this got to do with Joxer? The guy with the funny armor, remember?''

''Ah—yeah, sure, I remember. He was one of the last, and Klomes wanted to just run him through, pin him to a tree. I think Denos did, too; the guy was maddening. Then he announces himself as Joxer the Mighty, and Denos grabs Klomes and goes into the corner with him, talking real low, so's I couldn't hear—I *swear* to you, I didn't hear what was going on!'' he added urgently as both women eyed him in open disbelief. ''Anyway, they come back, Denos gives him the badge that'll get him in to see the king when he reaches Sparta, and *then* after he goes, Denos says, 'Let's allow the fool on his way, and see where he goes first.' No explanation why we're doing this.'' He eyed Xena warily, Gabrielle with growing resentment. ''I shoulda known it was because of something like *this*. Like *you*. Some of us got more brains than to go against you, Xena. *Or*—or *her*,'' he added lamely.

"It's Gabrielle." The staff wove a pattern just above his nose before she pulled it back and leaned into it. "I'd remember that name, if I were you." She glanced at Xena. "So now what?"

Xena shrugged. "So now we go back to camp and get you dry and fed, and you can tell me what Joxer said to you about all this." She got to her feet and, almost as an afterthought, reached down and hauled a gibbering Botricas to his feet. "And you can come with us," she added with a smile. It wasn't a nice smile. "No sense you upsetting Denos when he finds out you've been talking to me, right?" From his expression, apparently Botricas thought so, too; when Xena released him, he meekly followed Gabrielle back to camp.

2

They skirted the edge of the lake, Xena leading, a nervous Botricas next, his attention divided between the leather-clad warrior and Gabrielle, who was right on his heels, her staff digging angrily into the narrow track as she walked.

In her absence, the fire had caught properly. The younger woman snatched up a blanket and a small clay jug of hair-herbs and stalked off to find a reasonably clean corner of lake. When she returned, Xena and the old armsman were sitting on opposite sides of the firepit; the warrior smiled at her and fished a packet from the coals.

"Nice job on the fire." Xena sniffed, refolded the packet, and shoved it back into the fire with a booted foot. Gabrielle drew the blanket around her more closely; the sun was nearly down, the air now relatively cool against damp skin and wet hair. Xena tugged at the cloth and drew herself down next to the fire, then tucked the thick fabric closely around her. The warrior drank

from a small leather bottle. "Want some of this, Gabrielle?"

"Not if it's your usual stuff," Gabrielle said. "A nice
warm cider, now . . ."

"Over there." Xena pointed to a dark ewer positioned
close to the flames.

"Great. Ahhhh—how's the food?"

"Getting there. The bread'll be better warm, if you
can wait."

Gabrielle nodded. "I can wait. Let's talk." Her narrowed gaze fixed to Botricas, who flinched. "No, excuse
me. *You* talk. Because, frankly, none of this makes
sense. King Menelaus sends these creeps all the way
from Sparta to find guys like *Joxer?* And then, to stop
me from—what? Keeping him from leaving us? From
finding out where he's going? From going with him?"

"Joxer was one of several they picked," Xena said.
"But he wasn't typical. Mostly, Denos seemed to want
boys, and they all were more of the same type: a little
like your friend Orion . . ."

"Homer," Gabrielle corrected her absently. She considered this, shook her head, and began rubbing her hair
to dry it. "Wait. Now it makes less sense than before!
Homer's isn't a warrior, he's a bard! Xena, I sincerely
doubt he's ever hit anyone in anger in all his life!"

"Most of the boys chosen didn't look as if they had,
either," Xena said. She fished warmed bread from the
firepit, unwrapped it, and tore it, handing half to Gabrielle. "Keep that inside the blanket and pull off bites
to chew; it'll warm you twice, that way. There's a pail
of stew, too, but I'll have to fetch it and put it on the
fire. You watch him." Her eyes locked on Botricas's.
"And *you* don't get any. We didn't expect guests for
dinner and I watched you, Denos, and Klomes eat at that

22

inn—and not pay for what you ate.'' The old soldier looked resentful, as if he wanted to say something but decided not to. Gabrielle eyed him as she ate bread. Botricas wouldn't meet her eyes; nor did he look up when Xena returned with a small, lidded metal pail. She shoved this into the fire, fished the ewer of cider out with a bent stick, and poured some into Gabrielle's mug, then settled down cross-legged as the younger woman drank deeply.

"Great. I think I'll live now. How long until the stew's hot?''

"Finish your bread, Gabrielle. The stew was hot when I left the inn, but that was a while ago. And I got another loaf to go with it.''

"Good.'' Gabrielle shoved wet hair off her forehead. "Somehow, I seem to have worked up an appetite.'' She chewed, swallowed, and tore off another bite. "So, what exactly *were* these guys doing back in that village—and where did Joxer go, anyway? Not that I care, of course . . .''

"Of course,'' Xena replied evenly. "I've been thinking myself lately, he keeps tagging along with us and neither of us has strangled him yet—but there's gonna come a time.''

"Right. Me, too.'' The women eyed each other, sidelong. *Sure*, Xena thought, and sighed quietly. If she'd really wanted to get rid of Joxer, there'd been opportunities—and she had ways that would make certain he'd stay gone for good. If all else failed, she could have run him through, that first chance meeting, or later, when his foolish desire to become Callisto's warrior had nearly gotten Gabrielle killed.

The old Xena would have gutted him without a second thought, she knew. She leaned forward to shove wood into the fire and glanced at her companion. Gabrielle was still on the same bite of bread, her eyes now fixed on the deepening gloom across the clearing. *Wondering if it's somehow her fault Joxer's gone,* Xena decided. Maybe feeling as she did—partly glad for the quiet without him, his tinny armor, loud voice, and constant, clattering accidents as he tripped over his own feet, stones or logs . . . Xena tested the side of the bucket of stew with the backs of her fingers, shoved it deeper into the fire, and leaned back.

"I wonder where he is, right now," Gabrielle stated quietly, her own thought clearly on the same path as Xena's.

"Gabrielle, you know you can't be responsible for Joxer," Xena began.

"I know. It's just that—he's been giving me so much mouth lately," Gabrielle said with a heavy sigh. "I mean—did you know he's composed *four* new verses to his 'Joxer the Mighty' song? Xena, if I hear that, 'Gabby as his sidekick, fighting with her *little* stick' one more time!"

"Yeah, I know. Me, too," Xena said. She shrugged and slewed around to meet Gabrielle's eyes. "I happen to remember a verse we both heard recently, do you? Not one Joxer sang?"

Gabrielle sighed again, shook her head. "You're as bad as he is, I swear, Xena! Or as bad as I am, trying to figure out what makes a guy like that be the way he is—I remember when his nasty brother Jett started in with that, 'Joxer the tidy, never goes out-sidey' stuff. Picking on him for—"

"For not being like his parents or his brothers," Xena put in as Gabrielle hesitated. "Not a heartless killer, not an assassin, not a—well, whatever their other brother turned out to be."

Gabrielle shuddered. "No one I'd want to know, from the sounds of things. Except?" She considered this a moment, then laughed. "Wouldn't it be funny if he turned out to be, oh, like some kind of politician?"

"Could be bad," Xena agreed. "Menelaus is a politician, after all."

Silence for some moments, except for an occasional cautious creak of metal when Botricas shifted his weight and the crackle of flames. Xena tested the stew, shoved the bucket still deeper into the fire, and lowered herself to the ground, shoulders braced against a chunk of log. "All right," she said finally. "About that village. I headed straight for the inn, 'cause I figured if Mannius and his blind buddy were anywhere about, that was the place I'd hear about it. So, I figured, buy a couple mugs of ale, find a dark corner, blend in—what?" she demanded in an aggrieved voice as Gabrielle spluttered with laughter, but her companion merely shook her head and waved her on. "But I got inside and the dark corner was already taken—by Denos, Klomes, and our stable-boy here." Her eyes rested briefly on Botricas. "Denos had two village boys across the table from him, both of them wide-eyed like they'd just found the Golden Fleece, and he was talking fast but low—I couldn't make out a word, and his mouth wasn't moving enough for me to figure that way, either. Eventually he got up, handed each of them a new copper coin, and sent them out, with Klomes right behind them; even if I'd wanted to catch up and quietly ask them what was up, there wasn't any way I could have done it without drawing everyone's attention. So, I stayed put. Another boy came in—someone called Beronias, I think. Local weaver's son. He was the one reminded me of your Homer."

"How so?" Gabrielle asked as the warrior paused.

"Well . . . the eyes, mostly, I think. You know: seeing everyone as a friend, all the world as good. Or at least worth trusting, just in case good might come of that trust. Anyway, Denos barely spent any time with him, the boy gave him a salute and left. I would have gone out and flattened Klomes then and there, except Joxer came in next." She considered this gloomily, finally shrugged. "If I'd moved, he could have seen me. I didn't think it was such a good idea."

"No, probably not," Gabrielle said after some thought. "But I still don't understand, why Joxer—?"

"Gabrielle, if I knew that—!" Xena slumped down and rubbed her shoulders on the log behind her. "All right. All I can tell you is the impression I got, watching Denos and Joxer." She looked up. "Gabrielle, remember that story you told me, about the quest for the oil lamp of—I forget her name?"

"Ahhhh—Psyche?" Xena nodded. Gabrielle frowned at her hands. "Okay. Psyche was kidnapped by Cupid, who supposedly had an incredible case of the hots for her. And he swore he was gonna marry her, but he couldn't allow her to see him. Now, personally, I can see it: If his mom—if Aphrodite found out her fair-haired boy was goofy for a mortal, especially one as pretty and femmy as Psyche . . ."

"Gabrielle," Xena growled warningly.

Gabrielle cast up her eyes. "Ah—okay, skipping ahead, Psyche got curious and late at night lit an oil lamp to go see what kind of monster this was—some monster; he was sleeping by himself, you know?"

"*Gabrielle!*"

"*So*-ree! Anyway, she finds where he's sleeping and it's a gorgeous blond boy with muscles to die for and *wings*, and the wings catch her by surprise, this has gotta

26

be a god, and all she can think is, it isn't old gray and grizzled Zeus. And then she gets a *good* look at him and starts shaking, and some of the hot oil splashes on *him*. So, he's peeved because he's got splotches on his perfect shoulder muscles, and then Aphrodite gets involved because her boy has been marked by a mere mortal—one who might be considered prettier than *she* is, mind you, and—"

"Enough," Xena said hastily. *Poor Cupid, yeah, right.* Every low trick he *and* his self-centered mother—and his spoiled baby son—had played on her over the years, she didn't feel one bit sorry for him. Even if Gabrielle's tale wasn't just another story designed to make people feel comfortable with their all-too-human gods. "About the lamp, tell me that part again."

"Ahhhh, okay." Gabrielle finished her bread and thought a moment, head tipped to one side. "The lamp. There really was a Psyche, you know. And probably some kind of truth to that Cupid story. Because, long enough later that she was married to the king of Rhodes, and a grandmother, there was some problem with the royal line, no sons or something. She and the old king consulted the priestess, and the priestess said they needed to retrieve the oil lamp from its confinement by Cupid, that it was important, and had to be with Psyche and her family. But the priestess couldn't tell them exactly where to find it—"

"—what a surprise," Xena murmured sarcastically.

"You know how these things go," Gabrielle said with a faint smile. "Anyway, the king announced a quest, and word went around for any available heroes to come hunt for the lamp . . . Hey!" She sat up straight. "Some kind of a holy quest? You think so? But *that* doesn't make sense! I mean, what would *Menelaus* want . . . ?"

She subsided, still mumbling to herself. Xena shrugged, ate the last of her bread, and turned to give Botricas a cool, measuring look.

"Maybe you'd like to tell us?" the warrior inquired softly. The old fighter licked his lips.

"Look, Xena, all I know's what Denos told me, and that isn't much; I mean, look at me. I'm a soldier-servant, I take care of the horses for the officers, wash their linen, polish their boots, and I go where they say and do what they tell me." Silence. She continued to eye him. "Xena, you know me! What for would a man like Denos talk to me about his plans? Or the king's plans?"

"I also know men like Denos ignore men like you unless you're needed. You could have overheard—"

He gestured frantically. "Nothing! I swear it, Xena!" She waited. "All right." His arms fell to his sides. "I knew Denos was up to something; why else would three of us be this far north? There's nothing much here, the king wouldn't want anything he could trade for here, and he wouldn't want Thessalonika."

"Oh?"

"Anyone in the Spartan army knows *that* much," he replied. "The whole country's peasants and herders; men like Denos trade bad jokes about the locals here. Look, I only know Denos was up to something the king came up with on account of not being all the way asleep a few nights ago. Denos was talking to Klomes about Thessalonikan heroes, and they were both laughing, and then Denos said something about, all the same, they'd better deliver someone who could find the king's sacred treasure."

"Sacred treasure?" Gabrielle looked up; she was dishing fragrant stew into two bowls.

"That's what Denos said. Way he said it, it didn't sound like he meant—" Botricas paused and scowled at his fingers. "Sounded like he was being sarcastic, you know, like whatever this treasure was, it didn't come out of the king's storehouses. Or maybe, like the king thought it was valuable, but Denos couldn't see it? That's all I know, I swear it."

Xena offered him a faint, lips-only smile. "That isn't very much—is it, Botricas?"

"I swear by—by Ares himself!"

"Swear by your mother—if you had one," she replied evenly. "I might even believe you, then."

"By anything you want!" he yelled. "Denos needed someone to take care of the horses, do the dirty work; that's the only reason I got out of the king's stables at all!" He eyed her resentfully. "Since Troy, I spend mosta my time forking stuff into horses and forking up what they leave. Thanks to you and people like you, and Menelaus losing the war, and—" He sucked in his breath as Xena's eyes narrowed thoughtfully. Silence. He finally broke it when she made no move or sound. "Here I thought this'd be a good change. And what'd I get? Denos kicks me around, Klomes kicks me around— *she* kicks me around!" He glared at Gabrielle, who scowled at him over the rim of her bowl. "And now *you're* ready to—You think I'da ever left Sparta if I'd known I would run into *you* again?"

Xena smiled; this time her eyes were amused. "Nice to see you haven't forgotten me, Botricas. So, you're sure that's all you overheard? No names, nothing like that?" Silence; the older man stared at his feet.

She retrieved his javelin, still in its leather hood, but still said nothing. The silence stretched. She tossed it up, caught and reversed it, and held out the haft to him. "All right. I believe you. You can go. But if I were you, I wouldn't even think about going back to Sparta. Since Denos will get there before you do, and—'' She caught her breath sharply as the leather hood rippled, then leaped to her feet, snatching the weapon free and flinging it behind her so she could shake the hood two-handed.

Gabrielle froze; something small and tawny-colored was finally shaken loose. Xena dropped the hood and seized the little object before it could hit the ground.

Gabrielle had a brief, slightly confused image of a long stem and a fist-sized wad of straw or rough fur that seemed to be swaying in a light breeze—if there had been any breeze. Xena's face twisted in disgust; she dropped the object and stamped on it. A flattened round lay squashed in the mud. But when Gabrielle would have moved closer for a look, Xena held out a warning hand, slammed her foot onto it, shoving it deeper into the mud, and began scraping muck over it with the side of her boot, squelching it down as hard and deeply as she could. She finally stood still, glaring at the flattened patch of mud as if defying it to move. It didn't. ''Not good enough,'' the warrior muttered under her breath, and found a large, flat-bottomed stone to drop atop the ruined object.

Gabrielle looked from her friend to the old fighter, who was curled in on himself like a bug and whimpering nonstop. ''What was that?'' she asked finally.

''Stop that noise,'' Xena snapped; Botricas ignored her or was beyond hearing. She rolled her eyes. ''That, Gabrielle, was a *rhodforch*—they're created by a certain kind of priest, it lets them hear things at a distance . . .''

''It—you mean someone could have been listening to us, just now?'' Gabrielle shoved to her feet, staff in hand, and turned to eye the woods around them.

"Distance," Xena reminded her. "Maybe even all the way from Sparta, if the priest is good enough." Silence, except for the panting Botricas, who was now mumbling to himself. "Or bad enough," she added ominously.

"I—see." Gabrielle nodded. "I think." She glanced down at the squirming Spartan. "But it sounds like *you* know who that priest is."

"Menelaus only had one priest in his household after Helen left him, only one who'd stay with him." Xena gazed down at the rock with loathing, then stepped past it to nudge Botricas ungently with her foot. "How about it, old man? You want to explain to me how a *rhodforch* just happened to be in your possession, and how you were the only one who didn't run?" Another nudge, harder. "Botricas, the *rhodforch* is destroyed, whatever Menelaus and his pet priest heard before, they aren't gonna hear anything else you tell me. *Talk to me!*" She waited. The elderly fighter slowly uncurled and gazed up at her, blinking rapidly; his mouth moved but no sound came. "It's Avicus, isn't it?" she asked finally. Botricas nodded. "Did he give you that *rhodforch* to carry, instructions on what to do with it?"

He was already shaking his head frantically, and now he scrambled to his knees, shoving himself as far away from the firepit and that flat-bottomed stone as he could. Xena let him go a few paces, then came around to cut him off. "I didn't—I didn't—!"

"Didn't what?" But he had scrabbled his way around to stare at the rock covering the unpleasant little implement. Xena sighed faintly and squatted next to him. He flinched as her hand gripped his shoulder. "Hey, take it easy, okay? I know you couldn't have been aware you were carrying something like that. You'd have been

31

dead from fright halfway out of Sparta if you'd known about it.'' He turned to give her a wide-eyed look; she nodded. ''Anyone would. Just tell me one thing: Does King Menalaus still keep an oracle's temple, and is the priest in charge called Avicus?'' She waited. He swallowed, finally nodded.

''He'll kill me now,'' Botricas whispered, and his voice trembled. ''I—I've only seen him once or twice, at a great distance, enough to know by his robes and staff. Men like me don't ever earn temple duty. But we know what he's like.'' He swallowed hard. ''Denos, he headed the inner guard detachment, last two moon-seasons, at the temple. It's a special assignment, you get extra privileges, more dinars, things like that. Fancy mess where they provide girls, feed you decent food. So—I sort of wondered, when he and Klomos came for me, why Denos wasn't still at the temple, if maybe he'd done something wrong and been given this job as punishment.''

''All right.'' Xena patted his shoulder and got back to her feet. ''I get the picture—enough of it anyway. But Avicus won't kill you, Botricas; that's not his style.'' It was, but Botricas didn't need to hear that, just now. *Poor old stableboy, in over his head and not his fault, for once,* she thought sourly.

Botricas slowly uncurled. ''It's not?''

''If anything, Avicus will be angry with Denos for picking the wrong horse tender or for letting you get caught.''

''Oh.'' He edged back away from her, got cautiously to his feet. ''I—did you really mean I could go?''

''I meant it.'' She retrieved the now-empty bag, shoved it over the metal end of his javelin, and handed it to him. ''But if I were you, I wouldn't go back to

Sparta. I'd go back toward that village and keep walking toward the setting sun. About five days steady travel, you'll be in Ithaca."

"Ithaca? But, that's—King Odysseus's land, isn't it?"

"The same. There's a guardsman in charge of King Odysseus's palace, on the island Ithaca, man named Lemnos. He's a friend. Tell him I sent you." Botricas clutched his javelin, incoherent with relief. Xena hauled two coppers from her belt, shoved the coins into his hand, and closed his fingers over them. "Here, you'll need food between now and then—go on, go!" The old armsman shoved the coins into his own belt, clutched the javelin hard, and stumbled as fast as he could, off into the darkness.

Xena waited in silence until she was certain he'd gone for good, even though she knew the old fool would never dare to double back to eavesdrop on them. She shoved a skinny log into the fire and settled down next to Gabrielle. "Warm enough?" she asked.

Gabrielle nodded and held out the other bowl of stew; her own was nearly empty. She mopped up the last of the broth with a chunk of bread, ate it thoughtfully. "I'm warm, I'm fed—and I am *very* confused."

"All right," Xena said mildly. "You fought, I'll talk. Can I eat first?" Gabrielle grinned suddenly; the warrior grabbed hold of an end of blanket and vigorously rubbed wet red-blond bangs to dry them, then caught up her stew and bread.

Gabrielle rinsed out her bowl and began combing the tangled ends of her hair. Xena ate steadily, finally set the bowl aside, and leaned back on her elbows, feet propped up on the stones surrounding the fire. Gabrielle fished her comb out of her pack. "I hope one of us can make sense of this,'' she said finally. ''All I know is, Joxer's gone on what *he* says is a hero's quest, that three men jumped me when I tried to follow him, and that Botricas was carrying a forky-looking thing that scared him half to death, and that you killed. And that you let him go.''

Xena recrossed her feet. ''It's a *rhodforch*, and I didn't actually kill it. It's not alive, Gabrielle, not the way you or I understand alive; it's a priest thing. Some of them, especially priests who serve Apollo, can either create a *rhodforch* or petition Apollo to create one for them, I don't know how it's done. Mostly I've heard of them in connection with the high priest who tends the Oracle at Delphi. Each of the hairs in that wad is able to move, to sense sound, and the more of them there are—the denser the hair, the greater distance it can work at. Also, something to do with the length of the stem—I don't know. Anyway, the priest stays safe in his temple and eavesdrops on people. A device as dense as that one: It could be a very, *very* long distance.''

Gabrielle stared at her; a corner of her mouth quirked. ''You're making this up, right? A—a magic furball that could listen to us all the way from *Sparta*?''

Xena raised an eyebrow. ''What, you can believe in Psyche, but not that thing?'' She jerked her thumb toward the rock and the object buried under it.

''Well, all right. But it doesn't sound particularly evil,'' Gabrielle said. ''You acted as if it was.''

''It's neutral. Supposedly it can be used for good or for bad. But think about it, Gabrielle. Do you really want someone listening in on what you're saying?''

''Ahhh—don't think so.''

''Exactly. Besides . . .'' Xena sat up to drink a little ale from the leather bottle, then settled back flat, so she could stare up at the deep-blue evening sky and the few emerging stars. "Yeah. My brothers used to give me nightmares, when I was little, telling me stories about the gods standing next to your bed, listening to everything you said—hearing all your thoughts, and you wouldn't know because they weren't visible."

"Thanks," Gabrielle said lightly. "I have a nightmare like that tonight, and I'm waking *you* up."

Xena smiled. "Feel free, Gabrielle." The smile faded. "But it stands to reason if the king of Sparta's involved with something like that, it's not for any good reason. And you saw how terrified Botricas was when he saw that thing. It wasn't the king he was afraid of, either. It was Avicus." She stared into the flames for some moments, finally roused herself and gathered the pots and utensils together, to one side of the fire, and began shoving wood into the side nearest their blankets.

"Okay," Gabrielle gave up on her hair and shoved the comb back into her pack. "King Menelaus I know about—kind of. Married Helen, mostly because everyone else wanted her because she was beautiful and rich, right?"

"He was old enough to be her father," Xena said, but Gabrielle shook her head.

"Not old enough to be *her* father, if the stories I've heard are true. You know, I've always wondered how Leda—I mean, how would you try to explain to anyone that you'd slept with a *swan*? Except it was really Zeus?"

"Probably Leda didn't even bother. Why would she? And just because the story's well known doesn't make it true. Some jealous rival of Helen's might have made it up to explain why she was so beautiful, don't you think?"

"Possible," Gabrielle allowed. "So Menelaus was a lot older than Helen."

"And like a lot of the men his age, he never bothered to get to know her beforehand. He just got her father's permission, married her, and carried her off to Sparta."

Gabrielle's brow furrowed. "You never did say how you got to know her?"

Xena shrugged, shoved the last piece of wood into the fire, and began pulling off her boots. "I didn't. I was in Sparta a few years ago; that's when I first met Menelaus. I saw her, at a distance. I didn't get close to her, never spoke to her until Troy. Don't remember much about it, really."

Doesn't want to talk about it, she means, Gabrielle decided, and stayed quiet.

After a moment, the warrior shrugged again, and went on, "Even from a distance, though, you could see the way Menelaus looked at her, the way he looked at any man who talked to her, smiled at her—even the men who smiled just because she was so beautiful. They couldn't help themselves. He didn't even want to share any part of her: Not a kind word, not her beauty, not a passing smile. Certainly not her intelligence—he didn't know that existed because he never even got that far. I thought even then that if he could've kept her in a treasure chest, he'd have done it. If there'd been a way, she'd never have left the women's rooms in his palace.

"I heard at the time that he wanted her to wear a veil, even just around the servants, in her own private apartments. She refused, just as she refused to stay in her rooms. But each time she went outside, he discovered how she'd left, and he closed that way to her."

"No wonder she ran off with Paris," Gabrielle said softly. "Except—Paris wasn't that much better, was he?"

"He gave her freedom within Troy, but he was still obsessed with her beauty. Even after ten years with her, he couldn't see anything else. He didn't bother to look."

Silence. Gabrielle settled on the far side of the blanket. Xena gazed all around them cautiously, listening and looking. All she could hear was a distant owl and Xena's golden mare, Argo, shifting from one foot to another a short distance away. She stretched and yawned, then lay down next to her companion, tugging the blanket across her shoulder.

Gabrielle sighed faintly. "I wonder where Helen is now."

Xena settled the blanket under her and turned her back to the fire. "I don't. Way I figure it, the less I know, the better."

The girl came up on one elbow. "Why?"

"Because if that *rhodforch* I destroyed had powers beyond just understanding speech, if it could read thoughts, it still couldn't learn from me where Helen is. Menelaus can still find out somehow, of course. But not from me."

Gabrielle turned to study her friend's face. "But— those things can't do that, can they?"

"I don't know, Gabrielle. Only a priest or a god would know that. But the less I know, the less likely Menelaus will ever learn anything from me. I'd like to keep it that way."

The younger woman rolled away and started to settle down, then eased over onto her back again. "Wait a minute. You think all this—with Denos and Joxer and everything else—you think it's about *Helen*?"

Xena sighed faintly. "Gabrielle, I don't know. And that's why we're going to have to find Joxer—and soon. I know Denos. He really would literally die before he

37

told me anything, and he wouldn't trust any of his companions with any information he didn't want shared."

"Joxer, on the other hand," Gabrielle said grimly, "we can persuade." Xena yawned neatly, rubbed her shoulders against the blanket and resettled, one hand under her chin. Gabrielle shifted one way, back the other. "But, Xena, if Menelaus is really looking for Helen, why would he want Joxer, of all people, to—?"

Xena reached over to lightly tug her companion's hair. "Gabrielle? Go to sleep."

The warrior seemed to doze off between one breath and the next. Gabrielle levered up onto one elbow to gaze down at her relaxed face, smiled faintly and shook her head, then rolled over and resolutely closed her own eyes.

Xena lay still, half-open eyes fixed on the fire, her thoughts busy. What *was* Menelaus up to? She finally shrugged that aside and closed her eyes once more. She'd find out—and soon.

A short distance from the lake, the trail Joxer had followed joined into the rutted, ill-kept road out of the village where he'd been chosen by Denos. Nearly an hour's steady walking brought him to where another road joined in and the jointway turned south. For some distance, the surface was smooth and level, except where a caravan of market carts had recently worn two deep ruts in the mud. Now dried and rock-hard, they made for hazardous walking.

But just short of a league south, the road forked; the cart tracks went left and downhill, toward the sea. So did any semblance of a tamed path.

Joxer sighed in disgust as he looked up the way he

must go. "Right fork, sure, my luck," he mumbled. He'd already turned both ankles in the cart ruts and they ached.

The road ahead would have killed a cart within twenty turns of the wheels: Heavy rains had eroded what little dirt there had ever been, and sharp-edged rocks were everywhere.

He sighed again, but there was no help for it: Nightfall here would be extremely uncomfortable. There was no wood anywhere nearby and no place large and flat enough for a fire and a blanket, and the wind was already cool. Besides, the captain who'd chosen him for this quest had said he must reach Sparta in three days. The only way to be certain of that was to cross this ridge and reach the main south road before midday tomorrow.

"I should've brought a map," Joxer mumbled, then swore as his already sore toes slammed into another stone. He steadied himself, paid attention to the surface of the so-called road for some moments. "Not that I'm so good at *reading* a map, but I could have . . . could have . . ." He tripped again, flailed and caught his balance, shut his mouth resolutely and made the top of the ridge without further incident.

It was definitely cold out here. He could see the sea—deep blue water dotted with white—and feel the steady, harsh wind blowing straight up from the water. There was a nasty drop to his left; he swallowed, eased away from it, and only then turned to look downslope to see where the road went.

It dropped even more steeply than it had gone up, in a series of uneven, demented-looking steps. But after perhaps forty long paces, it bent to the right and vanished into tall brush. Joxer scrubbed suddenly damp hands down his britches and began slowly easing his way from stone to stone. He only fell twice, but the second time took the wind out of him. He lay still for some moments, narrowed eyes fixed on the darkening sky, rubbing a throbbing elbow. "This is all *your* fault, Gabrielle!" he shouted angrily. No answer except the wind, of course. He finally sighed, eased into a splay-legged sitting position, and considered the view all around him.

No one in sight. He tittered nervously and slowly eased his way down to the brush on his backside. Darkness found him squeezed into a hollow between two bushes, huddled under his blankets and wondering whatever had possessed him to listen to the Spartan king's man in the first place. His attempts at fire hadn't taken, the little bread he had with him was hard and green along one crust, the water in his bottle old and leather-flavored. "F-f-f-ortune and guh-glory, hah!" he stuttered, and rolled into a ball. It was going to be a very long night.

3

Gabrielle woke just after sunrise to find Xena already quietly and efficiently breaking camp. As she sat up and yawned, the warrior crossed to the fire, squatted, and fished out breakfast: a quarter loaf and a steaming cup. "Thanks," she mumbled sleepily. "I think." She tested the liquid, then downed the herb tea in one long swallow; Xena doused the fire. Gabrielle shoved herself back to the far and still shadowy end of her blanket, pulled her feet under her and began tearing bits off the rather tough loaf. "Xena, *please* don't tell me you're going to become one of those annoying people who wake up before the sun and tell people like me how we miss the best part of the day." Xena smiled and leaned over to ruffle her hair.

"Oh, no, Gabrielle, I wouldn't dream of it. Because the best part of the day for you is gonna be when you finally catch up to Joxer and get him to tell you just what he thinks he's doing."

"Joxer," Gabrielle mumbled, peering blearily into her cup. "Joxer? Why would I want to—?" The words sank in; she sat bolt upright and shook her head. "Oh, no! Oh no, oh no! No way! I already *tried* that and look where it landed me! And—what's this *you* stuff?" She tipped the cup back, too groggy still to realize she'd already emptied it. Xena silently took it from her, refilled it from a small, blackened pot, and held it out. Gabrielle eyed her warily but snatched the cup and drank deeply. Xena stayed where she was, crouched motionlessly on her heels, visibly waiting for some kind of answer. Gabrielle's eyes narrowed thoughtfully. She eyed the contents of the cup, glanced at her companion, then settled back to savor the rest of the liquid. After a silence broken only by loud, long, contented slurping sounds, Xena snatched the mug with a wordless snarl and flung the last few drops across the fire.

It was Gabrielle's turn to smile—a wicked, arch, "gotcha!" kind of look. The warrior laughed. "All right, Gabrielle, you win, we'll talk about it. And I'm not *that* crazy about this early either, but ya gotta do what ya gotta do, right?"

"Maybe," the bard replied cryptically. "What's this *you* business?"

Xena sighed. "I said you, and I meant just that. Look, I know you'd like to strangle Joxer every time he opens his mouth. *I* would like to strangle him just for breathing. Sometimes." *Most of the time,* Xena thought evenly. She bit back a sigh. *Until I realize what kind of family would turn out a kid like that—self-centered, odd, a hero wannabe with absolutely no skills to get him there. And an inflated vision of himself that that has nothing to do with what Joxer really is. And—he knows all that.* She stood and angrily shoved dirt over the still-smoking fire with the side of her boot. She knew all that herself and *still* wanted to strangle him.

Still, he managed, not only surviving all the fights, battles, and other messes he'd waded into, and still remaining—on balance—innocent. Ready to cut his way through dragons to protect the helpless. Of course, the helpless would be on their own, and probably ready to wring his neck.

She shook the thought off as pointless. Gabrielle was still waiting for an answer. "Gabrielle, you know why we're up in Thessalonika. I need to find Mannius, and I've got to pass that message on to Hercules. Personally. You know how much is riding on both."

Gabrielle sighed. But after a moment, she said, "Yeah, I know. A king's pardon for Mannius, and a salaried position as one of King Theseus's advocates—*and* a jail guard's job and pay for his pal Flyer." She shook her head. "Ridiculous name for a blind cyclops, if you ask me. I know; no one asked."

"I don't care either way about the cyclops, but Mannius is a friend. If I can help him get out of some warlord's camp, I owe that to him."

"I know. And I realize he has a price on his head; he has no reason to trust a message offering him all that. And then Hercules . . ." She frowned. "Why would King Nestor send all the way up *here* for Hercules and Iolaus? Nestor's as far south as you can get—and still keep your feet dry. And he has his own army, doesn't he?"

"Not much of it left, since Troy, Gabrielle. Nestor wants Hercules because I turned him down. He wanted me—us—to protect his city and his treasury from Sea Raiders."

"Oh." Gabrielle shook out the cloth that had held bread, sending crumbs flying, refolded it, and shoved it in her bag. "And, of course, *you* told him you don't work for governments, you don't work for money—and you wouldn't—"

"And I wouldn't work for *him*," Xena finished flatly. A grin tweaked the corner of her mouth. "Exactly, Gabrielle. Also, I know how much you love sea travel, especially this time of year."

"Huh?"

The smile broadened. "Waves three times your height, and the water's too cold; the squid catch is *way* down."

Gabrielle wrinkled her nose in distaste. "*Thank* you for sharing! So you have to deliver that message—Xena, you could send that one, you know. I bet Nestor has a dozen or more messengers out there right now, looking for Hercules. At some point, he's gonna get found."

"I know. But remember, Nestor lost a son at Troy. He's still grieving and not thinking clearly, and he's just remarried. Imoueye is young, ambitious, beautiful to look at, and utterly without morals. She also has access to her father's wealth, and she's thinking about a dynasty at Pylos that revolves around *her* sons, not Nestor's grown boys."

Gabrielle held up a hand for silence. "Let me guess: She's altered the messages, right?"

"She's altered the messages. Last thing she wants around Pylos is a pair of uncorruptible heroes. That's why I need to find Hercules and *tell* him exactly what Nestor asked for, and let him know what the family hour's like in Pylos, these days. It's tricky and it's important."

"Because of—" Gabrielle began readily, then hesitated and shook her head. "Because, why?"

Xena stirred ashes with a broken stick and held her hand over the doused coals. "Because of several things. Nestor was the noblest of the Greek commanders; he stayed above the infighting and kept his men from killing nonfighters. He went to war only because he'd signed the bargain that Menelaus insisted on when he married Helen: to war against anyone who'd take her from Sparta. Nestor kept a cool head and resolved the fights caused by treasure, or bruised pride . . . He was, and is, a good man.'' Xena sighed heavily, shoved to her feet, and slung her pack over one shoulder. ''And for that, because he stayed neutral, most of the Greek commanders wound up hating him.''

Gabrielle shoved the rest of her loose goods into her bag and got up. ''I heard about his wife. Imagine, getting home after so long, and she barely lived to see him. Then having to fight off Draco's army before she was even properly buried.'' She waited while Xena adjusted Argo's trappings and strapped blankets behind the saddle.

''Add to that, he lost his eldest son in battle. He wasn't in any condition to think clearly when Imoueye's father offered him a new wife.'' She rubbed Argo's golden throat and murmured against the mare's ear. ''So that's why I can't go south right now. But I think it's important someone stops Joxer before he gets to Sparta, and Menelaus—and Avicus—get hold of him.''

''Why? I mean, besides that even though I'm ready to murder him, why don't I want them sending him out to get killed?''

Xena settled her sword so that it would come free if she needed to draw it but wouldn't go flying at a full gallop. ''Yeah, I know, Gabrielle. But he's made us his family. Maybe it wouldn't have been my choice, or yours, but—'' She shrugged. Gabrielle sighed heavily. ''And remember this: A lot of people know Joxer hangs around us. Maybe Menelaus is using this whole quest as a smoke screen to cover what he's really up to. It could be his whole purpose was to get his hands on Joxer." Silence. Gabrielle nodded; her attention seemed fixed on settling something deep in her bag. "Now, I checked back in the village; there's a boy going south to Katerini with a pair of horses, they should get you on the main south road ahead of—Gabrielle, what's wrong?"

Gabrielle blotted her eyes with the back of one hand and smiled brightly. "Nothing! Why should something be wrong? I mean—" she swallowed. "Just because every single time we've separated lately, something really *exciting* has happened, why would it—?" She choked and turned away. Xena took hold of her shoulders, turned her back, and enveloped her in a fierce hug.

"Gabrielle, hey, it's all right. Honest, just listen, will you?" She waited; her companion finally nodded. "The times you're thinking about, that was my fault as much as anyone's. I tried to—to shove you in a corner like a bag of grain, something to get out of the way and collect later. I had my reasons, and mostly, they were to keep you safe. But you had every right to resent it. And when you had to make decisions, you didn't have the information to make good ones, because I didn't tell you anything." Silence. "Gabrielle, this time I'm not just shoving you aside, I'm asking you to use your mind and your talents, to be an equal partner in getting things done. Nothing's going to go wrong."

A muffled, small voice finally answered. "You can't know that for sure."

"You're right. Things can go wrong, every single time they can. Let's say I'm not worried about you. You know when to fight, when to talk—when to run, and how to get out of trouble. Besides." A corner of her mouth went up. "It's your turn to beat up Joxer. I got him last time."

Gabrielle laughed shakily and rubbed her eyes with the bread cloth. "Yeah, sure." The laugh faded. "What about this priest, though? Menelaus's priest?"

Xena shrugged. "Avicus? You're no worse off against him than I would be. Just stay away from him; he's bad news. But if you catch up with Joxer, search him for anything like that *rhodforch*, okay?" Gabrielle's face twisted with distaste; Xena mounted, gathering the reins together. "I won't be that far behind you, Gabrielle, I promise. Bet you an eel dinner I ride in before you get the fire going tonight! If not, it's your decision, but whether you wait in Katerini for me or keep after Joxer, leave me a message, so I can find you." Before Gabrielle could form a suitable retort, Argo was gone.

She sniffed quietly, blotted her face again, and sighed as the last hoofbeats faded and were gone. "All right," she mumbled, and shifted the bag so her staff was free if she needed to use it. "Great. She *knows* how much I love riding—probably a big old bony-backed thing with a lopsided gait." Well, Katerini wasn't that far, anyway. "My luck, Joxer's been and gone already."

Maybe not, though. Maybe Denos'd be with him and she'd get another chance to flatten him good. She smiled grimly at the thought. The smile widened as she neared the village—little more than a few huts, a small inn and adjoining open stable, and a stone pool for washing and watering beasts. "I almost forgot the good part. *My* turn to beat up Joxer. Boy, he's earned it this time!"

The sun was still behind the mountains eastward when Joxer woke, stiff, cold, and hungry. The partial loaf he'd carried with him was hard and would need water to soak in before he dared bite into it—but his water bottle held only a few drops, just enough to remind him how thirsty he was. At least he could see a stream just down the trail, once he eased free of the bushes—but the trail itself had deteriorated even from the previous evening. Joxer sat down and stared at it blankly. "He calls this a road? Something carts use? *Goats* would fall off this thing!"

He held the water bottle close to his ear and shook it, but of course it was still empty. He looked over his shoulder; brush blocked most of where he'd come down the night before, but he could see enough of the slope to know going back up was *not* one of his choices. He scowled at the jumble of cracked stone and rubble under his feet; an idea occurred to him, suddenly. "Did he say, *right* at the fork, or left? I thought he said right—didn't he say right?" Too late to worry about now. At least there was no one around, not even a goat, to watch him easing a very cautious way down the hill on all five: hands, feet, and his backside.

He reached the stream without incident, settled at the base of a gnarled oak, and filled his water bottle, drinking it empty twice before working his way through the bread; it hadn't been very good to start with and water didn't improve the taste. At least it filled his stomach— mostly. Now, clinging to the tree for support, he eased cautiously to his feet and gazed downslope. The trail still looked bad from here—at least for a short distance. After that, it began crossing back and forth across the slope, and the surface looked as if someone had tried to smooth it. In places, there were even stones edging the downhill side.

He looked back uphill one last time, rather wistfully. "Sure," he told himself resentfully as he splashed through shallow water and started out again. "Xena and

Gabrielle are gonna be along any time now to haul you out of this mess. Sure they are. Dream on, hero." He set his jaw, tightened the straps on sword and helmet and the pack holding his blanket and the empty food bag, and began working his way down to where he could stand up again.

It was midday before Xena reined in at the edge of Samnis—a regional market village that served a dozen or more outlying, smaller collections of huts and herds. She'd expected to find Hercules and Iolaus in one of them—there was supposedly a chimera in the crags somewhere above the outlying Krono, but the village elders had directed her here instead. She rode slowly, Argo picking her way neatly through a broad avenue made narrow with carts piled high with goods, bales, small shops selling everything imaginable, and lines that criss-crossed the market, a dyer's bright-colored skeins hung out to dry.

Someone nearby was cooking fish cakes, and another stall just behind that had fresh bread. Her stomach rumbled. Small children playing some kind of tag bolted past her, an old woman held up a sheer scarf edged in beads; a man, black as Vulcan, offered a shining array of daggers and spears. A girl, all thick black hair and enormous blue eyes, sat behind a table, a fan of fortune-telling cards spread before her.

The usual stuff, Xena thought dismissively. But a lot of it, and plenty of aggressive sellers. Probably it would be a good idea to get through all this before stopping to ask after Hercules.

In the end, she didn't need to. Emerging from the broad market street into an enormous square, she could see him and Iolaus, talking to someone on the far side of the central fountain and pool.

The someone turned out to be Salmoneous. She rolled her eyes heavenward, dismounted, and came up behind Iolaus, who sensed someone there and turned sharply, hand on his sword hilt. He relaxed at once. "Hey, Xena! What brings you this far north?"

Hercules turned; Salmoneous scurried around him, smoothing his robes—rather plain ones, Xena thought in surprise. Not just for him, but for anyone. A heavy brown apron covered most of his body, and a smooth cap of matching fabric covered his hair. "Xena!" he cried and caught her hand in both of his. But just as his lips would have made contact, she snatched it back.

"Please," she murmured. "You trying to kill my appetite or something?" She eyed Hercules. "What's *he* doing so far north?"

Salmoneous forestalled the hero's answer. "Cooking! This—" he gestured broadly—"is it, Xena, the thing that's gonna make me rich beyond belief and famous all across the land!" Xena looked where he indicated: A woven fence of skinny slats enclosed an area perhaps twenty paces on a side and held half a dozen small tables, two long ones that could probably hold twenty in comfort. Garishly colored cloths covered them, and other pieces of fabric were rigged as shades here and there. A few ratty flowering plants in chipped jugs were placed at random around the courtyard, and others surrounded a water bowl with greened rim. Behind this splendor, a small, whitewashed hut with a sagging door.

She glanced at the excited little master purveyor, back at the shabby open-air inn. One eyebrow went up. "You're starting a chain of inns that don't attract customers?'' she asked dryly. Hercules's mouth twitched; Iolaus laughed.

"Very funny, Xena,'' Salmoneous said evenly. "I'm laughing, I really am. It's an open-air inn, people can sit outside, watch the market move past, enjoy the view . . . eat my special cuisine . . .''

"What,'' she asked dryly, "sour wine and tough goat haunch?''

"Everyone's a comic,'' he muttered. "For your information, Xena, it's just a little more specialized than that! I have personally—''

Hercules's hand descended heavily to his shoulder, and the resonant voice cut him off. "Salmoneous, you want to spare the poor woman? It's not important right now; saving this place and your life is.''

The would-be entrepreneur seemed to shrink inside his clothing. "Ah, sure! In fact, if you don't mind, I think I'd better check on my most recent delivery, gotta be sure the tomatoes are fresh, you know . . .'' Still bab-bling, he vanished into the small hut. Xena watched him go, shifted a mildly curious gaze. Hercules smiled.

"It's good to see you, Xena.''

"I'm always glad to see both of you,'' she replied. "What's up?''

Iolaus shrugged. "We aren't sure. Salmoneous found out we were over in Krono and sent a message, some-thing about life and death, death threats—''

"So far as I could get out of him,'' Hercules said mildly, "he's had a death threat on account of this inn of his. He either doesn't know who made the threat, or he won't say, and if he knows what form it's going to take, he hasn't said that, either.''

Xena looked over the brightly colored collection of tables and winced at the mismatched hues. "Seems to

51

me he isn't much competition for anyone, is he?''

"Oh, you might be surprised," Iolaus said. "When we got here, the place was jammed, people waiting outside to get in, it was amazing. Once we found out his deadline on getting out of Samnis was midday and that the threat was against not just him but the entire inn yard, we cleared everyone back into the market."

Xena turned all the way around, eyeing the broad square with a fighter's eye. "You've checked the tables?''

"Everything," Iolaus assured her. "I was about to start on the fountain and the rest of the square; Herc's gonna check out the windows in line with this place, and—" A wild scream cut him off; Salmoneous came flying through the door, straight for them.

"Birds!" he shrieked. "They're out there, I could see them through the back, coming right at my kitchen and storage room! They're huge and black and they smell like—smell like—" Words failed him. Xena grabbed Hercules's shoulder and pointed: An enormous flock of huge, screaming, long-beaked birds were stooping on the building; more came across the roof to attack the shade cloths.

"Stymphalean birds!" Hercules yelled, and drew his sword. Iolaus already had his blade out; he half-turned to bow Xena ahead of him. She grinned, tore her own sword free, and pelted between the tables, through the doorway, Iolaus right on her heels.

The smell hit her like a blow: like rotting meat and putrid fruit all together. Birds were everywhere, fighting over the long table, pecking frantically at the barred door that apparently blocked the pantry, underfoot and swooping down on each other. Two people in this small area, both swinging swords, were as much a danger to each other as to the birds. Xena yelled, "All yours, pal!" and backed out. Hercules had things mostly under control in the courtyard. Xena kicked her way through fallen, odiferous birds and disgustingly oily and grubby loose feathers and came up behind Salmoneous, who was wringing his hands and whimpering. He yelped as she snagged a handful of robe and apron and pulled him close.

"So, tell me, Salmoneous," she murmured, "who'd you upset, and how'd you do it?"

"I don't—I didn't—!"

"Don't give me that. Who hates you enough to pull in that kind of favor from the gods? Who'd set the Stymphalaen birds on your operation here?"

"St—?" He gasped, turned, and tore loose from her and pelted through the tables and into the kitchen, snatching a frying pan off the wall to swing wildly at the nearest birds. Iolaus stared at him, then backed away. Xena grabbed his arm.

"Don't hit them with *that*. You'll never get the stench out. And you're in the way, you're gonna get stabbed." He seemed to be beyond hearing and beyond reason. Xena wrested the pan from his grasp, dumped it in a basket, and hauled him away. "Come back out here and talk to me, Salmoneous." He would have resisted, but when she switched her grip to a handful of his hair, he gave up and went meekly. Once outside the fence, she eased her hold but didn't completely let go. "Who?"

He dithered until she glared him into silence. "Well— you know," he stuttered finally, "for a town the size of Samnis, there really weren't that many options, unless you like grabbing something on the run in the market, eating it while you walk—what's the pleasure in that?" Talking, as always, seemed to relax him. He smiled.

"What you need is a theme, something people can recognize, something special in the way of food and drink . . . you know, Xena, what you need, is to try my special."

She rolled her eyes. "I'm almost afraid to ask."

"Funny," he growled. "No, really, I serve tea, my own special blend of leaves with a froth of whipped goat's milk on top. Bet you never ran across *that* before! And Sal-mooshes!" he finished triumphantly. She stared. He tittered, nodded. "It's this great new thing, I came up with it by accident, but aren't all the great inventions discovered like that? It's—you take your meat, your tomatoes and onions, peppers, whatever, a little spicy yogurt, and you *moosh* it between two pieces of bread! It's a whole meal in one hand, and by Sal-moneous! *Sal*-Mooshes, get it? Xena, I'm telling you, you're just gonna love it."

"Not with today's supplies, I'm not," Xena said flatly. "And maybe not ever. You're telling me people actually pay money to eat that?"

He glanced toward the kitchen, where Iolaus and Hercules were joking and piling up odiferous feathered carcasses, and was suddenly very sober indeed. "Xena, I'm making more money than I know what to do with. I'm thinking of setting up businesses in other towns, you know, have people pay me for the right to use the Sal-moosh name, pay for the recipes for the teas, all that. I don't understand this—this *vindictiveness*, though. I mean, the only other sit-down eatery in all Samnis is run by the Brotherhood of Silenus, and—" He yelped as her grip tightened. "Xena! If you *don't* mind, I would really like to keep what hair I have?"

"Let me get this straight," she murmured close to his ear. "You set up a business like this against the Brotherhood, and you *don't* expect retribution like this? Don't you know they have a reputation for repaying even the smallest slight in a big way?'' She tapped on his forehead with her knuckles. "Anyone at home in there?''

"Ouch! Um, well, but—but this particular branch of the Brotherhood is a little odd, Xena; they have a creed that goes—let me see—you know,'' he said suddenly, "I could think better if you'd let go of my hair!'' She released him so suddenly that he staggered into the nearest table and fell into a chair, where he remained, glowering at her from under his eyebrows. "It's not my fault,'' he said finally. "They've got some head priest who believes all life should be a minor torment, or else you'll never rise above the petty nature of man. Something like that. So, their food is uniformly bland, unless it's spoiled. The ale is always warm and sour, the fruit overripe, the meat two days past being fed to the dogs, and the tea—well, forget the tea.''

Xena shook her head. "Doesn't make sense. They thought people were going to beat down their door for bad food?''

He shrugged broadly. "What can I say? People did. Some still do. But a lot of the ones who did—well, they come here.''

"Great.'' She looked up as Hercules and Iolaus came up and held up a hand. "We can talk just fine from here, I don't have time to wait until you two bathe, Okay?'' She quickly passed on her messages. Iolaus stirred.

"Funny you should mention the king of Sparta,'' he said. "We—actually I had a message from him, a few days ago. Man in Spartan armor came through Krono, had been looking for us for days, he said. The message didn't make a lot of sense to me; something about the king only just realized he was missing a family heirloom from the funerary goods; they buried one of his uncles a short while ago and the thing was missing. According to the messenger, the king's worried that Helen might have taken it, when she left with Paris—it looks like a necklace but it could be dangerous to anyone who isn't a blood kin of the ruling family. He wanted me to find Helen and persuade her to give it back.''

"He *said* he wanted you to find Helen and persuade her to give it back,'' Hercules corrected him gravely. Iolaus smiled.

Xena considered this. "I guess it could be true,'' she said dryly. "Funny no one's heard of this thing before, though.''

"We talked about it,'' Hercules said. "And we came to the conclusion that Menelaus didn't dare just ask either of us to go find Helen for him. Since we know you, and we wouldn't be fooled by the message he sent Theseus.''

"Oh?''

"Yeah,'' Iolaus said with a broad grin. "Seems he's turned over a new leaf, he's changed, he'll do anything to prove to Helen that he wants to try again, love and adore her, make the marriage work—that he'll even respect her as a person. Pretty sickening.''

"He must think Theseus is a bigger fool than Joxer,'' Xena said. She glanced at the sky. "I'm reminded, I gotta go, I promised Gabrielle.''

Hercules smiled. "What? You don't want to help us talk to the Brotherhood about what the words *open market* mean, and all that?''

She glanced at Salmoneous; a corner of her mouth twitched. "Sorry, this is your problem boy. I've got one of my own to deal with.'' She moved to grip both men by the hand but stopped short as the overripe odor of Stymphaleon bird engulfed her.

Hercules shrugged, grinned. "It's the persuasive part of the talk." Xena gave him a sidelong, wary look, then vaulted onto Argo's back. People were starting to emerge from hiding, and others were coming from the market. She eased through the growing crowd and headed back south.

The sun was only beginning to drop from midday when she passed through the small village, pausing only long enough to be certain Gabrielle had gone ahead. "By now, she should be in Katerini," she told Argo. The mare's ears swiveled toward her voice; Xena leaned forward to rub her neck. Warm as it was, Argo hadn't broken a sweat; she'd be good for a long afternoon. There were no signs to Katerini from here, but the instructions had been so simple that anyone could remember them. "Stay left," Xena reminded herself as they reached the first branching of ways. Left every time, who could go wrong?

The pre-midday sun was hot and the air sullen when Joxer finally stumbled off the steep hillside and onto a decent track. Hedges lined it, separating road from grain fields, or a few fat goats, a few skinny-looking, recently sheared sheep, and the snub-nosed girl who kept them together and who eyed him curiously as he passed. On the opposite side, a tight-woven enclosure held pigs. Joxer's nose wrinkled, and he picked up the pace until the ripe odor of pig was behind him.

Down the long slope and away to his right, he could make out the clean little town of Katerini: Sun glittered on its whitewashed buildings. At least an hour's walk from here, he thought gloomily. His stomach hurt. But around the next bend, in the shade of an enormous olive tree and not that far from the sea and the protected port, was a tavern—the kind of small house that would attract the sailors as well as the local herders and farmers of an evening, where food and ale would be nothing special, but always familiar tasting and the atmosphere would be comfortable. He sighed happily and felt his hidden store of coins. "Great." There was enough and to spare, especially since he could count on Spartan hospitality two nights from now. Enough for a decent meal now, and for food to carry with him. Just maybe, this heroic quest stuff wasn't so bad after all.

4

The horse Gabrielle rode—a black-mane-and-tailed bay mare called Nessa—wasn't a rack of bones, but that was small consolation: The saddle and pad were poorly stitched and lumpy, and the beast had a trot that could loosen teeth. It was also clumsy and headstrong. At least Grytis, the boy who was taking the brutes south, took no more pleasure in riding than she did. *Listening to him sing their praises or coo love at them, now...* That would have been unbearable.

They rode at a steady, ground-eating pace for the most part, stopping frequently so both could walk around and stretch out—or, in Gabrielle's case, limp. Before she'd even swung up into the saddle the first time, Nessa had stepped on her foot. Fortunately, she'd yelled and shoved before the stupid mare could shift all her weight over, and nothing seemed to be broken, but it throbbed constantly.

The whole morning did nothing to improve her temper. *I could be spending a little time with Iolaus and Hercules, but no. I get to go haul Joxer out of trouble.*

She didn't begrudge Xena the ride north, though; the warrior had probably put Argo to a full-out gallop most of the way, and once she'd found them and passed on her messages, she'd turn around and come straight back south.

The boy was quiet for the most part—shy or just not good at small talk, she wasn't sure which. Mostly, he spoke only to suggest a stop or that they start again; once or twice he pointed out landmarks. For her part, Gabrielle's mind was full of the problem set up by Denos and his boys. No matter how carefully she worked out what Menelaus might be planning, it still made no sense. Why Joxer? *Unless Xena's right, and it's some plan of the king's to find out what she's up to. What we're up to.*

But that didn't make sense, either: *We aren't up to anything. It's not like we're hiding Helen or anything!* And at the most, Joxer knew only what Xena wanted him to know; he wasn't the most closemouthed person around, after all. The warrior put up with his presence, dealing with his sulks or fits of giddiness alike mostly by ignoring them. Anyone with half a wit would realize within minutes that Joxer couldn't possibly be in Xena's confidence. No. *If Menelaus actually wants to know what Xena's doing, he should've found a way to get my attention.* Not a pleasant thought; she'd barely seen the Spartan king when Troy fell, but he'd struck her as a bully and a brute.

But, of course, getting Gabrielle into his clutches wouldn't help him much, either. Xena had changed a lot since a very young and virtually useless Gabrielle had tracked her all the way to Amphipolis and persuaded the warrior to accept her company. Xena still kept her own confidences on a lot of things. Probably most things. *As if I'd tell him anything, anyway.* If the choice were hers, of course. She shivered and decided it was time to think of something else. But her mind kept picking at it throughout the morning.

The king and his priest wouldn't know that about me—that even if I wanted to tell them what Xena's up to, I don't know that much. Xena could have found Helen a refuge and if she didn't want me to know about it—. She shrugged that aside. Joxer could tell them even less, if that was the king's plan. She could only hope, if she didn't catch up to Joxer on the road, that he'd keep his big mouth shut and not make up a bunch of important-sounding things. As if, she thought sourly. Probably he'd already added another verse to his "Joxer the Mighty" song, so's to impress the Spartan ruler.

She sighed, shook her head, and came back to the moment; the boy was some distance ahead of her, and Nessa was exerting pressure on the reins, trying to shamble over to the side of the road where the grass and vetch were a thick, green tangle. Gabrielle dragged back the other way and used her heels; the mare's ears went back flat to her skull, but she finally moved. Gabrielle leaned forward to make eye contact. "Don't you *start* with me," she growled. The mare's ears flicked.

She had her hands full on the road down to Katerini; it was steep and winding, and Nessa kept snapping her head down, trying to rip the reins from the rider's hands. Gabrielle gazed at the dark ears with loathing and finally gave up: At this point, they weren't moving any better than a decent walking pace anyway. She hauled back hard, dragging the mare to a reluctant halt, threw her leg over the saddle, and dropped to the ground, clinging to the saddle momentarily so that she could put full weight on her uninjured left foot. Grytis eyed her curiously as she held out the reins and gingerly took a few steps.

She turned, freed her staff from the saddle loops, and leaned against it. "Look, Grytis, I'm really grateful for the chance to get so far, this early in the day. Don't get me wrong. But I can walk from here, if you want to go on ahead."

To her surprise, he grinned, rather shamefaced. "I kept hoping you would dismount, miss. Riding down this road terrifies me, but—well, you know."

But he didn't want to look bad in front of her. "Your secret's safe with me." Gabrielle waited until he dismounted, handed over her set of reins with something like relief, and freed up her water bottle. "What's Katerini like?"

Grytis took the bottle, drank, wiped his mouth, and recorked it before handing it back. "Clean. A nice town. Quiet."

Gabrielle took the bottle back. Her right foot still ached, but only like an old bruise or older sprain—bearable. Better than her backside would feel in the morning. "You mean, it's a boring place, and there's nothing to do, right?" He grinned again and ducked his head. "I know; I grew up in a place like that. They have their good points—but not when you're young. What kind of inns are there?"

He wound both sets of reins around his hand. "There's only one tavern, the Blue Bull."

"Just one for a town that size?"

"A distant cousin of my mother's owns it, white-haired old grouch named Numinos. It *could* be a pleasant enough place if he didn't snarl at people all the time."

Gabrielle gazed down at the sprawl of whitewashed,

thatched buildings. "And there's still only the one? One tavern for the whole town?"

The boy shrugged. "Numinos is rich. And he doesn't like competition, so he can usually find a way to not have any. Besides, his food and drink really are good." He hesitated. "Actually, there is *one* other tavern in the area; just over the hill, a—well, it's mostly the poorer fishermen who go there. And a few—ah—a few women—"

"Never mind," Gabrielle said hastily. "I get the idea." Something like the tavern hosted by good old Meg, a remarkable Xena look-alike: There would be cheap drinks and cheaper girls. The kind of place that had what *she'd* once thought of as "atmosphere."

The boy was following his own thoughts. "Mother says Numinos wasn't always like that, but all those years fighting at Troy changed him, she says. I only know him from after he came home. I was too young when he left for the war. He had a pocket full of gold coins when he returned, they say, and that was how he could buy the Blue Bull. And his ships, of course. My mother wanted to apprentice me to him, but my father said no, thank the gods. He snaps at everyone, but he's especially hard on his sons and his help." He shrugged the subject aside and pointed out the few boats inside the breakwater, describing those who owned them, when they'd changed hands, for how much coin. Gabrielle smiled, nodded when he paused or glanced her way, and more or less tuned him out. Her eyes followed his finger absently; one pale blue boat rocked idly back and forth on the low waves. Gabrielle swallowed and resolutely sent her gaze inland.

Gold from Troy, huh? she thought. Stolen money, then; soldiers who took only the pay they earned didn't

63

come home from war with a pocket of gold coins, not even from a war as long as the fight for Troy. It would make her angry if she let it—but there wasn't any point. *It's between him and the gods, when he's judged. Meanwhile, you can eat his food, drink his cider, and ignore the rest,* she told herself firmly. Besides, it might not be true. Stories like that were often nothing more than family gossip; people in small villages like Grytis's didn't have much to talk about except each other. Which, of course, was how it should be. *Better than talking about who survived the last raid or how they're going to feed their families on what some warlord left them of the harvest.*

The sun was much lower in the sky when Gabrielle finished her meal and swallowed the last of a tall mug of excellent new cider. Grytis had brought her to the Blue Bull and introduced her to his uncle—who eyed her clothing and fighting staff with tight-lipped disapproval—then taken himself and the horses off. *Good riddance,* Gabrielle thought, narrowed eyes on Nessa's ample flanks. Nice boy, rotten mount. The horse's ears twitched.

She turned back to smile at Numinos, but he was already halfway across the large room, snapping his fingers for one of the several younger men to show her a table and yelling at two others who were behind the long counter filling mugs. Not fast enough to please the landlord, apparently.

Gabrielle kept her eyes open as she ordered and waited for her meal. Grytis wasn't wrong about Numinos: The man snarled at one or another of the help, when he wasn't yelling at them. Sons or other kindred, she decided, by the look of them. The few other patrons in the whitewashed room were well dressed and quiet; an older man and his wife, a woman with thick black hair and two small boys; three men who looked as though they could be guards or the village watch. At least, their hardened leather breastplates all bore the same small token—blue badge, white ship.

She checked with the boy who took her order, the one who brought her drink and the youngest one, who arrived shortly with food: None of them had seen anyone anywhere in Katerini who even remotely resembled Joxer. *He's gotten lost, back up in the mountains,* she decided with a sigh. *No way he got in front of me, unless he walked all night.* In which case, he was probably dead, a mangled heap at the bottom of a cliff. *Serve him right,* she decided—not completely honestly—and turned her attention to her food.

One bite and she forgot her surroundings—and even the problem of Joxer—for the time being: Grytis had, if anything, underspoken the quality of the food. She lingered over seasoned, slow-roasted strips of boar laid neatly atop a bowl of chilled young peas and other greens; there was a smaller bowl of fiery, coarse-chopped sauce for the meat and a smooth, tart yogurt to spread over the greens. A fresh sprig of mint came with her cider.

Halfway through the guard-sized meal, she became aware of the landlord's astonished gaze; she ignored it with ease of practice. *I had nothing but dry bread before the sun rose, and not nearly enough of that,* she reminded herself grimly. *And I worked for this; I earned it.* Of course, a man like Numinos—the older and more set-in-his-ways type who'd scowled at her clothing that way—would assume a woman her size ate like a dryad: One small nut here, one smaller berry there . . . She finished the last strip of boar, washed it down with cider, and shoved the empty vessels aside.

The landlord's youngest son was at her elbow immediately. Again. Gabrielle bit back a sigh; his eyes were wide and admiring; a faint smile twitched the corners of his mouth. He could just possibly be her age, but she doubted it, and he acted like a boy ten years younger. And he was betraying signs of an enormous crush—maddening. *How come I get this all the time? It's not like I've got the leather, the legs, the blue eyes . . .* He cleared his throat, regaining her attention. "I—I hope that—yuh—you liked that. But if—if you desire any—anything else?"

"I'm stuffed," she assured him cheerfully. "But I could use some information."

"But, I already told you, there's been no one in Katerini who looks like—"

"I know. But someone told me there's another inn—over in the next village, Bacchia, is it called?" She paused inquiringly as his eyes went even wider and he went red to his hairline.

"I—well, yes, there's—I mean, it's a tavern, not an inn, but it's—I—you can't go *there*!" he finished urgently. Gabrielle smiled, and held up the staff; he stared at it, slack-jawed.

"Well, yes, actually, I can—ah, what's your name, anyway?"

He blinked. "Um? Oh, it's Briax, I'm sorry. You—I mean—that's a fighting staff! But that's not—not the point, you can't go into a place like that! People would—they'll—I mean, they'll think that—"

"Well, Briax, you know what? I don't exactly care what the people in Bacchia think, or the people inside the tavern. I have someone to find, and it's important. I'm just trying to figure out how he would have got over to Bacchia without anyone in Katerini seeing him, unless he came through town last night, after dark." It wasn't

66

likely, considering the distance Joxer'd had to travel, and the time he'd left her—and that he was most likely afoot the whole distance. But Briax was shaking his head.

"The guard would have seen him—after you asked my older brother Magris, he asked Chelemon over there, with the guard's patch. They watch the road after dark, keep an eye on things. They'd have seen a stranger. Unless he managed to sneak through town—"

It was her turn to shake her head. "Oh, he could have tried. He'd probably have awakened the entire village, though. So, that means he didn't come through Katerini, but I was told there's only the one north-south road. Which means, somehow, I'm ahead of him, unless—he went directly to Bacchia." She looked up at him; he blushed. "This is possible?" she asked crisply.

"Well—" Briax winced as his father's bellow temporarily silenced the inn's main chamber, and two of his brothers or cousins scrambled to clean one of the tables and sweep the floor. "Well, I suppose he *could* have come down the old road. But it's not very likely."

"No? Why?"

"Well, if you came down from the high ridges, you'd've seen it, up at the very top, where there are no trees, not much but stone?" She nodded. "You can see what looks like a—a trail, except the rocks are all standing on end? It goes to the right, the main road to the left and downhill, toward the sea?"

She considered this, nodded again. "It didn't look even a little bit like a road to me, though. Maybe a goat trail."

"Even the goatherds don't use the old road. Though it used to be a regular path, it went through the old olive groves and into Bacchia. But since before the war with Troy, it's been unused. Now if you want to go to Bacchia from Katerini, there's a narrow road and a path along the ridge that's much shorter but no good for carts.'' He winced again as his father bellowed for his elder brother. ''The old road has been in bad repair since I can remember, but the past year or so, it's deteriorated to the point that you'd have to be a total idiot to take it.''

''Total idiot—well, at least now I know which way he went, don't I?'' Gabrielle snarled under her breath. She looked up; Briax was eyeing her with that 'O! Beautious Maiden Thou, Beloved of Artemis!' blindly adoring look she found highly unnerving.

''Lady—'' he began breathily.

''That's Gabrielle,'' she put in as he hesitated.

''Guh—Gabrielle. You—'' He drew himself up with a slightly shabby dignity that oddly—and touchingly—reminded her of Perdicas when they were children, the time he'd lied to protect her from a beating over stolen corn. ''You really can't go to uh—a place like that. People—they'll think that you—that—''

She laid a hand on his arm, silencing him. ''Briax, I understand. And it's all right, really. They honestly won't believe I'm part of the—ah—entertainment. And I won't be there long enough for it to matter.''

''You'd—you would risk so much for this—this Joxer?'' His father's bellow cut through the small room again; the boy winced and began scrubbing at the table with a dampish rag. He glanced up at her from under his brows, and said rapidly, ''What is he to you that— that I couldn't be?''

She stared at him, momentarily stunned into silence. ''Ah—Briax? Look, it isn't like that. He's—he's a friend. Kind of,'' she added honestly. ''But he gets himself into trouble a lot, and this time, it's my fault—well, kind of, it's my fault. And I'm trying to keep him from getting into even worse trouble, and the only way I can do *that* is to stop him from going on this stupid quest, and—''

''Quest?'' Briax stopped scrubbing the table; the cloth fell unnoticed from his hand; his face shone with eagerness. ''There was a priest of the sun god, Apollo. He came here when the moon was a sliver, days ago, and talked about a quest! He said there was need for puhpure young men.'' He suddenly went beet-red, and he no longer met her eyes. ''That they were seeking—well, he said not to tell anyone about it, but that it—that they—''

''Briax?'' Gabrielle laid a hand on his arm; his sudden smile dazzled her. ''Briax, that's the same story Joxer was told, and it's not true, okay? There's no quest, believe me.''

His mouth took on a stubborn set that reminded her of Joxer's. ''But—but the priest said that a holy vessel had been taken, that it once belonged to Persephone, and that it—''

''Briax, listen to me. I'm a bard—''

''I thought you said you were a fighter,'' he broke in.

''Well—I'm both.'' His mouth twitched. ''Really and truly, I *am* a bard. I've been a bard of sorts since I was a young girl, and I can tell you right now, there is no such thing as a holy vessel of Persephone. Any bard worth her salt would know about it if there was such a thing.'' She looked at him; he stared back sullenly. ''I'm just trying to save you a long walk for nothing.''

''But what if you're wrong about that? What if—''

She sighed faintly, got to her feet. ''I could be, but I'm not. Trust me.'' She looked up and the boy stepped back as the innkeeper came stomping over. He gave her and her staff a sour look, then grabbed Briax's shoulder and gave him a hard shake.

"There's work to be done hereabouts, you! I don't pay you to moon about, do I?"

"N-n-n-no, sir."

"Well, then?"

"Y-y-yes, sir." Briax cast her one last, brief look she couldn't begin to fathom and hurried off. Numinos transferred his glare to her—and the bellow.

"And exactly what were you telling my boy, just now?"

You can't argue with his kind, Gabrielle reminded herself. The mere fact that she was young, female, and traveling alone—instead of home tending half a dozen howling brats and waiting on a brute of a husband— would be enough to anger a man like this. She smiled brightly and enumerated on her fingers. "What was I telling him? What would you think? Wonderful food, good service, but the floor show needs a *lot* of work." He frowned. She gathered up her pack. "All that bellowing while people are trying to eat; you'd have more customers without it and probably keep your help around longer." His mouth sagged; his eyes narrowed, but before he could begin yelling at *her*, she added sweetly, "I need to leave a message, in case a friend of mine shows up here. Her name's Xena, and if you'd tell her I'll be back here before full dark, and not to leave without me?" She waited; he nodded blankly. He was still staring when she turned in the doorway to wave at Briax, but the boy was fiercely scrubbing away at a pile of dirty cups and didn't see her.

The tavern in Bacchia was definitely a dive, Gabrielle decided. A few tough-looking men huddled over cups in a far corner; near the entry, two blowsy barmaids joked with some older fishermen. The woman behind the counter, polishing cups and handing out ale, looked as disreputable as Joxer's friend Meg, but not a tenth as pretty.

Even with one wall open to the sea and a shaded patio with more tables and benches, the place reeked of cheap ale, raw onions, and fried meat. Gabrielle's excellent meal rebelled briefly; she breathed through her nose and crossed the room to the counter.

Joxer wasn't here; she'd seen that already. He'd *been*; three scarcely clad women near the entry were drinking and giggling and not very tunefully warbling about a "very tidy" warrior. She bit back a groan and headed straight for the barkeep.

"Joxer, huh? Cute guy, very original armor, sweet smile? Your boyfriend, honey?" the woman asked cheerfully, sending a mixed blast of onion and sour beer in Gabrielle's direction. "Listen, he's adorable, you know? Sense of humor, fun laugh, and a real flirt. Brave, too, if half the stories he told are true. I was you, I'd keep a closer eye on him. Someone's gonna snatch him up when you aren't lookin' and *then* where'll you be? Sweet little thing like you, hardly any decent curves, you won't find it easy to replace someone like that Joxer."

There are no words, Gabrielle decided grimly. She merely shook her head, found out how long since he'd left (hours, if she gathered correctly), and managed to stem the barkeep's ecstasies long enough to leave her own message for Xena: "I'll be back in Katerini just long enough to pick up some food for on the road. If I'm not at the inn, it's because I've gone south. *Meet me.*" She made the woman repeat the message twice, then left quickly. The earlier breeze had died away and the stale air inside the tavern was curdling before her eyes. *Besides, I hear one more word—just one more!— about Joxer the Mighty! I'll Joxer the Mighty him when I get my hands on him!*

Unfortunately, two of the women had very high, carrying voices; the song followed her all the way to the ridge.

The sun was dipping near the line of western hills when Xena finally found Mannius and passed on King Theseus's message. By the time she'd convinced him the king wasn't merely setting a trap, the last rays were lighting the tops of the tallest trees. Time to leave, she decided. There'd be enough moon to illuminate the road for some hours, and she needed to get a head start on the next day's travel. Gabrielle would worry, and she might need help. *With Joxer running loose, she probably does need help. Or will by the time I reach her.*

Mannius walked her from the countinghouse where she'd finally found him, out to where Argo was waiting. "This is great, Xena. I can't tell you how much I appreciate it. But I wish you'd stay, have dinner with me. We could talk."

She smiled: He'd gotten rid of the beard, but the curly brown hair and warm dark eyes hadn't changed; nor had his smile—a little wicked at the best of times. "I'd like that, too, old friend." She gripped his shoulder. "But I have other things to do and besides," she glanced beyond him, well down the track where the cyclops sat on a high stone ledge, swinging his feet back and forth, "I bet your pal Flyer hasn't learned table manners yet, has he? I'll see you in Athens one of these days, all right?" She vaulted into the saddle, waved, and was gone.

• • •

A long night and morning later, she reached Katerini and Numinus's inn, to find no Joxer, no Gabrielle, and an infuriated landlord, though she noticed he was careful not to bellow at *her*. "Comes in here half-clad like that, gets my boy Briax making a fool of himself, drooling all over her. Well, she eats, leaves, leaves that message for you, then later comes back and leaves another—what I just said, about she'd set up a camp along the Athens road—and not *that* long after she's left for good, I look around for Briax and *he's* gone as well!"

The warrior's eyes narrowed. "You're not gonna tell me that my friend ran off with your boy, are you?"

A suddenly pale Numinus swallowed and shook his head. "Ahhhh, no, of course not! It's—I mean, he was already full of these tales of fortune and glory some priest brought here, some days ago, but when *she* came in, he—I mean, he—"

She sighed heavily. "Never mind. I get the picture. I don't think it'll do much good, but if I see him—Briax, is it?—if I do, I'll try to convince him to come home. If it helps, Gabrielle already knew there's no quest; she would have told Briax that, if she knew what he was up to."

"No quest? But the priest said—"

"Numinus, you're old enough to know priests lie as good as other men. No quest." She thought a moment. "You might spread the word, Numinus. In case any other would-be heroes want to leave Katerini. *There is no quest;* it's some scheme of the Spartan king's."

"King Menelaus." The older man nearly spat, only just remembering it was his own just-swept floor he'd be dirtying. "I know him; I was in Troy, you know. Fighting under Agamemnon, I was, ten years and some, gone over there. Long enough to know the leaders for what they really was. For all they called King Odysseus

73

the trickster, it was the Spartan we all knew to distrust. And that priest of his—priest. Wait.'' He was silent for some moments. ''If that priest who came here was one of *his*—Avicus, it was, I think?'' He eyed her; she nodded. ''Avicus. If *he* sent that priest to Katerini . . .'' The anger went out of him in a gusty sigh, and he suddenly looked old, gray and anxious. ''Tell the boy to come home, if you see him, will you, warrior? Tell him—tell him the old man doesn't mean to—'' He shrugged helplessly.

A faint smile turned the corners of her mouth. ''I understand, Numinus. And I'll tell Briax, if I see him.'' She started to leave, then turned back. ''You saw nothing of the other one I'm looking for?''

''Your girl already asked,'' Numinus said. ''I'd've remembered *him*. Likely he went over to Myla's, in Bacchia, by the fleet cove. More to a—single man's taste, if he's not too fussy about his food and prefers strong drink.'' She was already on Argo and ready to head west when the innkeeper came out, waving his damp cloth. ''Nearly forgot; my eldest boy said he saw the girl in town just at dusk yesterday, hour or so after Briax went. She was just leaving the baker's, heading south.''

At the branching of ways, Xena hesitated but finally decided to take the detour through Bacchia. Of course, the two were long gone, but Gabrielle's message gave her a little more information.

It took time: The barkeep wanted a nice, long gossip, her two servers had come up with a new verse to ''Joxer the Mighty'' that they wanted to share, and none of them was sober enough to properly remember exactly what Gabrielle had said, until the warrior grabbed two handfuls of skimpy dress and hauled the barkeep halfway across her counter. "I need to know what's going on," she snarled. "I need to know when my friend was here, how much earlier Joxer was here, and if you've seen one of the boys who works in the Blue Boar in the past two days. Tell me that, and I'll leave *before* I get mad— not after. Get my drift?"

"I—if you'd let a lady *think*!" the barkeep snarled back, and yanked free. Cloth gave with a loud rip that silenced the room momentarily. She rearranged tatters of fabric over her bosom, shifted her skirts around, and settled her fists on her hips. "I mean, who died and made you Ares?" Xena's eyes narrowed; the woman backed away, tittering nervously. "All right, honey, don't get your leather in a bind. I'm thinking, aren't I?"

"You got me," Xena said softly, but the barkeep was counting on her fingers, staring blankly at the far wall and mumbling under her breath.

"All right. The hero showed up well before midday, while it was still fairly cool out and custom was slow. He stayed a while, ate, had a drink or two, talked real nice to the girls and taught them that cute song of his— have you heard it?"

"Spare me," Xena said wearily. "All I need to know is he was here before midday. And?"

"And he left before the heat of the afternoon, with a loaf and a bag of wine. Oh—and you know, I forgot to tell that girl of yours, he said to leave a message for Xena . . ." She caught her breath in a squeak. "Xena. That's—omigods, that's—you're you! I—I mean—!" She clapped both hands over her mouth, and her eyes were wide. Xena cast up her eyes and waved her on. "I—let me think, okay?" A frown creased her forehead. "You know," she added rather absently, "I thought you'd be taller . . ."

"The *message*?"

"Oh, ah—sure, the message. He told me, Myla, he said, you be sure to remember this—" The warrior snarled; the barkeep hastily recited the message. 'Xena, I'll be in Athens in two nights and in Sparta the night after, and I'm sleeping close to the road in case anyone gets in trouble and needs my help, and you and Gabrielle don't need to bother about me, I don't need *your* help this time.' "

"I see." Xena sighed quietly. It was as straightforward a yell for help as they'd get out of Joxer. She wondered briefly how long he'd known he was in over his head, then dismissed it as unimportant. Myla was eyeing her avidly. "All right, anything else?"

"Your girl said she'd go back over the Katerini, to the inn . . ."

"All right, never mind, I know the rest—"

"You *did* ask about Numinus's boy, too. Don't you want to know about him? Numinus is gonna be furious. Two of my girls were down waiting for the last fishing boats to come in when they saw him—the youngest, Briax, I think it is? Anyway, he went on down to one of his father's two-man boats and last they saw, he had it out around the breakwater and was heading south."

5

I've lost count of the days, Gabrielle realized as her gaze fixed on the sliver of moon just cresting the rugged peaks east of Sparta. It did nothing to improve her mood. "That makes it at least seven, or more probably nine days since I let Xena talk me into this—this—" She shrugged sourly and went on.

The journey south to Athens had been frustrating—no sign of Joxer, though it was obvious she never did miss him by much; those arrogant-sounding little messages he left for her and Xena that didn't fool her one bit. *He's in over his head, and he knows it, and he's scared silly—sillier than he normally is, that is*. Not that he'd ever admit it, turn around, and head back, oh, no!

From Katerini south, she'd seen the insides of more shabby or downright unpleasant taverns than in all her early and totally notionless days with Xena; she'd been pinched four times (and left all four pinchers moaning on the floor, wishing they'd thought before reaching for an armed young woman, however small and helpless she might otherwise appear). Twice, she'd left an entire common room full of thugs flat on the floor, one land-lord angrily ordering her to move on, the other on the floor, whimpering in chorus with his customers. *Been there, done that*, she thought tiredly.

The food had ranged from almost as good as the Blue Bull's to something even a starving cyclops wouldn't touch. She'd been ordered out of yet another inn for suggesting the woman change the name of her place from Phoenix Rising to Stymphaleon Death Wish. *People were actually eating that stuff, bad as it smelled—*. All right; drunken people. She grinned crookedly; it had smelled worse than her first whiff of raw squid, aboard that ocean-going eternity of Cecrops's, before Xena'd found a way to break Poseidon's curse.

One good thing on the whole journey south, trying to catch stupid Joxer: At least she hadn't *eaten* any of that woman's food; raw squid had been bad enough coming up.

Ordinarily, travel from Athens to Sparta involved two fairly walkable roads (or so she understood, having never been to Sparta before). Unfortunately, Joxer had for whatever reason taken a ship across the Gulf of Saronica, which meant that unless she cared to chance losing him after this long a journey, *she* had to take a ship as well.

The sea was every bit as rough as Xena'd predicted; she came ashore with a raging headache, a queasy (and empty) stomach despite pinching her earlobe nonstop during the crossing, and she *still* had to deck two of the common sailors who thought what a very seasick young (armed) woman (who wasn't wrapped in a blanket from nose to ankles) needed was an amazingly simple distraction they'd managed (how astonishing!) to think up all by themselves.

Yeah, she thought angrily as she remembered the extremely direct approach made by the older man. She slammed the staff end into the road, digging into the dirt and leaving gouges with each step. *Like nobody every thought of that one before, and like anyone would be interested in theirs!* Well, one of them would have a long-lasting reminder not to come up with such an "original" notion in the near future.

Unfortunately, land—once her legs had adjusted to land—hadn't been that much better. Apparently Menelaus couldn't spare troops or be bothered with the land more than a league away from his chief city and his palace: The Spartan maps should have had "Here Be Bandits" printed all over them in large letters. Fortunately, most of those who preyed on travelers stayed close to the ships' landings, but by the time she was certain she'd left the last bands behind, it was nearly dark, and the landscape had taken on the look of bear and chimera country.

There hadn't been a chimera—none she had seen or heard, at least. And bears didn't like fire. She knew that much, because she hadn't slept a wink that first night, and she watched at least one enormous, hairy brown brute out beyond her camp, drawn by the smell of bread and fish but not willing to argue with the long blazing brand she kept handy.

Another two nights saw her high into the mountains, mostly above the forest line, though a few stunted trees somehow managed to survive the cold and the harsh wind. One more night of utter desolation in a high, narrow pass that seemed to hold the complete hopelessness of a battle fought against horrific odds—and lost. She tried twice to set up camp, and each time moved on, unable to bear the sensations of fear, loss, remorse, and death that pressed around her.

The next day, the path wound down, and by dawn she was again in trees, protected from the constant icy blasts of wind. Worn out, she'd slept the entire day, only to waken with a start at sunset to the distant but unmistakable echo of Joxer's voice. Nearly impossible to gauge direction, but she thought he was on the same road as she, some distance ahead of her. Now and again throughout the evening hours, she heard him—or an echoing refrain as he tried to firm up yet another verse of his wretched little song.

I'll Joxer the Mighty, he'll cure your plighty, him! she thought savagely as she reached blessedly level ground and a nearly straight road that widened as two more joined it. One of those two, she was willing to wager, was the direct route from Athens.

The sun's last long rays rested on the city gates and the armed guards flanking it, as she came out of the belt of trees separating wild country from tilled fields and herds. There were no houses out here, no huts except what might be grain storage, and certainly no inns. But Sparta had always been a walled city, and whether there was still need for siege mentality, Menelaus obviously practiced just that: The setting sun picked out heavy metal reinforcing the gates; the walls were high and smooth and appeared to slope outward.

Her attention was caught by movement just in front of the gates. "Joxer!" she snarled under her breath. He was a tiny figure in the distance and against the massive Spartan wall; so were the two guards who blocked the narrow opening with crossed spears, and the third, who wore one of those ridiculous horse-crested helmets: He moved behind Joxer, sword drawn to keep him from retreating. Gabrielle ignored aching feet and picked up her pace. "Hold him there for me, boys, that's right." But before she'd made it past the first narrow fields and crossed the first irrigation ditch, the three had made room for him and pushed the loose gate enough for him to enter the city. The would-be hero went in, and the guards hauled the gate shut—and resumed their stations.

"Aaugh!" Gabrielle slammed the butt of her staff into the road so hard it bounced. She stood where she was for several moments, breathing deeply. "All right," she said finally. "At least I know where he *is* now." As she started forward again, the sun dropped behind the craggy peaks behind her, and an icy wind sprang up. She shivered and picked up the pace. "Not that I ever heard anything good about Spartan cooking, but bread's bread and at least I'll be warm."

Warm—if she could get through the gates. Unfortunately, the guards weren't eager to admit her. In fact, Gabrielle decided as the two circled her, eyes narrowed, they were downright unfriendly. She leaned against the staff as if its only use were for walking and propping up an exhausted body and managed a smile for them. "Look, if we could finish talking about this inside, a friend of mine's here, I'm sure he can vouch for me, if you'll just—"

"No one enters the fortress of Sparta between dusk and dawn," one of the two intoned. She smiled at him; he blinked, but otherwise his face remained a blank: dull brown eyes, a full-lipped mouth that sagged slightly open so that he could breathe through it when he wasn't talking—*make that, reciting,* Gabrielle thought, and smiled some more, taking in both of them this time. The other guard didn't look any brighter, or any less bored. Or any more capable of thinking for himself.

"Well, yes, I can see how that would be a good rule. But sometimes, rules can be bent just a little, especially for one lone woman traveler out here by herself, someone who's out of food, hungry, and—you know, I've heard such good things about Spartan cuisine! People sing the praises of your soups all the way to Ithaca, and I've come so far, just hoping to—"

"No one enters the fortress of Sparta between—"

"I know, dusk and dawn," she finished hastily. "But it's not like it's that dark out yet, is it? Look, up there, there aren't even any stars out yet, to me that says 'not quite dusk,' don't you think?"

As if, she mentally added. Neither one looked able to think. They eyed her warily, glanced at each other, and began in unison, "No one enters the fortress—"

"... of Sparta between dusk and dawn, OK, fine!" The smile felt tight. "Nice song, dull lyrics. I'll talk to you boys tomorrow, sometime after sunrise, all right?" She turned and strode off, back up the road toward the distant line of trees. After maybe a hundred steps, she glanced over her shoulder—they were watching, all right. Suspicious. Probably they were gonna watch her all the way back to the trees. Gabrielle swore under her breath, turned to give them a bright, toothy smile and a little bow, then spun away and walked off.

"Okay," she mumbled to herself. "What would Xena—no, never mind that, what is Gabrielle gonna do now?"

Obvious answer: get inside, somehow. Now. How was another matter.

Once she reached the line of trees and blended back into shadow, Gabrielle moved off the road to examine what she could see of the walled city, a task made easier by encroaching night and the torches lit upon and behind the walls. The two guards now paced before the gates, which were flanked by lit torches—and above them, she could see the horse-crested officer—Denos, perhaps; if not, the one who'd welcomed Joxer or another. Beyond that impressive display, to either side of the gates at a distance of maybe fifty paces, there were towers, a torch on each and what might be stationary guards. And at least northward, where she could see best, no more towers and no guards. Few torches except what light shone from down inside the city. And several places where the walls seemed to be under repair or simply lower for some reason.

"Could be guards posted there, too," she mused as she started across stubbly fields and squeezed through a prickly hedge. Well, if there were, too bad. She spun the staff in a neat twirl, tucked it under her arm in a slick, well-practiced move, and picked up the pace, angling north as much as possible to put as much distance between herself and the gates by the time she reached the walls.

Once there, she leaned against still-warm stone and listened, letting her breathing get back to normal and waiting for the sound of anyone nearby. Nothing, not even wind at the moment. A burst of distant laughter from well inside, and high and away to her right, a gravelly voice cursing—apparently someone was dicing and rapidly parting company with his month's pay.

"Fine," she muttered. "They're on duty and playing games; they aren't too worried about being attacked— or snuck up on." She moved along the wall, checking for the best place to climb quietly, and finally found a section where there'd apparently been a recent earthquake: Recent at least, if this really was a walled city because the stones were all out of line with each other and much of the grouting was loosened or gone. If Menelaus really considered Sparta a fortress, he wouldn't permit damage like this to stay unfixed for long. She wedged her staff through her belt, snug against her back, settled her pack over one shoulder so that the strap was tight across her body, and began slowly and quietly working her way up.

She paused now and again to listen, but there was no indication she'd been seen. *Smart soldiers would just wait down inside the wall and grab me when I landed*, she thought. Not a pleasant notion. And the Spartan army might actually have a smart soldier or two.

She edged flat onto the top stones and stayed put for a while, catching her breath once more. It was dark down there, but not so dark she couldn't make out the immediate area: A narrow alley ran along the wall, and if there were doors along the opposite side, she couldn't see them. Light some distance to the left, and from there more laughter; probably a tavern, but possibly a barracks. She could smell a stable, but not close by.

Still, she hesitated. "It's hardly a drop at all," she whispered to herself. It wasn't the drop; she knew that. It was coming down in a locked-up city full of Spartan soldiers. There were plenty of nasty stories about the Spartan prisons. Add in the Spartan king and a twisted priest . . . "Nothin's like that's gonna happen," she ordered herself flatly. "Cause no one's gonna see you. Provided you get down there and out of sight."

"Not a bad idea," came a throaty murmur against her ear. Gabrielle drew a harsh breath and tried to pull her staff free; one long arm dragged her close, the other hand clamping down hard on her mouth. Familiar—she went limp as she recognized Xena's hands, the feel of her armor and her unmistakable scent: a mix of soap, leather, the herbs she used on her hair, and the polish she rubbed into Argo's saddle and the grip on her sword. The hand against her mouth relaxed. "You picked a good spot to go over the walls, Gabrielle: There's nothing down there but a back street leading to the old barracks; nobody's around here, most of the time." She let go of her companion, eased to her hands and knees. "Come on," she said quietly, and let herself over the edge.

Gabrielle cast her eyes skyward and ground her teeth. "Was it something I did? I mean, is there some god's curse on me for something I did?"

"Gabri*elle* . . ." Ominous whisper. "Geddown here." Gabrielle swore tightly under her breath and began the descent.

It was quiet and dark where she finally landed; Xena's hand gripped her shoulder as she righted herself; the warrior's breath was warm against her ear. "Turn this way, stay close to me. There's an old stable just up here. Better shelter and we can talk if we're quiet about it." Behind them, muted sounds of yelling and cheering. Gabrielle turned to listen; Xena tapped her arm, hard. "Come on, that's just a buncha drunk Spartan soldiers busting benches and heads. Place has even more atmosphere than *you'd* like."

"Thanks," Gabrielle hissed, but Xena was already moving. Give it up, she told herself, and followed.

The stable doors hung ajar, creaking in the fitful breeze that reached this sheltered spot, and there were visible holes in the roof. Still, it was reasonably clean: a mound of straw in the nearest boxes, a few straps hanging on hooks near the entry. Xena pulled her on into the darker regions, scooping up an armful of straw as she passed. She dumped this in one of the farthest corners. "Here, sit." She plopped down herself, settled her assortment of weapons, and pulled the sword and sheath free, dropping them in front of her crossed legs. Gabrielle could barely make out the gleam of teeth as the warrior grinned. "So, how was *your* trip?"

Gabrielle scrambled onto her knees. "I just wanna know when I collect on that dinner," she hissed. "Do you know—do you have *any* idea how many messages I left for you? And in case you've forgotten, I don't *like* taverns with atmosphere anymore, you know how many of *those* I went through trying to catch up to Joxer?"

The smile was gone; Xena's eyes narrowed. "Matter of fact, *yeah*, I know how many messages, because I not only got all of *yours*, Gabrielle; I also got most of Joxer's, *and* I heard from probably every last person who talked to you about the whole mess. You got any idea how many people that is?"

Gabrielle waved that aside. "I have been—I have been cooed at, I have had the scum of the earth *and* Tartarus pawing at me! I have eaten some of the filthiest—no, I don't want to know what any of it was, it'll spoil my appetite for that dinner you owe me! I—did I mention I have been *pinched*? Have I mentioned lately that I *hate* being pinched?"

"Gabrielle," Xena began warningly; she shifted suddenly, then pulled the girl down into the straw with her. "Guard!" she hissed. Gabrielle, who had somehow wound up on the bottom, was too winded to more than nod when the warrior edged back up and finally whispered, "Okay, must be a regular, he didn't even look in here. Gabrielle?" She tugged at her companion's arm, helped her sit up, and brushed straw off her. "So, I'm guessing Joxer's already in here, huh?"

Gabrielle tugged free and finished brushing herself off. Now that her eyes were adjusted to the gloom, she could see Xena smiling that bemused smile that meant, *What? What'd I do?* As if she didn't know, Gabrielle thought, shaking the last loose bits of straw from her top, one-handed, as she leveled a finger at Xena's nose. "Don't you start with me," she began flatly. To her astonishment, her companion clapped both hands over her mouth and rocked back, spluttering with laughter.

It was infectious, as always. Gabrielle fought to contain her own laughter but finally gave up. Xena grinned at her. "You're scary, Gabrielle. You're starting to sound like me."

"Naah! I can't get my voice that low, hurts my throat." She shook her head; amazing, still, how little it took to neutralize ordinary anger between them. *Ordinary—sure.* She shoved that aside and murmured, "Yeah, Joxer's in. Got here before sunset. If that isn't a Spartan ploy to keep single women outside the gates."

"They lock them at sundown," Xena said. "And a single woman in Sparta isn't someone to protect; she's someone to carry burdens, do all the work, and bear sons, remember?"

"Nice guys," Gabrielle said. "Helen must have *loved* this place."

"Why d'you think she left with Paris, because Aphrodite was having a hissy-fit? It probably wasn't that, and it for sure wasn't his great manners. But even a self-absorbed pretty boy was a step up compared to Menelaus. At least the Spartans are no longer keeping a count of girl babies to boy babies and exposing the excess girls," Xena added flatly.

Exposing—such a nice-sounding word for laying a naked newborn out on the rocks and leaving it to die. Her throat suddenly tightened. *No!* she ordered herself fiercely. *Don't!* What she could see of Xena's face mirrored her own feelings. Too soon, too close—despite everything they'd been through, there were still some things that couldn't be set right with words. Some things that would need time. *Don't leave it there; you can't just leave it there.* She reached, caught Xena's hands in her own, and just held them. Xena's grip was hard, almost painful. Reassuring. Finally, she let go; Gabrielle cleared her throat, sat back on her heels, and fought for something normal to say. The thing that popped into her mind surprised even her.

"You know? I keep forgetting to ask you—how come that thing's called a *rhodforch?* It doesn't look like a road, a fork—what gives?"

"Huh? Oh—that." Xena shrugged. "You know about the island of Rhodes, right?"

"I know there *is* one."

"Know about the statue?" Gabrielle shook her head. "Enormous thing, huge brute of a bronze male in full armor, with a foot on each side of the channel where the ships go out to sea. The common Rhodsians say he's 'forking the channel' ..."

"*Not* going there," Gabrielle said hastily.

"Yeah, me, too." Xena grinned. "Rhodsians have a really earthy sense of humor. And I have no clue what they mean by that. But the possibilities ... never mind. Supposedly the statue was imbued by Apollo with the ability to test those aboard incoming ships, to feel out whether they meant good to the island, or not."

"I get the idea. Although the move from a bronze brute to a little hairball ..."

"Both look like something that wouldn't be a weapon, don't they?" Xena asked reasonably.

"Point," Gabrielle conceded. "All right. Joxer got in just after the sun went down." For a wonder, her voice was back to normal. "I had to wait to make a move on the city walls until those two idiot guards couldn't see me out there; they were watching, too." She considered this. "Hey, you don't suppose—?"

"I don't think they were necessarily watching for you—or for me, Gabrielle. Men who guard Menelaus's gates aren't picked for their brains; they can be taught to follow orders, and they don't question anything they're told to do. Let this guy in, keep everyone else out, no one in after dark—anything more than that would just confuse them."

"All right. Fine. So, I guess we need to find out where the palace is, and—"

"I've been there, remember? Well," Xena considered this and finally shrugged. "I've been in the palace. But somehow, my company wasn't good enough for the king's table."

"Probably your manners," Gabrielle replied gravely, but her eyes were wicked. "I keep telling you, Xena, you just can't do stuff like pick your nose at a banquet."

"I know," the warrior replied drearily as she got to her feet and held out a hand for her companion. "You only get to pick your nose after dessert, right? Come on, let's get this done and get *out* of this city," she added flatly. "Sparta gives me the creeps."

It wasn't that far in a direct line to the palace, or so Xena later told her. The route they took followed every back road across uneven bricks and over nasty, muddy potholes, via long-unused (but not de-scented) sewer pipes, and along what had to be every last single skinny passage between buildings in Sparta. Oh, of course, there was plenty of room for passage, Gabrielle decided halfway through their cross-city trek—if one turned sideways and didn't take a deep breath. She emerged from the last such passage scratched, hot, and bruised; her hair had caught on every splinter, shard of stone, metal bar, and other encumbrance, and now hung down her back in a massive, dirty tangle.

Xena was waiting to grab her wrist as she had so often the past hour or so and haul her on—this time across open ground and into a low mass of bushes. Something jabbed her shoulder; she fought not to yelp in pain and slewed around to free herself. Thorns—a heavy, heady scent . . . ?

"What," she hissed angrily against Xena's ear, "is the king of Sparta doing with *roses*?"

"Gift to Helen when they married," Xena hissed back. She sounded merely annoyed by comparison. "He still has them tended because they cost so much when he bought them. Lucky for us; there's nothing else anywhere close to the palace to provide shelter." She eased cautiously up onto one knee and listened for some moments, then let herself back down. "It's OK; the guard pattern's the same as I knew it and one went by a short while ago. We're fine for maybe an hour."

"Fine?" Gabrielle freed her skirt from another welter of thorns; the fabric ripped. "Fine? Xena, this is a whole *new* way of defining *fine*, as far as I'm concerned!"

"We won't get found," the warrior corrected herself with obviously strained patience. "*If we don't start yelling and calling down the guards*! All right?" Silence. Gabrielle slewed around to sit cross-legged, staff across her legs, and waited. "All right, fine. Now, look over there, where the lights are. We're at the back of the palace. The pale yellow curtains over there? That was Helen's apartments. The dark opening beyond it was Menelaus's—probably still is, he's too cheap to change rooms for anything less than an earthquake. That way,'' she eased her companion part-way around and pointed, ''where you can see torches? That's the main reception— probably where Menelaus and Avicus are interviewing heroes. If,'' she corrected herself dryly, ''that's really what they're doing.''

Gabrielle shrugged gloomily. ''I've given up trying to figure it out. What next?'' Xena hesitated; so long, that Gabrielle turned to eye her with rising suspicion. ''I said, what next?''

''You wait here, I'll go get Joxer—and if I can't catch him in there, *you'll* have to follow him, so I guess— damn, I'll have to show you how to get around to the main entry . . .''

Gabrielle shook her head fiercely. ''Oh, no! Have we been there and done that before? He-*llo*! Yes, we have, and oh, no, you don't, Xena! I am *not*, for your infor- mation, waiting anywhere while you go somewhere else—or the other way around! In fact, I—'' A deep masculine voice broke the flow of words.

''Hey, what's this? Get up! Hey, you, girl!'' He prod- ded a startled Gabrielle with his foot. ''I said, get—'' Before she could bring the staff around, he went limp, nearly landing across her legs. Xena knelt beside him, grinning widely.

''Funny,'' Gabrielle said shortly as the warrior hauled the unconscious guard aside and shoved him under a rosebush. ''I *thought* you said they—''

''Okay. They changed the rotation, so? Now you've got another hour before someone comes looking for *him.*" She rose to her feet, squeezed Gabrielle's shoulder, and was gone.

"Xena! You come back—oh, Hades," Gabrielle snarled under her breath. "She's—" She broke off, startled, as the warrior suddenly dropped back next to her and pulled her down flat. Her nostrils were suddenly full of dust, compost, and rose petals. "Xena, I can't *breathe* down here, do you mind?"

"Gabrielle, will you shaddup?" The girl nodded cautiously; Xena released her and helped her sit up. "I just saw Draco, over by Helen's old windows—" She squawked breathlessly as Gabrielle snatched at her armor and hauled the warrior down flat on top of her.

"Draco? Xena, tell me you're kidding."

"You really think *I* could mistake Draco, even in the dark?"

Gabrielle snorted, clearly irritated. "I'm *not* going there!" Her fingers tightened, her voice rose to a squeak. "Xena, don't let him see me!"

"Gabrielle—it's dark enough out here, no one could see you unless he tripped over you!" the warrior whispered. It was her turn to sound irritated.

"Well, golly gee, I'm *sorry*!" Gabrielle didn't sound sorry at all. "But if you happen to remember, the last time I saw him was when we were trying to protect all those virgin priestesses, and he—ah, he—"

"I know, Gabrielle. He decided you were the hottest thing since Vulcan's forge, right?" Xena bit back a smile; Gabrielle clearly found no humor in the entire incident. Nor had she ever fully accepted Xena's explanation about Cupid; his son, Bliss; all those arrows, the most unlikely types falling for each other. Draco and Gabrielle; no more likely than a village boy and his neighbor's cow . . . "It's been a while since Draco went nutty over you, Gabrielle. Maybe he's lost interest."

"As *if*. If you don't mind, I'm not taking the chance," Gabrielle retorted. "Listen, I've changed my mind; show me how to get around to the front of the palace in case I need to. You go get Joxer and bring him out, okay?"

"If you insist," Xena replied gravely, but she quickly gave the necessary instructions, then turned away, her mouth twitching. "I'll be as quick as I can, Gabrielle, and I'll get him out. But just in case I don't—stick with him, will you? I mean, he's Joxer, but, still?"

"What, do I get another dinner out of this?" Gabrielle demanded sarcastically. The guard moaned and began scrabbling around; she brought her staff around and down on his head, hard. Xena winced, then waited as the silence stretched. Gabrielle shoved the staff aside, where she could reach it quickly at need and sighed heavily. "Xena, I—all right. I understand, it's important—"

"Gabrielle," the warrior said quietly, one hand on her shoulder. "It really is. Do you think I'd put you at even the least bit of risk to keep *Joxer* safe? If there wasn't an incredibly good reason for it?"

"I—all right." Gabrielle smiled up at her. Their eyes met; the smile faded. "Xena?"

"Yes?"

"I—be careful in there, will you?"

Xena came back to one knee and drew her friend briefly close. "Gabrielle, it's me, remember? Careful isn't part of what I do. But I'll be all right. I won't leave you alone, not here or now."

"Good." Gabrielle swallowed hard. "Don't, all right? Not now. Not—any time soon, if you don't mind." She forced a smile. "I mean, it's so hard to get you to pay up on these meals."

Xena grinned broadly, wrapped an arm around her friend's shoulders, ran hard knuckles across her bangs. "Yeah, I know. Especially when it's eel, right?" Before Gabrielle could find anything to say besides "owwww!" or "cut it out!", the warrior was gone, crouched low and moving in utter silence. Gabrielle caught one brief glimpse of her, sliding past the darkened windows of the king's apartments, and then she was gone.

Behind her, the guard stirred again. She cast her eyes heavenward, clubbed him back into Lethe, land of forgetfulness. *Or, is it a river?* she wondered. Didn't matter. By the smile on his silly-looking young face, the dream must've been a good one.

Xena moved quickly and quietly, gliding from shadow to shadow, easing her way through the formal gardens until she stood on the low balcony to Helen's apartments. Once there, she froze, holding her breath, listening for any least sound. Nothing. Still, she decided finally not to chance it: With all these supposed heroes crowding the palace, Menelaus might have left a guard inside the chambers, to keep his motley assortment of guests from getting inside to savor the atmosphere and perhaps gain a vision of some kind. Of course, Avicus might actually encourage that kind of thing; it would fit with his supposed service to the god of visions. In which case, again, the chamber wouldn't be empty.

She rolled her eyes heavenward, leaned against the wall. "I hate second-guessing a lousy priest," she snarled under her breath.

All of that supposed that Helen was the goal. "Who knows, maybe Menelaus really has started collecting expensive and pointless little bits of pottery and gold." She sighed. "You'll know soon enough. Go." She stalked quietly past the billowing curtain and moved on.

Draco had been a familiar, backlit form two balconies farther along from Helen's. *Odd,* Xena thought as she eased her way along the deeply shadowed wall, pausing now and again to listen intently. *He's a warlord, not a prince. Why house him in a royal's apartments?* This palace had plenty of guesting chambers, but most of them had the least favorable northern view, and they were some distance from the west-facing suites.

As she had good reason to know. *No reason to tell Gabrielle that I spent a night in one of those chambers, while Menelaus tried to convince me to use my army against rebel forces high in the hills.* He hadn't convinced her, of course—even though he'd offered her a fortune for the job. Even then, she had felt no urge to put her men at the beck and call of the noble and powerful, who were often no better than the warlords she called allies or enemies. *They're still scum and pigs. They just dress better.*

The corner of her mouth quirked; if not for Menelaus trying to use her the way he used almost everyone, she possibly would never have seen the fabled Helen at the supposed height of her beauty. Even though, as she'd told Gabrielle, she never did get to sit at his table. *My table manners were bad back then, my taste in food worse . . .* Menelaus's real reason, of course, was that he didn't want gossip to spread, or word to reach the rebels about his potential ally.

A Spartan banquet was never anything to brag about, anyway.

She let that go, eased beyond the king's long balcony, waited silently on the far side for some moments. No sound from within, but at an hour like this, the rooms would be empty: servants using their little free time to eat or relax, the king entertaining guests or closeted with his commanders or his priest.

She moved on. The drape where Draco had been was just another dark shadow. In the distance she could hear a horse moving quietly toward the gates, two guards passing in the distance, their spears clattering against their bronze-clad legs. Menelaus's guard-captain was getting lax; she shouldn't have heard those two until they were right on top of her.

Behind her, a sudden, sharp *clack!* that might be a hardened wood staff slamming into another guard's hard head. Xena sighed. Gabrielle was certainly in a sour mood—though she had reason for it. It would definitely be a good thing if they made it out of Sparta together, Joxer firmly in tow.

Unless I learn something in here that changes all that. The king's garden would not have been the best place to explain such a strategy to Gabrielle, though—not while she was so angry. Some of *that* little problem could be solved by a decent meal and some serious sleep. She glanced back toward the rose garden: nothing to be seen there but plant shadows, moving in the light breeze. At least it was quiet.

You're stalling, she suddenly realized. *What, you're afraid of Draco?* She grinned wickedly, flexed her hands, checked her weapons to be certain nothing was too loose or too tight, and pushed past the curtain, immediately backing against the nearest wall so her eyes could adjust to a deeper darkness. But it wasn't, really, that dark. There was a small oil lamp set in a deep niche against the far wall; it cast very little light her way but illuminated most of the room—enough that she could tell she was the only person in it. The main room itself was large, with two smaller alcoves flanking the niche.

97

The walls had been whitewashed, and the furnishings were of quality but plain—which was useful. No gauzy drapes, no tables set at awkward intervals with flowers, baskets, or vases atop them, no heavy hangings around the bed or anywhere else, except the single cloth across the balcony opening. Useful, since it meant there was nowhere anyone could be hiding in here.

She waited another long moment anyway, to be certain the alcoves—a privy and a linen store—were also empty, then edged along the wall, eyes moving between the double doors on the inner wall, the curtains over the balcony entrance that billowed out as the wind shifted, and a small pile of goods on the room's single table— a simple black slab of wood, highly polished. She crossed to it. At one end, a flat gold-and-black–worked dish on a pedestal held a small bunch of fruit: a few cherries, some dry-looking dates, a brownish banana peel. Some long, crisp-looking grapes. She broke off one of the grapes, bit into it and let her eyes close as she savored it: It was sweet, fragrant, and crunched under her teeth—pure bliss. She snatched up the rest of the bunch and squatted to check out the goods at the other end of the table as she ripped the individual fruits from their tethers and popped them into her mouth.

The pack was Draco's, she'd know it anywhere—it and the black leather vest strewn carelessly onto the floor. The room smelled faintly of the oil he rubbed into his muscles and the stuff he used on his hair, anyway. She closed her eyes briefly, inhaled. *Nice.* Even if the entire package included Draco—his arrogance, his swagger, his absolute self-assurance of how pretty-boy cute he was, never mind his utter certainty, she'd come back to his side of the coin, return to her old, dark ways—she'd spent some extremely pleasant hours surrounded by that scent.

Get a grip! she ordered herself, half amused and half irritated. She shook her head to clear it, dropped the empty grape stem next to the banana peel, then crossed to the door to listen. Somewhere, faintly away to her left, she could hear armor clattering—another of the king's crack guard squadron, no doubt. But it was probably sound coming from the other side of the palace, if not on the grounds outside the north-facing windows: The notoriously cheap Menelaus had never bothered to post guards in his household quarters and in fact was known to dislike having soldiers around the one place where he could close himself off from the world and relax. She began counting on her fingers, ears still attuned to the world beyond the doors: The last time she'd been in Sparta, there had been a barracks of no more than fifty to patrol the walls and man the gates and another, larger barracks half a day's ride away, guarding the frontier to the southeast, near the sea. Most of his fighting force was kept there or in the beacon towers that connected his mountainous realm. Ten or so guards were all that were needed to keep peace within the city walls—which included the men who made an hourly circuit of the palace—and about that many again who dealt with the farmers, herders, and minor nobles outside the gates on what little arable land surrounded the city.

And another ten—sometimes fewer, and all of them older and specially trained—who served inside the palace. Menelaus wasn't the type to have patience with young, awkward armsmen who couldn't keep from tripping over their pikes.

She edged the doors open slightly, listened, and finally peered out. The hallway was as she remembered it: long, narrow and straight, the ceiling high and vaulted. A few large decorative clay urns dotted the tiled floor along the plain walls, no apparent pattern to the arrangement. Other than the urns, and oil lamps or torches set every twenty or so paces, there was no ornamentation—no place to duck out of sight.

Which meant, if a warrior wanted to remain as unnoticed as she had her last trip through this end of the palace, she'd better move quickly, once out in the open.

She paused another long moment, reviewing what she recalled of the palace layout: The main reception, with its massive circular fireplace, the king's throne—and a small, secret chamber just behind that throne for the king's priest—were to her right. Left: The corridor that led to the guest apartments, and to the priest's grubby little single chamber. *I won't trust that last one; Avicus probably has his own royal suite these days, across from the king's—with hidden doors and a tunnel to connect them.*

The clatter of armor came again—this time she could place it, outside the palace, moving back toward the main gates. *Good*, she decided. Unless it was the guard she'd left with Gabrielle. *The mood Gabrielle's in, I very much doubt he'll be awake before midday tomorrow.*

The next question was how to find Joxer, which way to go first? She considered this, finally opted for the right. Chances were good that at this hour, Menelaus was in one of the public chambers, possibly eating with his potential heroes or testing them, and that would mean one of the banquet rooms or the reception.

And Joxer might be just about anywhere in this warren of hallways and rooms. *Unless he's back in that tavern near where we came over the wall—or another. You don't know Menelaus is keeping them in the palace, or even why Draco's here. It might be he's here for something completely different—another bunch of rebels to be smoked out of the hills, maybe.*

Joxer could even be somewhere here in the royal wing, set up in style like Draco. *There's a picture, Joxer wrapped in silk, sprawled across a rich man's bed, choosing which fruit to devour next . . . Now, that's scary!* Worse: It would give him inspiration for more verses to that ridiculous song of his. The verses she'd heard coming south, trying to catch up to Gabrielle, were bad enough.

She looked both ways one last time, checked the release on her chakram, and slipped into the open, moving sideways as quickly as possible, back to the east wall, glancing often back the way she'd come.

Spooky, she decided as she slid into shadow near the main reception. *It's been much too easy getting in here. Hope that doesn't mean it's gonna be a lot harder getting out.* Because it would be better to get out unnoticed, if possible. She bared her teeth in a mirthless grin as she eased into a darkened corner, behind an enormous, badly done gold statue of Apollo—the god's shoulders weren't the same height or size, and he had a definite squint.

There were guards at the main double-doored entry, of course. But she knew there was another way: the hidden vantage Helen had sought on the evening a younger Xena was staying in this palace and had decided it was only sensible to learn as much about the building—and its owner—as possible. Apparently, the queen used the ancient and forgotten opening to learn what Menelaus was up to.

I shoulda talked to her, then. Should have . . . It didn't matter, at this point. The warlord Xena hadn't had any patience with the notion of a young pedestal bride, es-

101

pecially one as slender, honey-skinned, and incredibly beautiful as the extremely feminine Helen. *As if I hadn't known even then that no woman of her class gets to choose the man she marries.*

The heavy curtain still lined the north wall and covered the narrow passage that ran behind the reception; it unfortunately could not have been shaken out or dusted since the last time she'd seen it. Pinching the bridge of her nose with one hand, the other moving constantly to keep cobwebs out of her hair and eyes, Xena covered the narrow little passage in record time.

At its far end was a window opening at waist height— a now-interior window that might once, when the palace was much smaller, have been part of the outer wall. Xena eased up onto the broad sill, drew her legs in close so that they couldn't be seen if someone should just chance to glance down the passage, and eased down flat, edging slowly forward until she could see down into the reception.

The room was an enormous square: The ceiling was flat, relatively low, held up by rows of plain stone columns. Directly across from her, Xena could see the glow of fire some distance away—a thin, flickering ribbon of it in the enormous circular fireplace that was open to the outdoors on one side and overhead. Previous kings had doubtless held banquets around the hearth or allowed their trusted soldiers and officers to cook skewers of meat over those flames, as a sign of favor or as a reward for some special service. As a way to bind men to them with more than a pay packet.

She'd been at one such meal in Pylos, when a distressed Nestor had tried to get her to resolve the disappearance of Helen before war was declared. *Yeah, you couldn't have made a difference, even if you'd wanted to, back then,* she told herself sourly. *When hard men want to go to war, there's no force can stop them.* Nestor was one of the old kings; he should have known as much.

Menelaus left his own great hearth cold and dark most days of the year, or so she heard. *Too cheap to send men to bring in the wood for it; too mistrustful of his men to allow them even the pretense of that kind of trust and closeness between a ruler and his protectors.*

So far as she could tell—it was difficult to see much, for the rows of pillars and the shadows everywhere but the central rank that led from outer doors to throne— there were only two men in the room at present.

Menelaus stood half-turned toward her. He was unmistakable: tall and gaunt, a granite shard of a man. He still dressed in his favored blood-red knee-length tunic under bronze and leather armor, and even within his own house, he wore a broad-bladed sword and two thick-hafted knives in a wide, black leather belt. But the once-dark brown short beard and moustache, and the close-cropped hair, were shot with gray.

The king suddenly began to pace, gesturing broadly, angrily; his brows were drawn together. Something, apparently, not going as he wanted it to go.

Facing him, a study in stillness and confidence, arms folded across a bright sun-yellow robe, the priest Avicus stood in midchamber, only his head moving to keep Menelaus in view as the king paced. At his back a tripod of wrought black metal and atop it, a black stone bowl filled with water or oil—liquid of some sort that oddly gave no reflection from her vantage, though it should have at least shown the shadows as Menelaus paced.

Xena's eyes narrowed and her fingers curled into the stone sill. *Avicus. All these years, and you haven't changed one bit, you bastard,* she thought flatly. At least, not from this distance. The priest was a full head shorter than his king and in much better condition: there was good muscle under that robe, she knew from their last enounter—and indeed from their first. But it was obvious: expensive, filmy fabric clung to impressive shoulders and upper arms. *Avicus, you've come up in the world since you ran the god-machines for the Athens theater, deceiving the public with your tricks and cheap magic. You're wearing silk.*

His neck was as solid as ever, and it was clear he still tapered from a muscled torso, much as Hercules did, even though the priest was noticeably shorter. This was a man who kept himself in top fighting condition, even though Apollo never asked that of those who served him.

His light brown hair was cut like the king's—battle-short. Pale, intense blue eyes were hooded at this distance, but she could readily see the slightly upturned corners of his mouth; she'd seldom seen him without that half-smile in place, in his eyes if not on his lips. He stood with his back to the black stone bowl, flanked by two lanterns that suddenly spluttered, then began to burn with a bluish flame. They cast odd shadows and made strange shapes across the liquid, which itself moved as if a faint wind blew across it. Xena wrenched her eyes away from the fascinating surface: So far as she could tell, there was no air moving at all.

Two angry voices out there—one harsh, the other genial, even, slightly resonant and higher in pitch. She eased herself even flatter, fingers clinging to the stone as she edged foward, ears straining to make sense of their conversation. There seemed to be a trick to the air in this niche, though. No wonder Helen had used it, because once her chin rested against the inner ledge, she could hear nearly as well as if she stood between the two men.

The king's harsh Spartan accent and the priest's habit of speaking quietly and quickly would require total concentration, though. She glanced behind her to make sure the area behind the niche was still dark, then fixed her whole attention on the chamber below her.

". . . and I still fail to understand, Avicus, why you chose to send *my* men on a personal mission for you, to find this person, this—this—surely no grown man could possibly be called Joxer? What kind of name is that?"

"It was either his mother's sense of humor, or his own, Highness," came the smooth response. "I didn't care enough to find out; what matters is, he's here."

"You're mad, priest! Even I have my resources beyond my dead brother's lands, and I know this Joxer travels with—"

"—with Xena, and the nattering little companion she seems to have traded for a dark army, Highness. Yes, I know that also, are you surprised?" The priest widened his pale eyes; the smile stayed where it was, small, neat and secretive. "Don't be—isn't that why you recently moved me from that hellish, narrow little chamber the size of a tomb, all brown rough walls and badly woven brown goat-hair carpets, and put me in surroundings where I can more properly work the god's wonders, and interpret his visions? I mention that to remind you that I realize my indebtedness to you, Highness." His eyes crinkled at the corners; the smile broadened. "But in this matter, I'm hardly practicing insurrection, Highness. I knew of the man Joxer, I knew he could be reached and suborned if he were dealt with in the right way, of course, and so I had your men approach him—and they in turn sent him on to you. A—a gift, if you will."

"No, thank you. Priest."

"He could be useful, Highness." Silence, as the two locked eyes. Finally, the priest shrugged. "Well, yes, he *is* traveling most days with Xena. And he seems to have a child's concept of truth, right, and good: There aren't any in-between areas where a lie is bad here and good there, if you will. Still: If he's given the right vision, he'll be ours. And if you recall, you were the one who wanted an insight into the warrior princess's actions. Because of her journey to Troy, those last days, and her—"

"Because it was Xena who stole *Helen* from under my nose, you needn't lesson *me*, priest!" Menelaus spun away from his companion and began pacing between the throne and the end of the length of carpet leading to it. Avicus watched him steadily, his expression giving away nothing. "All right," the king snarled finally. "He won't know anything useful, you realize. Unless the woman's changed greatly, she'll hardly be confiding in an oaf."

"She hasn't changed that much, Highness," the priest replied steadily. "I've *seen* her recently, her and the girl. You might be amused to hear—"

"Gossip, Avicus?" the king broke in harshly. The priest shrugged broadly and turned away; his eyes, Xena thought, were full of dark secrets; involuntarily, she shivered. She'd seen eyes like that before: the Furies, the Bacchae. She shook herself back to the moment; Menelaus was speaking again, less angry this time. "It doesn't matter, I don't care what the woman does, so long as she leaves me alone. Bringing this Joxer *here* will scarcely assure that—do you think?"

The priest's voice was suddenly sharp edged and commanding. "Hear me out, so please you, Highness. The facts are simple: You want Helen back, and Xena is no fool. Even if you cloak your search for the woman under the guise of a quest for the Ewer of Persephone, the box of Pandora, or the flaming cloak of Medea, you won't confuse *her*; she would eventually hear of it, and she would know your goal is Helen. And she will move to counter you."

"She'll fail," Menelaus gritted out between clenched teeth; his color was high. "Because nothing will keep me from fulfilling the promise I made before Troy—the promise I made when I wed the woman and brought her here." His eyes went distant; he paused, staring off into darkness. "Do you remember her, Avicus? When first I won over her family and brought her here? She was slender as a reed, with eyes that could drown a man in their dark pools, beauty that had even my cold-blooded brother Agamemnon ready to give over his wife and children and challenge me for the right to wed her." He snarled a curse under his breath. "As if he or any other man could have won her or taken her home, once I saw her! As if any other man in all the world had earned the right to call her his wife! I knew from the very first moment I set eyes upon her that bastard child or no, daughter of Zeus or no, she was mine and would never be any man's but mine!" He considered this, laughed briefly; his voice sounded like chill water over pebbles. "Agamemnon knew; he understood when he saw us together, and *still* he would have taken her, if he could— why do you think I made that pact, that any man who stole her from me could expect to see all the suitors and all their armies march against him? Did you think I meant it against Odysseus, all devoted to his whey-faced Penelope and their newborn whelp?"

"Your brother has paid," Avicus pointedly reminded the king. "Not just for his lustful appreciation of your *wife*, but for his choice of measures to set the fleet against Troy, and for his choice in Trojan captives.''

The king snorted. ''My brother thought with his loins, and his desire for glory blinded him to what good things he had. He had a good family and he had Mycenae in all its fertile glory. For him to sacrifice his only child in order to turn the winds, when there might have been another way—ah, blast it to Hades!'' he snarled, and turned away, fingers tight against his nose, clasping his tight-closed eyes.

Xena, in her hiding place, raised both eyebrows. *What: The bloodless, heartless Spartan king just possibly cared for his brother's daughter?* The girl had come from Mycenae expecting to marry one of the Greek heroes; she'd died as a blood sacrifice, because men believed they'd never reach Troy otherwise. At least Helen hadn't known about that. She could hope the woman didn't know.

Xena closed her eyes briefly, swallowed, then turned her attention back to the matter in hand: Learn what Menelaus was up to; get Joxer out of the middle of it. Do all she could to be sure the king didn't find Helen . . . *Though how I'm gonna do that, when I don't even know where she is . . .* She was no longer sure ignorance of the queen's whereabouts was her best course—but she could worry about that later, once she and Joxer were out of here; once she had Gabrielle safely out of Sparta.

Agamemnon . . . you died too easily, ugly as it was. I hope you rot in Tartarus! She eased back from the opening to draw a deep, steadying breath, counted to twenty, then moved back where she could see and hear.

King and priest had moved on to other matters: Menelaus now sat on his throne, and Avicus moved seemingly at random—up the three steps and down again, over to his brazier or mirror, back to the steps, a few paces down the carpet, back again. "Remember that if we are to succeed, we need to keep the entire plan, my king."

"I plan to," Menelaus replied shortly.

The priest stopped on the second step. "You have the purse, then?" Menelaus merely looked at him, the set of his jaw stubborn. "I thought as much," the priest went on evenly, and produced a large leather pouch. He tossed it up, caught it one-handed; it jingled agreeably.

"I fail to see the reason I would *pay* those who fail to pass the test," Menelaus growled.

"For the same reason you and I will both gently let down those who do not pass it. Remember whom I serve, Highness! Despite your choice of allies in this last war, He has chosen to back you in this.

"Achilles and my brother, fighting over a chit of a girl—"

"Over a *virgin priestess* who served Apollo, Highness." The priest's voice hardened; the king eyed him narrowly. Avicus shrugged. "It doesn't matter; Apollo will feel as he chooses about the matter, and our feelings regarding this 'mere chit' count for nothing to him. He does not care greatly for Greeks, and not at all for Sparta." Silence. The king finally gestured for his companion to go on. "My reasoning is practical: Young men who are not chosen to quest for wonders will feel ashamed. But they will more likely return quietly to their villages and homes, and perhaps speak of the gracious king of Sparta to their friends and families, if they are treated well. Those who are scorned by such a king and sent upon the road without any hint of the ancient Greek courtesies—they will complain loudly and bitterly, and for long.'' The priest fixed his ruler with a chill eye. ''You have many enemies outside Sparta's boundaries, Highness, and not just those who resented your battle against Troy—for a mere woman. Do you really want them to learn you are about to embark upon another mission to seize that woman?'' Silence again; a chill one this time. ''Remember you were given this throne by Helen's father, when he chose you as her mate—do you believe Tyndareus will allow you to . . . ?''

''Allow? *Allow?*'' Menelaus slammed both hands flat on the arms of his throne with a ringing slap. ''How dare you suggest such a thing, priest? Remember that although *you* serve Apollo, there are others who do so as well!''

Avicus inclined his head, but when he brought it up again, Xena could see no submission in his eyes or the set of his jaw, though the faint smile was gone. ''Perhaps so, Highness,'' he murmured. ''But if you wish this quest to begin any time soon, I would suggest you utilize the tools you have, and not seek for others. They might be some time—some years—in arriving.'' Menelaus stirred; Avicus held up a hand. ''I don't threaten you in saying that, nor does the god. Practically speaking, it would be difficult to find a priest of Apollo who *would* serve the king of Sparta, whatever the god bade.''

''We waste time,'' the king growled finally. ''Everything takes too long, every day she is away from me, I know she grows older . . . a day less beauteous . . .'' He drew a deep, steadying breath and the fire went out of him. He settled his chin on one hand and waved the other. ''Bring in your candidates, priest. I remember as well as you the plan we created, and why. I won't break it.''

For answer, Avicus turned away and strode swiftly

down the aisle between the throne and the great doors, pushed one aside, and stepped briefly out of sight. When he returned, he was still alone, but just as he reached the dais and took his place behind the tripod and its odd bowl, the doors opened to a pair of household guards clad in impressive red and bronze, fully armored and armed. The boy between them looked very young; his clothing and the roughly cut thatch of reddish hair proclaimed him a villager. Round brown eyes stared in awe around him; the guards had to nudge him to get him moving.

It was Xena's turn to stare as Menelaus rose from his throne and came down from the dais to hold out his hands. The boy stared at the fabled king, at his extended fingers; one of the guards had to nudge him and whisper something to him before he held out his own hands, which the king clasped. The second guard approached the king and murmured something against his ear. Menelaus smiled. It wasn't a nice smile; probably he didn't *have* a nice smile, but the boy seemed dazzled. "My thanks, Eteocles, that you braved the roads and took such a journey to come to my aid. I can only hope that the sun god will read your heart truly and accept you as his own, for I have need of all such strong young heroes."

Behind them, unnoted by any but Xena, Avicus's mouth twisted slightly, and he cast up his eyes. But he was all smiles, charm, small pleasantries as the boy was brought over to him, to stand before the bowl. Eteocles's color was high; as the priest spoke reassuringly, the blush faded and the boy seemed more at home. Avicus brought him around to stand facing the bowl and across it, the king's dais; behind the boy, he made a small sign, crossing last and next-to-last fingers. The king inclined his head the least bit. The priest meanwhile was talking urgently and in a voice too low for Xena to catch more than a few isolated words: "... vision ... and if you ... pure of heart ... fitted for such a quest ..." His voice rose suddenly. "Understand, such a quest is not for everyone, and we could not tell if you were qualified until you came to this place. And that is why you were asked to travel here in secret, so that the god might test you."

"And—um ... if I fail?" The boy's voice was too high; he cleared his throat. Avicus gave him a bland smile.

"You do not fail. There is no failure, though you may not be chosen for this quest. That you were picked to come this far means you have courage and heart and strength, and that doubtless the god will call upon you in the future. When he has need, and the quest is one suited particularly to you."

"Oh ..." The boy considered this; a smile twitched his lips. "Then—then I'm ready to try, sir."

Avicus passed one hand across the bowl. "Look at the water, think of nothing, and tell me what you see."

"Water," Eteocles began doubtfully, then caught his breath in a gasp. "I—it's my mother, my village! She's—she's fallen, on the street, the bundles are scattered everywhere!" He jumped as the priest touched his arm.

"Allow me, Eteocles," he said as he smoothly switched their positions, so he could stare intently at the water. "Your mother, you say. Has she been ill?"

"N-no. But I—when I was chosen, I didn't want to tell her. My father died in the war, sir, and there's only been me and my two older brothers to help her, and then last winter a tree fell on my eldest brother, Eponium,

112

and he only died after a long and horrid winter. Suh—
so, she's clung to me, and, and I knew if I told her,
she'd cry until I said I'd never go, so I made my brother
Markus swear not to tell her until I was half a day
gone—and not to tell anyone else, sir," he added un-
happily.

Avicus nodded absently; his attention was on the
bowl, where now Xena could see odd little flashes of
lights; she averted her eyes. "It was brave and right of
you to come, boy, and Apollo thanks you for such courage. The God bids me say, though, that this is not the
quest for you. He says that there will surely be another,
and it will be in your homeland, where there will be no
need for you to make such unhappy choices. The lives
of many, and not just your mother, will hang on your
actions."

He turned from the tripod, drew a small bag of coins
from the purse now lying on the dais nearby, and held
it out to the boy. "There is a room for you to rest for
the night, and food; the guards will see you safely there.
This is for your trouble, and for your journey safely
home." He smiled; the boy smiled; the king rose from
his chair and smiled. Xena's mouth twisted. *It looks like
one of those stupid comedies Avicus used to do the
smokes and flying gods for, all the actors wearing smiley
masks. Disgusting.* "Go in peace, and wait for your
glory, Eteocles; it will surely come to you."

The boy drew himself up straight; if he was disap-
pointed, it didn't show. "Sirs, Majesty—I shall." He
returned to the guards and went out with them. Avicus
watched them go.

"Village puppy," Menelaus growled as the doors
closed. "I hope they won't *all* be so green, Avicus. Allow me to applaud your *waste* of time and ten coins!"

113

"On the contrary, Highness. The boy entered this chamber as a village oaf, but he left a hero, awaiting a quest. You may hear of him one day." He drew himself up straight as the doors opened again, and another village boy with a rough-cut shock of hair—black this time—came in between the guards.

7

Several would-be heroes followed, in quick succession, and Xena fought not to doze on the ledge: It was warm and stuffy up here, and she'd had little or no sleep the past nights, trying to catch up to Gabrielle before her close companion reached the city walls. Fortunately, she'd learned years earlier how to sleep upright in the saddle—a trick made simple when the mare was Argo. It had helped on the long journey south—but it wasn't enough.

The men below her weren't helping, either; the pattern between king and priest was repetitive, slow . . . dull. Most of the hopeful candidates were cast in the same mold as the first village boy who'd looked into the liquid, most not even as likely, though a few at least wore swords that looked as if they'd been used—and used by the current owners. *I hope that bowl of god-water isn't making me sleepy!* she thought, suddenly apprehensive—but she had actually only looked at it the once, and if Avicus's voice was having any effect on her at all, it was only to make her angry.

An older man named Cadmus was chosen, as was a boy who called himself Helarion; at that name, Xena eased forward to get a better look, but it wasn't the gangly young Athenian thief who'd believed himself the son of Hermes. *Better not be,* she thought grimly. *As much as Gabrielle and I both did to convince him to stay home with his mother and behave himself.*

The guards went back out, and Xena could hear raised voices beyond the open doors. Avicus turned at the king's angry question; he shrugged and went to check. He returned moments later, himself and a boy who looked even greener than Eteocles, but unlike that first village boy, this one wore a grimly determined look and a battered sword in a worn leather scabbard—the belt had been cut for a larger man. He advanced to the dais and inclined his head; at the priest's whispered comment, he nodded and bent one knee. The king eyed his priest over the boy's hair.

"This is Briax," Avicus said mildly. "He was not one of those initially chosen. But he claims to have heard the summons and asks the God's judgment."

Silence. Menelaus transferred the blank look from priest to Briax, who stood and gazed levelly back at him. *Too young and naive to be afraid, too village-green to know how to address a king*, Xena decided. "Briax, are you?" Menelaus asked finally. The boy nodded. "And tell me, Briax, why should my priest give the test to one who has come here unasked?"

"But—but there *was* no asking in my village of Katerini," Briax replied in a resonant voice that wobbled a little and now and again threatened to break. "The priest of the sun god, A-Apollo, he came to the small temple we have, but not when he usually does, at midsummer. He—went among us early in the day, and he

116

asked s-some of us to come to the temple at midday. And—and he told us of this quest.''

"What did he say?" Avicus prompted when the boy fell silent.

"He—told us the king in Sparta needed help, that something of great value to him and—and to Apollo had been lost, and that he had come to seek out young men—unmarried, he said, because they should be puh-pure." He swallowed; his color was rather high. "And brave, he said. Because they—they would need to dedi—desi—*give* their lives over to Apollo, and that still only one would be the man chosen to find the Holy Ewer of Persephone. And—and then he gave us a prayer, and then he left.''

Avicus laid a hand lightly on the boy's arm. "If the priest named you to come to the temple that morning, then he chose you to come here, Briax. Didn't you realize that?"

The boy shook his head. "He didn't say. Besides, I am—" he spread his hands, taking in his appearance. "I am no hero, I'm my father's youngest son. I scrub tables and cups in a tavern, I milk his goats. It seemed—foolish to even think—"

"You wear a sword," Avicus said mildly. "Can you use it?" Briax nodded; his mouth quirked.

"I can use it. It was—*is*—my father's. He'll be very angry when he finds it gone. He and my oldest brother have given me some lessons with it. But I will not lie, sir; I am no swordsman."

"Apollo did not ask for fighters, boy, only for those who had the courage to seek a lost thing of great value to Him. And yet, you are here now. Why?"

Briax drew a breath, let it out in a long sigh. His face shone, and so far as Xena could tell, he was no longer

117

aware of his surroundings. "Because I must. Because a maiden came to Katerini, in search of a hero. Oh, she was wonderful—glorious! All golden hair and storm-colored eyes—a smile radiant as the sun itself!" He suddenly blushed, swallowed, and ducked his head. "She also spoke of the quest, huh-Highness. And it was at that moment I knew, as if the god himself had told me, that I *must* come, to serve her, to honor her, to somehow make myself—ah—worthy, in her eyes. A little. Even if she never knows of it."

Menelaus stirred and would have spoken, but Avicus held up a warning hand. "You would take up such a journey—for love? Even knowing that the object of your love is unaware?" His voice was sardonic. Briax didn't seem to notice; he nodded. "To encounter dangers, monsters, the ire of the gods—all the pitfalls of such a quest—and for a woman who does not even know you care for her?" the priest asked. The boy paled at that, but he nodded emphatically, wide eyes fixed on the priest's face. Avicus smiled faintly and laid a benevolent hand on Briax's head. "Such bravery should not be turned aside now; nor would I dare shame you so. You shall indeed face the test, and let Apollo judge you. But tell me two things: First, does this maidenly vision have a name?"

Briax smiled brilliantly; king and priest blinked and up on her hidden perch, Xena groaned. *Wait for it*, she thought drearily. "Gabrielle," the boy breathed. "Her name is Gabrielle, she has hair of red-gold, a mouth—uh, a mouth—" He stuttered to a halt, drew a deep breath. "She passed through my village days after the priest, and she is both a bard and a warrior, if you can imagine it. I can, for when she spoke, even my father, who fought for Troy, dared not answer her. And—and she is—she is the most beauteous maiden I ever—''

"I have no doubt she is all of that," Avicus broke in with a genial pat on the boy's shoulder and a warning gesture that stopped a red-faced Menelaus from bellowing out what would surely have been a very unpleasant remark. "Also, you say the priest spoke of a need for purity. Are you?''

Briax blinked. "Am I—what, sir?''

"Why—pure. Remember, we two men do not judge you, but the god does, and he sees your heart and mind." Briax blushed a painful red.

"I—my father was a soldier, before Troy. A—a hard man. He—he told me so often since I had ten winters, as did my older brothers, a man was not a true man until he lost his—uh, his innocence. I—uh—I mean, um—'' His face was very red, but suddenly he drew himself upright and announced in a rush, "Last year I spent one night with a woman at the inn in Bacchia. For—for two copper coins.''

"Two copper coins." Avicus was visibly fighting hard not to laugh; fortunately, the boy didn't seem to notice. "I see. Well, I believe the God will judge your heart pure, whatever your body may be. So, let us see, shall we? Come with me, and let us put you to the test.''

High on her ledge, Xena let her face down onto her forearm and groaned again. "It's the hair, the eyes, the smile—Hades, it's the damned little stick, who knows?'' Poor Gabrielle had scooped up another live one, and she wasn't even fishing. She shook her head and edged back to where she could watch—and clearly hear what was going on.

"Gladly," the boy said with a rather sweet dignity. He squared his shoulders and went with the priest to

119

face the depths of the stone bowl. At the priest's soft urging, he gazed into the water for some moments. "How strange! I see—it appears to be a dish on a pedestal, like the good dish my father uses to serve fruit to the well-dressed. But this is—it is not plain pottery. It shines." He hesitated, glanced sidelong at the priest, who went somewhere behind the king's dais and brought back a red-and-blackware vase, a ruddy background with black figures upon it—a wrestling match, Xena thought. Hard to tell at a distance. But Briax was already shaking his head. "No, this—in there—it was black, but a black that shone, and gave off odd-colored reflections, greens and purples and—" He shrugged as words seemed to fail him. "Black without any people, sir," he said finally.

"Ahhhh." The priest smiled; the boy looked up expectantly. "And within the dish? Was there anything— or nothing?"

"There was—" Briax closed his eyes, considered this, finally nodded. "There were three tiny pieces of fruit—pomegranate seeds. I have seen them, though my father won't put them at his table; he calls them common. Three bright red seeds—nothing else," he said finally. And stared at his feet, waiting.

"You," Avicus said softly, "have seen the Sacred Ewer of Persephone." Silence. The boy considered this with a frown.

"Oh," he said finally. "Was this Persephone a hero? My village has no tales of . . ."

"It is an old tale, only important because the god of the underworld stole Persephone, daughter of Demeter— ah, you *have* heard of Demeter?" he asked warily. The boy nodded; he seemed to be on safer ground here. "The girl ate a single seed of the pomegranate while she was in the dark god's keeping, and because of that, she could only return to earth three seasons of four—which is why we have winter, young Briax.''

Xena's mouth twitched. The priest made a smooth-voiced, half-decent story of the ancient tale, but he was clearly annoyed by the young man's ignorance. Mene-laus merely looked bored, his hand propping up his head and his eyes glazed. The smile—a toothy gash between nose and chin—hung there forgotten.

Xena's mouth quirked in an irritation of her own. *So he doesn't know the old stories. So what? He has a life, and memorizing all those tales about the gods wouldn't put food in his family's mouths. Come on, let's get this moving, get Joxer in here and back out again, so I can grab him and go!*

But the priest was finally finishing up with the boy; the king straightened and managed a slightly more natural-looking smile as Avicus gave the boy back over to the guards for escort to wherever they were keeping the winners of this little contest for the night. The doors closed behind the three.

Avicus sighed heavily and turned his eyes ceiling-ward. ''What do they teach them in those villages?'' he asked.

Behind him, the king snorted. ''I hope you had a good reason for that little show. You were practically cooing at that boy. It was obscene!''

''It was also useful, Highness. You heard what he said. Remember the name he spoke?''

''I wasn't listening. Why should I?''

''Fortunately, *one* of us was,'' the priest said evenly. ''How many blond warrior-bards named Gabrielle do you suppose there are? I know of one—and she travels with Xena.'' The king came halfway to his feet, but before he could speak, Avicus turned away; there was a commotion beyond the doors.

Menelaus was aware of it now, too. "Why are my guards *singing* out there? I don't permit that kind of noise! Avicus, see to it, shut them up!"

High above them, Xena gritted her teeth and moved back from the edge as the priest strode across the reception and flung open the doors. It didn't help much: She could still hear the horrid cacophony of untrained male voices bellowing out a familiar refrain—and overriding them, a reedy tenor voice shouting, "No, no, no! It's 'Joxer the *Mighty*'! Try it again, all—right?" The last word came out as a high squeak.

The warrior leaned against the wall and briefly closed her eyes. "That's it, I've had it," she snarled softly. "Nobody should have to put up with *this*. I'm gonna walk outta here, right now. I'm gonna go find a ship and sail off to—no, I'm gonna go find a lake, nice high-country lake, and I'm gonna fish for the next moon-cycle and a half!" She bit her lower lip, drew a deep breath, let it out slowly, and let herself down flat again to see and hear what was happening in the reception. *Sure, you're gonna do just that. Gabrielle's down in Helen's roses, waiting for you, and Helen's out there somewhere* . . . And even though Joxer probably deserved a good mangling, she couldn't just stand back and let someone else mangle him. *That's Gabrielle's job. But if we get through this and I find that lake, I'll throw him in and hold him down until he—naah, it would kill the fish.*

Down in the reception, Joxer had removed his ridiculous helmet and now bowed very correctly before the dais. Apparently, Avicus had given him a rough coaching on the way up the room, because he was surprisingly terse, answering questions with a simple, "Yes, Highness," "No, Highness," and "Joxer the Mighty, Highness." But even that last was delivered without fanfare, and he looked almost meek as he took his place by the bowl.

To Xena's surprise, however—and apparently to Joxer's—what he saw in the bowl wasn't the supposed Sacred Ewer. "I—it's a woman," he said, and he stared intently. "Gosh, is it ever a woman!" Avicus held up a warning hand, and Menelaus sank back onto his throne. "She's—there's a stone wall behind her . . ." He went on for some moments, then added, "Wait, it's—she's crying. I mean, I *think* she is. Maybe she's just got something in her eye . . ." Avicus hissed something against his ear, and he fell quiet for some moments.

"Tell me," the priest said softly. "What is she wearing?"

Joxer tittered. "Not much, that's for sure, because, you can see all the way down to—oh. I mean, it's a dress! Well, something white. And a necklace of some kind—"

"Describe it," the priest demanded.

"Well—it's gold, I guess. Long and skinny, with a big red stone at one end hanging right between her—"

"And the other end?" the priest asked hastily. Menelaus's eyebrows were drawn together and his knuckles white where his fingers dug into the arms of his throne.

"The—oh, I see it, it's kind of in her hair. It's a flat piece of gold with—with letters on it, or something. And—uh, it looks like a pile of wood or something, like a bonfire? Maybe?" He stepped back from the bowl as the priest pressed him aside; he frowned at the far wall, then transferred the perplexed gaze to Avicus. "So— who's *she?* I—excuse me, but I thought there was—it was this sacred bowl, or something? With three gold pomegranate seeds? I mean, if she had anything like that with her, I didn't see it.''

Avicus moved his hand, urgently indicating something to the king—probably Menelaus was supposed to say something at this point. But a glance let him see the man was fighting a full-blown jealous rage. The priest drew his latest bowl-gazer aside and said, ''That? The ewer, you mean? That was—a story we came up with to hide the real quest, Joxer. Only those the god Apollo blesses with a genuine vision—such as you—can be allowed to hear the truth. But you must swear first, here and now, to reveal it to no one.''

''Well—yeah. Sure,'' Joxer replied. He looked even more bewildered than ever.

''Swear,'' the priest said flatly, ''upon this.'' He held out a small disc, a golden sun in splendor that was half the size of his palm.

''Ah—okay.'' At the other's indication, Joxer laid his right hand on the thing, then snatched it back. ''Oww! That's hot!'' He sucked his fingers. ''What is it?''

The priest looked amused, Xena thought; his pale eyes were very wide and that secretive little smile turned the corners of his mouth. ''It is not hot, merely warm. A surprise, no doubt. It is Apollo's gift to you—and his warning. Remember the god sees everything, and he will know if you break your vow. The heat—well, the sun is hot, isn't it? Hot as fire? Which can shrivel a man to nothing but a pile of ash?'' Joxer stared down at the bit of gold and swallowed hard. ''Come,'' Avicus said, and now he also sounded amused. ''You need only swear the oath, and keep it, to tell no one—even those in the guesting chambers you see tonight, or later on your journeys. Remember that—easy enough, isn't it?'' Warily, Joxer laid his hand palm down on the priest's upturned one and mumbled the words. ''Good. Now.'' Avicus passed one hand over the badge and suddenly slapped it onto Joxer's shoulder armor, where it shimmered briefly, then faded to silver. All at once, unless she looked hard, Xena couldn't see it any more. From a much closer distance, by his startled expression, neither could Joxer.

"It is also a token of King Menelaus's trust in you," Avicus went on after a moment. "And there are those you may meet during your journey who will be able to see it and will name it." He glanced cautiously around, tugged at the ties of Joxer's leather jerkin, and pulled his head down so he could whisper against the taller man's ear. "Remember that word—but keep it to yourself! Apollo will not need the badge to cause you *great* pain, if you speak that word aloud to any, except the man who gives it to you first, do you understand?"

"Ah—got it." A rather pale Joxer nodded vigorously and loosened the ties a little. "I *remember* the word, but I don't *use* it, except if someone *else* uses it on *me* first—and if I get it wrong, Apollo hurts me. Right?"

"Exactly." The priest smiled at him. "By that exchange, you will know they are his men, or mine, and you can trust them. Though even to them . . . ?"

Joxer nodded as the priest hesitated. "I know, I get it, I say nothing—right? Except the word—except only after *they* use it?"

"Exactly." Avicus drew the erstwhile hero with him, away from the bowl and back over to the front of the dais. "You asked who the woman was. My king—Highness, I think you can tell him best."

Menelaus had control of himself again—more or less, Xena amended to herself as the king cast his priest a black look. His mouth twitched then, and he shielded his eyes with one hand. "That," he murmured in a broken voice, "was my wife. Helen."

Joxer stared for a long moment, his mouth slack; the priest nudged him and he blinked, then smiled hugely. "Ahhh—*that* was Helen? I mean, that was *Helen?* I mean—wow!" He thought this over; a nervous smile twitched his face. "I mean, that was your—*wife*, Helen. I—ah—well, you know, if I said anything that sounded a little, um, disrespectful. I mean—if you—I mean—" He probably would've gone on like that for the rest of the night, Xena thought tiredly. The priest allowed him to stutter to a momentary silence, then gripped his forearm to get his attention—a hard grip, by the pained look on Joxer's face.

"You did indeed see Helen, fairest woman in all the lands, and the queen of Sparta," he intoned.

Joxer nodded eagerly. "Yeah, and of Troy, too, right?" Avicus eyed the king sidelong and eased Joxer around, where he couldn't see Menelaus's suddenly savage face; with his free hand, the priest gesticulated sharply, a complex gesture. Menelaus clamped his teeth together, sat back, and began breathing deeply, eyes closed.

"Allow me to tell you—without interruption, please!—" the priest added sharply as Joxer drew a breath. He lowered his voice a little and drew his companion a few steps away from the dais. "King Menelaus was broken-hearted when he returned from Crete and found her gone—kidnapped by the Trojans. He still is. I know!" he said, as Joxer would have spoken again. "Ten years and more. But is it so hard to see?"

"Well—actually," Joxer began apologetically. Avicus gripped his arm again.

"Please. Close your eyes, let me create it for you. See yourself and the woman you love—or a woman you could love, the very ideal of woman—see her married

126

to you and then, suddenly, one day, you return home from a journey to discover the man you received as a guest has left your home—and taken your wife with him. Imagine your pain, your anger, knowing she is a captive, stolen by a younger man who believes all he must do is bed her, and she will come to love *him* instead. Imagine you cross the sea with a fleet of ships and all the allies you can find, to bring her home. But the other man also has an army and great walls to keep him safe while he works to turn your beloved against you.

"Imagine how long ten years are; you fight and sometimes you win ground and sometimes the enemy does, but at last the gods are with you, and you overcome the enemy's city." Joxer, eyes closed, was swaying in place, clearly caught up in the story. "And then, one of your allies creates a plan that will let you reach her with the least chance of harm coming to her—and only then do you learn that she has come to believe the lies her captor told her: that you married her only for the chance to be king of Sparta, that you cared for her only as an object of beauty, like an expensive vase."

"Even worse: Imagine they have hinted to her—your wife, who once loved you and came happily to your bed—imagine that now she believes their lie that you would have preferred the company of her brother Pollux to hers."

"You mean, Paris or someone woulda told her that Menelaus was—"

"Something like that," Avicus put in quickly.

"Wow," Joxer breathed. He considered this, his brow furrowed. "But, ah—you know, not to doubt your story or anything, but that's not exactly the way I heard it."

"Of course you heard another side of the story. From Xena or her companion Gabrielle?" Avicus smiled, man-to-man; Joxer's mouth twitched in a nervous smile and he shrugged. "Well, Xena fought for the Trojans, you know; she's hardly an unbiased source—she has her own reasons to make the king look bad, don't you think? And think about it. Xena's a warrior. This Gabrielle, wouldn't she be more likely to tell the story so it made Xena happy? Just how good would Xena look in a story where an older husband discovered his young bride stolen by a handsome young man—but after long trials, the girl returned home to her loving husband, to remain a happy wife? Especially when the older man is a man Xena hates as much as she hates King Menelaus?"

"She does? I mean—yeah . . . that makes sense, I guess," Joxer said doubtfully. Avicus smiled broadly and clapped him on the back, driving the air from his lungs.

"Don't take my word for it, Joxer; unlike Xena or her companion, I don't want a quick, emotional reaction from you. Just—think about it."

"All right." Joxer looked up. "So—what am *I* supposed to do about Helen? I mean, if she didn't come back from Troy, doesn't that mean—ah, well, you know?" He glanced at the throne and more or less discreetly drew a hand across his throat.

Avicus was already shaking his head. "I have my ways of knowing she lives. Trust me. But I also know she will not return to Sparta of her own will."

"Wait—I thought you said she was in love with King Menelaus?"

"She was and is. She has been lied to by the Trojans, and because she is young and was emotionally upset, she believed the lies. Once she learns they are lies, however . . ."

"So—what? Am I supposed to tell her all that? Or do you want me to *drag* her back?"

Xena bit back a grin, even though the overall situation was far from humorous. By the set of the priest's shoulders and the tendons standing out along the back of his neck, he'd had about enough of Joxer—and it served him right. But he somehow kept the tension out of his voice. "Of course not. King Menelaus's heart is broken, but he understands her fears, and he would never wish to force her in any way." *As if,* Xena thought flatly. "Though—if you would be willing to carry a message from him to her, I know he would be grateful." Joxer's brows drew together; Avicus spread his hands. "Merely a vow of his continued love and his hope that she will at least agree to meet him in some neutral kingdom, to listen to what he has to say.

"No, it's another matter entirely, something the king only recently discovered. The neckace she was wearing—the piece you described? It is not jewelry. It is an heirloom of the king's family, an artifact from ancient days—nearly as ancient as the royal house of Thebes itself. It was—a gift, from Zeus to the woman Europa, when he carried her away. For Europa, it was protection, but it only protects the Atreidae—members of the king's family," he added in explanation as Joxer stared at him blankly. "It was only recently discovered missing when I conducted a funerary offering for the king's dead parents."

"Oh—okay. But why would Helen want a weapon or whatever if it wouldn't protect her anyway?"

"Because—you saw it, warrior. It resembles a necklace. No doubt on Helen, it is very striking. She was drawn to it from the first and never accepted the king's explanations why she could not have it or even wear it. The danger, you see, is that—well, if Helen were to grow angry with her husband and the chain was around her throat? Even if she were a great distance away? It would kill her.''

"Ahhh—I see." Joxer considered this briefly, then cast the priest a wary look. "Um—and what happens to the guy who is trying to talk her out of it, if the guy says something about Menelaus and she gets mad?" Avicus raised one eyebrow. Both Joxer's went up. "He— gets, ah—he gets—"

"You have an excellent grasp of the situation," the priest said smoothly. "The trick will be to present the subject so she does not become inflamed—but that should not be a problem for a man so, ah, attractive to women as you are. The greater danger is that once you have the chain in your possession, there will be those who learn of it and want to steal it from you . . .''

Joxer dismissed the latter with a wave of his hand and a smirk. "That," he said loftily, "will be *their* problem. Not mine.''

"I see we understand each other," the priest said, and turned to walk back toward the dais. "Come, let us at least offer you food and wine before you return to your quarters for the night." He gave the king a small nod, then snapped his fingers. Two servants came from the curtained alcove behind the throne first with two chairs, then with a small table and refreshments. Another servant brought a separate table for Menelaus, poured him wine, deftly arranged a cut loaf and fruit and left.

When the three men were alone again, Avicus gestured Joxer into one chair and took the other, poured wine for both, and offered him a plate of sliced meat and bread. "A fighter of your class must have worked up an appetite, coming here," he said, helping himself to a single piece of bread. Joxer nodded; his mouth was too full for speech. "But I wonder that you would leave your two women comrades behind . . . ?'' He let the question hang between them and under cover of the table made a slight gesture in the king's direction that, to Xena, clearly said *stay out of this and keep your mouth shut!* Couched in less inflamatory style, obviously.

Joxer shook his head, chewed and swallowed, washing food down with a deep swallow of wine. It must have been a strong one: He fought not to choke as his eyes bulged. "Ah—companions? Oh—yeah. Xena and Gabrielle. Well," he shrugged. "They have *important* things to do, they don't need—I mean," he amended carefully, eyes fixed on the table now, "I mean, I left them attending to a few—minor problems that were too—ah, petty for me to bother with." He shrugged; a corner of his mouth twitched. "You know how it is, a man like me can't solve everyone's problems, I gotta keep myself free and rested for times when—"

"When?" Avicus prompted as his companion scratched his head, suddenly at a loss for words.

Joxer glanced up and gave him a cavalier smile. "Oh, you know," he said easily. "Like the time Draco tried to steal the virgin priestesses of Hestia, to sell to a slaver? Well—" he visibly expanded. "Of course, he had to get through *me*."

Avicus smiled; his light eyes were very wide. "Really!" he said. "You amaze me. I had heard that Xena—"

Joxer preened. "Of course, I let her take the credit. She likes having the reputation—*you* know." High above him, the warrior's eyes narrowed as her fingers dug into stone. *No, Joxer*, I *don't know—but* you're *gonna know.* "So," Joxer went on expansively, "anyway, I don't think there's any problem—if you really do need my services on this quest, I mean. Of course,

I'm still a busy man, you know, even with Xena and Gabrielle handling the—petty stuff for me."

"How odd," the priest murmured. Xena had to crane her neck to catch his words. "Because I clearly saw a vision last night: Gabrielle, passing through the village Katerini, following you."

"Katerini? Gabrielle?" Joxer started. "You mean, she's—"

"Behind you, yes. She might even have reached Sparta by now."

"Sparta?" Joxer echoed. His eyes darted nervously as he considered this; then he sat back and gave the priest a would-be worldly smile. "I guess I shouldn't be surprised. Not to—ah—speak out of turn, but frankly—" he lowered his voice, "—I can't keep her off me."

I'm gonna kill him; this time, I'm really gonna—no. The warrior smiled grimly. *No, I'm not. I'm gonna tell Gabrielle exactly what you just said, Joxer.* The smiled widened briefly; her eyes glinted.

"Ah, of course—hardly surprising. I understand." Avicus finished his wine and rose in one fluid movement; Joxer blinked up at him, then staggered to his feet, nearly overturning the table. The priest righted it; Joxer, who'd half-tripped on his boots to get out of the way or catch the table, flailed and righted himself. "Well, Joxer," Avicus went on blandly. "We will rest more easily, knowing you are laboring to resolve this terrible situation." His free hand gestured in the king's direction, but he had to repeat the sign twice—sharply indeed—before Menelaus was capable of speech.

The king finally cleared his throat. "Yes, we—certainly shall." Avicus glanced at him but Menelaus's face was suffused and he clearly wasn't going to say anything else—anything else in the program, at least. The priest shrugged faintly and broadly gestured for Joxer to precede him back toward the outer doors.

8

The night was growing cool, and a chill wind blew across Sparta from the northwestern crags, sending whirls of dry leaves across the king's courtyard. It sounded, Gabrielle decided uncomfortably, like someone trying to sneak up on her. *Great. Because right now, the way things have gone so far, someone probably is sneaking up on me.*

The guard who'd tried to arrest her stirred and mumbled something under his breath. Gabrielle rolled her eyes heavenward before cracking him one across the helmet with a short swing of her staff; he went limp and quiet once more.

What to do about the guard was beginning to bother her. Because unfortunately, he'd seen her—he'd possibly seen Xena, too. She couldn't simply let him get back on his feet and hope he'd keep his mouth shut. *Even back in Poteidaia, even before I met Xena, I was never that naive.* But she couldn't keep swatting him upside the head, either; already she was less irritated with the poor little idiot than she'd been when he first showed up, and a lot more sympathetic to the headache he was going to have when he finally came to.

Besides, she'd been hit like that more than once: The flat crack of wood against bone made her wince. Especially at a moment like this, when there was no ongoing battle, no "flatten or be flattened." *Hitting's okay—but not like this.* She sighed heavily. *Why am I worrying about some dumb Spartan? Would he care if I was there and he was here? Give it up!* she ordered herself. *You don't have any choice, okay? Pretend he's Joxer, why don't you?*

That helped. A little.

A better solution would be to find somewhere else to wait, somewhere preferably less open and not right in the middle of the guards' rounds. Somewhere she could could stay out of sight and still watch for Xena—and, yeah, also watch for Joxer.

She drew up her knees and gloomily settled her chin on them. Of course, she realized, at the moment, she was assuming that once the stupid guard woke up, he'd yell his head off, calling in every fighting man in Sparta to find her.

What if that weren't the case, though? She glanced at him, considered what she knew of Sparta and its armed-camp mentality, everything Xena had told her. It was very possible a guard who'd been flattened while on duty would keep his mouth shut—it wouldn't be the kind of information you'd want your captain to have. Especially after being caught off guard and flattened by a mere girl. Getting flattened by Xena herself probably wouldn't even be an excuse.

In which case, maybe she should go ahead and find somewhere else to wait for Xena. She considered this, hesitated. *Sure. You wanna take that chance?* she asked herself sourly. This guy had sounded too dumb to think all that through. *So, what would Xena—?* "Never mind that," she whispered to herself. "What are *you* gonna do?"

What Xena'd do was easy: head for the main entry, find someplace well out of sight and wait for Joxer to emerge. Xena knew Sparta, knew the palace; and if she said Joxer would leave by that set of doors, she was probably right. *If I'm not here when she comes out, she'll head there. She might go there first.*

But the main entry would surely have more guards around than here, especially if all these strangers were coming to accept this quest.

Another thought occurred to her: If those city gates really were closed for the night, where were all these hero wannabe types staying? The king wasn't likely to shove Joxer into the queen's old apartments for the night; probably there were guest chambers or barracks in there somewhere. *So I'm supposed to hide in the bushes until sunup? Great!*

Well, she and Xena could talk about that when the warrior came outside again. A safe distance from that entry.

Gabrielle shifted; rose thorns prodded her and one jabbed deep into her arm—for probably the tenth time. She swore under her breath, gently freed her skirt, and plucked the thorn out of her skin. The puncture itched fiercely; they all did. *Time to move,* she decided.

Besides, if King Menelaus had any brains at all, Joxer would be out on his ear momentarily, and she'd miss him. If she did miss him, by the time morning came, he could be anywhere from a cheap inn to halfway down the road to the coast or up into the mountains. If for some insane reason Joxer was chosen, it was just pos-

sible the king was storing his heroes in the common
barracks along the outer wall. *All the times you've
missed him so far, Gabrielle, you do not want to miss
him this time.*

If he did come out tonight, and she got hold of him,
she might have her hands full. Joxer's voice was *very*
carrying, and he didn't have the common sense to keep
quiet—especially if Gabrielle was trying to convince
him. *I can whack him one, and when Xena comes, she
and I can haul him over the city walls and beyond the
open fields.* And once we're out there, we can make him
tell us just what he thinks he's up to.

It made a satisfying picture.

At that point, it wouldn't matter if the guard came to
and yelled his head off. She glanced over at him; still
out cold. *And who knows? Maybe our luck will change.
Xena just could come back out that window any time
now. Sure, she will—as if!*

Gabrielle drew her staff close to her side, cast a practiced eye at the heavens: The faint blur of stars that were
the Pleiades—seven sisters pursued by Orion. *If Orion's
above the eastern sea, it's late: midnight, or close after.*
She considered this with a frown and counted on her
fingers. *All right: It's been nearly as long as you feel
like it has, Gabrielle, but it's still a long time until sunrise.*

It didn't really surprise her that the palace was so well
lit at such an hour. The same thing had been common
in Athens, where King Theseus and his family and
household had been up until the coolest hours of pre-
dawn, sleeping through the cool morning hours. No
doubt King Menelaus did the same, though the climate
here wasn't the same: At least, the past few days hadn't
been muggy and hot until middle night, the way it had

138

been in Athens. Here, it seemed to get downright cool as soon as the sun went down.

As someone who'd grown up in a village, Gabrielle still found this odd. The sun made a perfect sandglass: You rose with it, you ate as it set, you slept as the sky grew too dark for anything that didn't need light—and light could often be hard to work or expensive to maintain. There had to be better things to spend money on. Of course, most kings didn't think that way. Xena did; she and the warrior often bedded down at full dark and were up with the sun.

But royals and nobles could afford torches, candles, and expensive lanterns, people to keep them lighted; the fact of affording both the goods and the servants made them important, a part of the prestige. And Menelaus—a first-generation royal who'd only become king of Sparta when his new father-in-law granted him Helen *and* a crown—would no doubt take full advantage of such a status symbol.

Clearly, in fact, he was doing just that: Nearly every window of his palace shone. Even if the daytime temperatures were comfortable enough for conducting business, Gabrielle thought sourly, a man like Menelaus would prefer to eat and interview "heroes" for his quest at an hour like this. Late hours, such as kings keep.

If there really was a quest.

If Joxer has actually been— Her mind balked; she clutched her hair. *Let it go. It'll never make sense, okay?*

Another thought intruded: Had Xena really seen Draco? *He* was as unlikely a hero as Joxer! She let her head fall forward onto her hands. But why else would a warlord occupy a guest's apartments in the Spartan palace unless Menelaus was also planning on acquiring more territory and hoping to use Draco?

That didn't make sense, either. Draco had a reputation, and it wasn't one for being used. She shoved the matter aside. So long as *she* didn't have to deal with Draco again. . . . Especially not if he still had A Thing for her. "Cute, maybe—just *not* my type. Makes sense he'd be here, though," she mumbled. "Everything *else* has gone wrong, so why not?"

And to top everything, Xena was in one of her moods. *Like the day we went after that nasty giant and that stupid warlord on the same day—what was that scuzzy warlord's name?* Didn't matter; with a few exceptions like Draco, they were all pretty much alike in looks, actions, and everything else. This one had shaved his head, and a huge tattoo covered most of it. It was on one of her scrolls somewhere; not worth digging out.

What mattered was from the moment the two of them had been rudely wakened at dawn by half a dozen of Tattoo-Boy's men attacking their camp, Xena had been in that strange, giddy mood—hard to fathom, impossible to deal with.

Gabrielle sighed wearily. "At least there aren't any eels around here for her to toss at me; and she is *not* gonna get hold of my new frying pan to beat up Menelaus's guards." The pan was still a bone of contention between them: The new one wasn't nearly as good as the original, and Xena couldn't see what the difference— or the big deal—was.

A grin tugged at the corners of the younger woman's mouth. "At least no poor village sap's fallen in love with her *this* time—at least, that I know about," she added hastily, and crossed her fingers to ward bad luck. No sense tempting Cupid and his incredibly warped sense of humor.

She scowled down at the guard who just now

sprawled bonelessly at her feet, a silly grin pasted on his face. "Maybe if I could drag him over there by the palace, maybe even onto Helen's balcony—where he doesn't belong?" It might not work. But if he came to someplace really off limits, and if he was already disoriented and headachy, he might temporarily forget how he got the headache . . . It wasn't a good plan, just the best she could come up with at the moment. She finally shrugged, set the staff aside and bent down to snag him under the arms. A cloud of sour, wine-thick breath enveloped her. She wrinkled her nose in distaste and leaned away from him to catch her breath. Her eyes suddenly glinted. "He's been drinking on duty. Has to be! No one lets their guards get away with *that*. And I'll bet anything—" She drew a deep breath of fresh air and leaned forward to pat him down.

The wineskin was hooked to his weapons belt, hidden under the small leather-covered wooden shield. She tugged it free, shook it experimentally: It was not quite half full. She drew the stopper, then dribbled liquid along both sides of his mouth before emptying the contents on his neck, the bit of shirt sticking out above hardened leather torso armor, and his hands. She dropped the empty skin on his chest, dragged one hand up to cover it. He murmured something she couldn't understand, and his fingers closed over the empty bottle. Gabrielle got stiffly to her feet, stretched cautiously, and began casting about for the best way to get from where she was to where Xena'd told her to go. Behind her, the guard began to snore softly.

My legs are going to sleep, Xena thought gloomily. With Joxer out of here, maybe it was time for her to go as well. But there was Draco . . . *I should find out what he's doing here—if I can.* And Gabrielle could handle Joxer just fine. Then again, Gabrielle had been in one of those moods ever since Joxer'd gone off on his own. *Like the day I fried that rotten giant. I wish she'd quit giving me grief about her stupid frying pan. It's as pointless as me maybe giving her grief because she couldn't get Hower off me and I had to fix things between him and Minya myself.*

She shifted forward again as the king's voice suddenly rose. "Avicus, I tell you I have had enough! Enough fools and dolts, enough—!" He was pacing again, arms flailing as he bellowed at his priest. Avicus's eyes moved, and now and again his head, to keep his king in sight, but he was otherwise motionless. Menelaus finally stopped. "I," he said evenly, and in a clear attempt to rein in his temper, "am going to my chambers, where I will have food and wine brought to me. Good wine, a full pitcher of it. And nothing short of an armed revolt or Apollo's descent from the heavens will bring me back out tonight! If you wish more of these—these—" He drew a ragged breath, expelled it in a gust. "If there are more 'heroes' for this quest, then it is entirely up to you to choose them, priest."

But Avicus was already shaking his head. "My king. Highness. I agree that you should take an hour, enjoy a proper meal, drink a little wine. Relax. But remember what I told you about that bowl!" A gesture took in the tripod and its vessel. "It will only work correctly if we are *both* present." Menelaus sighed heavily and turned away. "And recall the bargain that was set, when you told me your desire, and I petitioned the god on your behalf."

"Yes, of course," the king answered impatiently. He

turned back. "I intend to keep my bargain with Apollo, priest."

"And the pact you and I made, Highness?" Avicus asked steadily. "I cannot pick your—ah—'heroes'—by myself; that is partly the god's decree and partly sense on my part. I will not risk your wrath if somehow this goes awry and if, because of a man I alone named, you fail to retrieve your woman."

Menelaus bared his teeth, slammed one fist into the palm of his other hand and began pacing again. "Then let us say we have enough! Enough heroes, enough idealistic young wanderers—enough of whatever you choose to call them! Because I refuse to deal with more village puppies and wide-eyed would-be Jasons!" He stopped short, drew another harsh breath, and let it out slowly. "Did you receive any message from that—what was his name?—the one who travels with Hercules?"

"Iolaus? No," Avicus said. "I scarcely expected to, Highness. Though there was just enough of a chance to make it worthwhile, sending the message. Hercules will have heard a different story from Xena, no doubt. But the god will see to it that those two don't have the time to interfere with us, if they won't join us." Momentary silence. "As to the other matter—there are two men left. I believe it—important to test them both."

"Another village boy—and the man Draco," Menelaus spat. "This Draco is a warlord, Avicus! Why should I trust him?"

"I'm not certain we should, Highness. But I am unsure enough to want the test. As for the other—I don't know," the priest said softly. He shook himself, brought up that lips-only smile. "We shall see—but not until after a proper meal, I agree." Menelaus looked wary, but he finally spread his hands in a conciliatory gesture and then waved his priest ahead of him.

Xena waited until the two men reached the outer doors before checking the passage behind her and gingerly slipping from her ledge. Her legs were prickly from being up there so long, but not too bad. *So— Draco's gonna go be a hero, huh?* She grinned as she stretched her back, checked her weapons. Well, it might be fun to watch him take that test, see what the priest had cooked up for him to see—but she doubted it would be that useful overall. It was enough to know the man would be out there, up to no good for Menelaus instead of just on his own account.

Gabrielle's just gonna love it, she thought; her mouth quirked as she eased back up the narrow passage behind the dusty drape and stood silent and still at the other end, listening for the least hint of movement in the hall. In the distance, the way she'd come, she could hear Avicus's voice and the deeper rumble of the king's, but the men were too far away for her to make out the words. Moments later silence, then a door closing. And then another, a little distance further on.

All right; time to leave. She glanced cautiously down the hallway toward the king's apartments, back in the direction of the reception. No one moving anywhere. With a little luck, she'd be out of here, back in the courtyard, before servants came with the king's meal.

Best way to do this, though . . . She eased back into hiding, briefly considered. Neither priest nor king had said how the two remaining men were to pass the time. Maybe food would be sent in to Draco and this boy, wherever they were waiting. Since Draco had not been in the apartments with his pack, he was likely waiting in one of the small chambers close to the reception. She knew of at least two used by the king to entertain a select number of close friends or allies.

The guards might send or return both to the rooms where they would sleep. Meeting Draco in that long, open hall would not be a good idea—not if she intended to keep her presence here a secret.

She could hear voices down that direction, suddenly: two bored-sounding men, an older woman with a high-pitched cackle of a laugh. A door opening and closing, then silence. Xena considered the possibilities briefly, decided that food had been brought for Draco and this unknown boy—and from the sound of things, also for the guards. She eased out of hiding, sprinted down the hallway in record time, and paused only to catch her breath when Draco's door was closed behind her. She leaned against it briefly, then crossed the chamber, listened just long enough to be certain no one was on the other side of that billowing drape, and edged around it, onto the balcony, where she crouched down and pulled the chakram from its clip.

She could hear someone moving, all at once: not the guard, and not Gabrielle, who could be almost as utterly silent these days as Xena herself. No, this was at least two men—she eased quietly back into deeper shadow, fingers tight around the circular weapon, her wrist cocked, and held her breath.

It was two men, dressed in full Spartan guard uniform, those silly horse-crested helms and all, and that incredibly uncomfortable full-face helm that covered everything but the chin, with a crossed slit for eyes and nose. *I'd go nuts inside one of those, she thought. Menelaus must be nuts, or whoever dresses his guards. How do they expect these guys to keep a decent watch with their vision and hearing messed up like that?* She held her breath again, listening intently as booted feet shuffled to a halt on the sandy path.

"Hey, Miklos!" one of them hissed. "Lookit! Isn't that—?"

"Sssst!" Miklos hissed urgently in reply. Xena watched as one of the two knelt, the other stooped over him. "Gods damn him to Tartarus, it's Meritos!"

"What—ya think he's sick, or something? That fish they fed us tonight, all that salt to cure it, and it still tasted kinda funny to me."

Miklos got heavily to his feet. "Thessalo, this is Meritos, remember? Put your head down there and get a whiff. And anyway, I can see the wineskin from here."

Thessalo swore under his breath. "Awww, Miklos? Ya sure? On account of, he promised me, he *swore* he wasn't gonna do that anymore, after the last time. I mean, he and I got stuck scraping skins for the tanner for so long I thought my nose had died."

"You mean you *wished* it had. He's drunk, Thes."

"Awww, *man*? What we gonna do with him, Miklos?"

"Get him out of the path, for one thing," Miklos said grimly. "And keep your voice down! You want to get caught out here, with him like this?" Silence. "Let's see. All right, you get that arm, I'll get this one—no, grab that Ares-blasted wineskin. You *don't* wanna think what'll happen, the next shift comes through and finds *that*."

"Ah—no. OK—awww, *man*, he's heavy! OK, I got it. Wait a minute, lemme get my breath, get under him a little better, OK?" Sounds of feet slipping on the path, a muted grunt or two, a startling and startlingly loud snort from the fallen man as they levered him upright. "OK. Where to? Ya know, maybe if we hauled him over to the cells, tossed him in for the night? Teach him a lesson, maybe?''

"Blessed Ares, are you *nuts*, Thes? We don't go within half the city of the cells, or the main barracks! We haul him off to the old stables, all right? And we keep him there until he's sober once more, OK? And we keep it *quiet*, you got that?''

"Well, yeah, I got it. I guess. Because, wouldn't he be better off if he finally had to see what happens to a guy, drinks while he's supposed to be on—''

"Nuh-uh. Nuh-*uh*! You know what Captain Celano would do to us, he found out one of us had been guzzling wine on watch? You know who they blame? Every last gods-blasted one of us, that's who, 'cause of, we're supposed to keep each other from doing something like this! Especially an idiot like Meritos! And then Captain Celano strings every last bleedin' one of us out on a barren peak for harpy chow!'' Silence. "All right, you got that side of him? Can you haul him up, onto his feet?''

"Geez, you asking *me*?''

"C'mon, Thes, we can do it. Blessed Ares, we'd better. Hey, brace up, c'mon, you can do it, all right? Slow and easy now.'' The three-headed, awkward, stumbling shadow turned away from the palace.

Xena watched the shadowy movement as the two dragged their comrade down the path and out of the rose beds. She was fighting laughter as they struggled off. *Gabrielle. She found wine on the little jerk and doused him with it. Had to be*, she decided. However her companion had come up with an idea like that, it was inspired. Better yet: It seemed to have worked.

Time for her to get moving; Gabrielle would be worried, which meant she'd be cross. *As if she wasn't cross enough already,* Xena thought. *So I'll make it up to her later—as soon as I can.* She eased to her feet and, crouching, ran across open ground, past the rosebushes, and slid into the deep shadow of a tall, prickly hedge. Around this, she could make out the main entry, still some distance away, but well lit enough for her to pick out familiar details.

The bronze gates on the inner wall were for show, she knew: Commissioned by an earlier Spartan king less miserly with his dinars, they depicted an elaborate battle between the Titans and the gods and would probably break in half if anyone tried to move them.

A broad path of crushed stone led from the gates to several low, wide steps and the torch-lit palace portico. The wide doors of the main entry were also bronze, but the doors were strictly utilitarian: plain, solid metal that needed a hard shove from a well-muscled arm and could easily withstand a direct attack.

Now: To find Gabrielle in all this. Xena kept her back against the hedge and let her eyes move slowly across the space before her. There wasn't much cover on the other side of the path, but Gabrielle wouldn't have tried to cross that expanse of open ground anyway. Most likely she'd have picked a spot where the ground was soft, the shadows deep. Far enough from the portico that anyone coming out wouldn't spot her; probably nearer the fancy gates, so she could grab Joxer as he passed her.

Her eyes lit on a likely candidate: a low tree with branches that swept the ground, closer to the path than to the hedge. The long, leafy streamers swayed gently as a chill breeze swirled over the palace grounds. Xena went back into a crouch and covered the distance quickly and silently. Once she could reach out and touch the nearest branches, she held her breath, listened intently. Someone was in there, a slightly lumpy shadow against the trunk, barely limned by the fluttering torches on the portico. Whoever it was, was breathing deeply and regularly.

Xena felt cautiously with one hand; her fingers closed on the end of her companion's fighting staff. Gabrielle started, clutched at the other end, and with a faint mumble subsided against the trunk. "Ssst!" the warrior hissed as she crawled forward. "Ssst! Gabrielle, wake up!"

"Hmmmm—huh?" The younger woman started again, and this time her eyes opened. She muffled a yawn behind her hand, the other tugging at the staff. Xena let go; Gabrielle caught her breath sharply as the end of the hardened, polished weapon slammed into her knee with a loud "clack." "Owwwwww! That hurt! What're you *doing*?" she demanded. Gabrielle snatched at the staff and slammed it down next to her thigh. "Xena! Do you have any idea how long you were *in* there?" Xena sat next to her, grabbed a handful of hair, and tugged, bringing the other's ear over close to her mouth.

"Will you keep it down? There's guards around here, remember?" Gabrielle scowled at her.

"I know there's guards around here, remember who got *left* out here with one of them?" she whispered angrily. "While you were in there—Hey—are you sitting on my staff?" She yanked; Xena shrugged and shifted her weight.

"Yeah. Wondered what that was." Gabrielle gave her a look and moved the weapon to her other side. "Anyway, keep it down, will you, Gabrielle? There's two more of 'em around here, dragging your little pal off to

149

hide him out until he sobers up.'' Silence. Gabrielle went back to rubbing her knee. "Good trick you came up with, that wine. I like it.''

"Yeah, well, I had to do something, with you being *gone* so long—''

Xena sighed heavily. "Give it a *rest*, Gabrielle. You seen any other guards out here?''

"No—no one.''

"You're sure you could've seen anyone? I mean, with your eyes closed—'' the warrior began. Gabrielle snorted.

"Are you saying I was *asleep*?''

"Did I say that? I just asked—''

"Not that I'd have any reason to be sleeping. It's only night and I've only had almost no sleep at all for the past five days, but—''

"Gabrielle, don't get started with me, all right?''

Gabrielle sighed heavily and cast her eyes heavenward. The smile she turned on her companion wasn't a friendly one. "Get started? Me? Why would I—?'' She drew a deep breath. "Look. Let's save this for later, huh? Is Joxer in there?''

"He was. He probably still is,'' the warrior replied shortly.

Gabrielle waited a moment in silence. Then: "That's it? Just—he was and he probably still is? Xena, do you have any idea how *long*—?''

"Gabri*elle* . . .'' Xena growled. "As a matter of fact, I do! Because I spent all of that time hiding on a ledge, *listening* to just about every single idiot King Menelaus and his pet priest talked to in there! *Including* Joxer! And you know what? When we get outta here, I'm gonna tell you exactly every lousy, irritating, annoying thing Joxer *said*, okay?''

Gabrielle eyed her warily, then laid a hand on her arm. "Look—all right, I'm sorry. Let's try this again—"

"Told you I heard something!" Large male boots, four of them, were suddenly visible just beyond the low-sweeping branches. The voice was familiar; Thessalo, Xena realized gloomily. And his pal Miklos.

"All right, we can just see you," Miklos said. He was, Xena noted, keeping his voice low and noncarrying, just as Thessalo had. She tapped Gabrielle's shoulder, gestured at the two dim shadows with her chin. Gabrielle drew the staff over her legs and nodded, then crawled forward, hissing as she put weight on her sore knee. Xena eased off to the other side, emerging in a low crouch, arms flailing.

It worked: The wild movement caught Miklos's eye, and he half-turned to see her, one hand pulling his short sword free. By then, Gabrielle had erupted into the open, staff already a high-speed blur. It caught Thessalo in the gut, driving the air from him in a harsh gust; back around, over and down, she slammed it rapid-fire across his throat, into the side of his helmet, and, as he finally sagged at the knees, hard across the back of his neck. He landed flat and hard and didn't move.

Miklos was no fool, despite being caught by surprise; he immediately brought his attention back to the leather-clad, dark-haired woman now rising to an impressive height. "You're Xena!" he snarled. "I remember you—from Troy!" He brought his sword up. "Well! This time you won't—"

"Won't what?" she asked softly. "Miklos, isn't it? Hard to tell when all you can see of a man's face is a couple of eyes and part of a nose. I saw you back there, picking up your drunk little friend." She glanced beyond him. *They haven't had time to get rid of him and get back here.* She couldn't be certain, but that low shadowy mound a few paces behind the two guards certainly looked like another unconscious man. "You know, I bet you'd like to keep things quiet out here—wouldn't you?" He stared, sword momentarily forgotten. "Well, Miklos, maybe we'd like to keep things quiet, too."

"Yeah, I'll bet you would," he spat, and winced as Thessalo moaned and Gabrielle snarled wordlessly and slammed her staff across his helmet. "But I got no reason to keep quiet about *you*, do I?"

"With your drunk little friend right behind you? Go ahead," she said throatily, a sly smile creasing her lips. "All I gotta do is yell, and then, guess what? Captain Celano shows up and—" He looked wary, all at once, then squared his shoulders and brought the sword back up.

"All I gotta do is kill you and her; Thes and me can deal with Meritos and then we can call the captain."

Xena bared her teeth; her eyes were wicked. "That's it, huh? Well, come on, then. Uh-uh," she added and held up a hand as he cocked his wrist. "You're not gonna use *that*, are you? Nasty sharp blade, make a big cut. Someone gets cut with that, they're gonna yell, right?"

"Ah—ah—" He stared at her blankly, then shook himself. Xena drew her own sword, set it on the ground, spread her arms wide. Half-dazed, the guard dropped his sword and kicked it aside, then drew a long-bladed dagger.

"You *really* don't get it, do you?" Xena asked, as if she really wanted to know the answer. "Long, pointy blade, big, nasty cut—loud yell of pain—? We getting through here?" She unclipped the chakram and drew two open daggers, then slipped one from her boot and

152

the other from her cleavage. The guard's jaw sagged briefly, but he grimly pulled his remaining blades, tossed them aside. Only then did he grin nastily as he hauled a bolos from his belt.

"Hold still," he snarled, "and this won't hurt much at all." But he was talking to the tree. As his fingers tightened on the waxed cord, Xena had already launched herself, completed a tight and utterly silent double back-flip over his head, to land behind him. Her arms slashed down, catching his neck in a savage double-blow that dropped him, already unconscious, in a boneless heap next to his comrade. The warrior's mouth twitched in a pleased little smile; she stepped over him and knelt to collect her weapons, one ear attuned to the fallen Miklos.

He still wasn't moving when she finally stood, sliding the small dagger back into her top and clipping the chakram at her hip. Gabrielle was gazing at her wide-eyed. "You are really something, you know that? I mean— what if that guy was—what if he'd yelled?"

Xena shrugged. "He didn't. What else counts?" She went to one knee, checked both men; neither was likely to regain consciousness for some time. "You got any more of that wine, Gabrielle?"

"What—when have I ever carried wine? Xena, this is me, remember? I drink cider?" Her brows drew together. "Why?"

"Your idea—I like it."

"There was only a bit in that one guy's skin, and I used all but a swallow. Xena, look, all you need to do is—"

"Gabrielle, I'm not gonna just drag them off somewhere to sleep it off. We could be here a while yet. They might decide to ditch their friend somewhere to sleep off the wine and come back—with reinforcements.

We're trying to keep our presence here a secret, remember?''

"*I* remember," Gabrielle replied grimly. Xena ignored the implied comment.

"So I heard them talking—those two," she nudged Miklos with one boot. "Their captain isn't the kind would give someone drunk on duty a second chance. They wake up smelling like the bottom of a wineskin, they aren't gonna do anything but hide out and clean up, right?"

"Maybe." She caught hold of Xena's arm as the warrior turned back the way they'd come. "Where are you going?"

"You stay with these two, make sure they don't wake up ahead of time. I gotta find some wine."

Gabrielle's fingers tightened. "Are you nuts?" she hissed. "You're telling me you're going back in *there*— Draco's rooms?"

"Unless you want to," Xena retorted with a wicked grin. "He's got cherries—"

"Cute."

"Hey—I try. There's also a full wine pitcher in Draco's rooms. It's close, and he's not there right now." *Well, he wasn't last time I checked*, she told herself, more honestly. "Look, Gabrielle, I won't be long, OK? Then we'll get out of here, all the way out of Sparta."

"Xena! Look—Xena, this isn't exactly safe, you know?"

The warrior bit back spluttery laughter. "Gabrielle, you know what? Being in Sparta is not exactly safe!" Momentary silence.

"You're going in there anyway, aren't you?" Gabrielle's grip didn't loosen, but now she sounded tired.

Resigned. "And if the two of us are getting out of Sparta, then what about Joxer?"

"I know more or less where he is, and I know where he's going. I know where we need to be to catch up with him. Fair enough?"

"There's something wrong with this; it sounds too easy," Gabrielle grumbled. She released Xena's arm, but before the warrior could move, she leveled a finger at the woman's nose. "Listen—don't let your creative juices get in the way of your common sense, will you? Just—promise me, all right?"

Xena caught the younger woman's shoulders between gentle hands. "I promise. But only if you promise to take a few deep breaths and relax!"

"Relax—are you nuts?"

"Relax. Look—Gabrielle. When did this little journey start getting to you—about the time Joxer walked away from camp up in Thessalonika, right? You should know by now, these things happen sometimes—"

"Yeah, sure. Every time *Joxer's* involved. Like when Aphrodite roped him in to break up that marriage—?"

Xena lightly tapped her forehead against Gabrielle's, silencing her. "Old story, Gabrielle. Forget about it. When things get this weird, you gotta let it go, all right? You find the laughs where you can, and you don't let it get to you, unless you want to turn into Fury bait." Silence. Gabrielle gazed at her; Xena gazed back, fingers tightening slightly on her friend's shoulders. "Besides, c'mon. You really want to waste a perfectly good hissy fit—on *Joxer*?"

"A—a hissy—? Xena, I do not—!" the younger woman began indignantly; her mouth quirked and she suddenly clapped both hands over her mouth to contain laughter. "Yeah, all right. You're right, I know that. Except—"

"I know." Xena's voice was warm. "You don't do hissy fits. I'll be careful, Gabrielle, and I'll come back to you. And I won't be long." She was gone before Gabrielle could find anything else to say.

As Xena eased silently across open ground, she could hear Gabrielle muttering something. Just as well she couldn't catch the words, she decided with a brief grin. The smile faded; the situation really wasn't amusing. *We get outta this mess in one piece, I need to do something nice for her. She doesn't deserve this.*

The rose garden was quiet and empty, darkness nearly complete here, and the wind had died away. There were still no visible lights through the drape separating Draco's rooms from his balcony, and though she held her breath and listened for some moments, no sound in there, either. With a swift glance around her, she loosened sword and chakram and slipped into the chamber, back set against the wall until her eyes adjusted. The lamp in its niche was flickering as if the oil supply were low. Nothing seemed to have been moved; the jug was where she remembered, right next to the fruit. She stole across the room, picked it up, and turned to leave, but a flat, expressionless voice stopped her in her tracks.

"Xena. I just had a feeling."

• • •

Gabrielle watched Xena vanish around the hedge, then sighed heavily. "All right, let's get this done," she mumbled. She leaned her staff against a thick branch, grabbed Thessalo by the wrists, got him turned the other direction, and dragged him across to where they'd dumped drunk Meritos, then went back for Miklos.

Miklos was unfortunately heavier. A lot heavier. By the time she had him sprawled out next to the other two, she was panting for air and her hands ached. Thessalo shifted and whimpered faintly; she retrieved her staff and clopped him one.

"All right, Xena," she whispered angrily. "As long as it took me to move those two idiots, you coulda gone to the outer gates for wine. Where *are* you?"

Xena bit back a sigh, but when she turned she was smiling, and her eyes were warm as they moved up and down the superbly muscled, dark-skinned man who'd just emerged from the linen storage, fingers absently twirling a dry grape stem.

"Draco," she murmured throatily. "You're looking— good."

He tossed the stem aside and leaned against the wall, arms crossed. "Save it, Xena. I want to know what you're doing in Sparta *and* what you're doing in my rooms—with my wine, I might add."

She gave the jug a surprised look and set it back down. "Doing? Here? Waiting for you, of course." She smoothed leather with both hands and crossed the room. "So," she said softly as she reached him. "You been in to see the king yet?"

He looked down at her warily and kept his arms crossed. "Yeah, just now. What do you care? You gonna

158

ruin another good deal for me? You still owe me for those Hestian virgins, you know.''

"They weren't yours, they were Hestia's. I didn't want to see you get in trouble with the goddess; that's all.''

His mouth twisted. "That's a laugh. I know you better than that. What's the deal this time?''

"Why would I ruin anything for you?'' Her hand slid up his left arm and along his shoulder; he watched it, rather as if it were a spider, then searched her face. Good, she thought, and licked her lower lip. *Keep that attention right here, fella.* Her questing fingers brushed Avicus's patch.

The little scrap of metal felt warm, and she kept her hand on it with an effort. It did nothing else, and Draco seemed unaware of it or her interest in it. Her nails pried it loose. When the warlord finally sighed and made a show of removing her hand from his armor, the device came with her. She stepped back, casually let her hands down to her sides, dropped the thing, and set her heel on it. Something made an unpleasant little ''squnch''; Draco glanced at her and then beyond her, frowning suspiciously.

She glanced over her shoulder, then raised her eyebrows and shrugged. *Worked—I think. Nasty little thing's gone, and he's no wiser.* "What?''

"Nothing—I guess. I thought I heard a noise.''

"Well, I didn't hear anything,'' she said, her voice a husky whisper.

He held up a hand. "Save it, okay? You're always up to something when you act like this, and it's never anything I'm gonna enjoy.''

"Me? Up to—?''

"I said, save it. Besides, I'd rather we just talk. Because I still haven't heard an *explanation* of what you're doing in Sparta, Xena.'' He leaned back against the wall once more. ''Don't tell me you're in this for the king, either; everyone knows how much he hates you. And I've heard enough to believe that you'd—never mind. Talk to me.'' Momentary silence; he suddenly seemed to remember something else and came away from the wall in one smooth move, eyes searching the gloom beyond her. ''Where's Gabrielle?''

''Gabrielle? Oh—her.'' Xena looked suddenly bored; she twisted a strand of hair around one finger, shrugged. ''I don't know. She isn't with me anymore.''

''That's bull—''

''It's not. We—well, all right, we broke up over you.'' She eyed him from under her lashes. ''*That* make you happy? 'Cause it sure doesn't please me; I gotta eat my own cooking again.''

''Too bad,'' he scoffed. ''Or it would be—if it was the truth.''

She tapped her breastplate with one long finger, gave him her best innocent smile. He rolled his eyes and waited. ''Aw, hey, come on, Draco—would I lie to you?''

He closed the distance between them with a bound and took hold of her shoulders. ''Is the sea wet? Are your lips moving? Where is she—out there?'' Xena shook her head. ''She's—she better not be with that *Joxer*! Is she?'' The warrior raised an eyebrow and shrugged. Draco's grip tightened. ''She is, isn't she?''

''How would I know?'' Xena broke free of his grasp with no effort at all. ''I guess she could be, but she wasn't the last time I saw her.'' Draco's mouth twisted in disgust. ''It's the truth—what d'you want me to swear by, huh?''

160

"She's with him. You can't lie to me, Xena. I can always tell when you lie! Where are they?"

"Why should I tell you?" Xena countered in a sulky tone. "I didn't come here to talk about Gabrielle." He started as her hand slid along his jawline. "I came here to talk about you—and me . . ."

She got no further; he covered her hand with one of his to hold it still as his mood shifted suddenly, as it always did around her. He broke into a low, throaty chuckle. "Yeah, sure you did. Xena, if I had a dinar for every time you've pulled that lousy trick on me, I could *buy* Ithaca from Odysseus!"

"I thought you didn't want Ithaca, and maybe it's not a trick this time. What do I possibly have to gain?" She took a step toward him. "And hey, just because we aren't allies anymore doesn't mean I don't—ah—appreciate some of your—ah—*finer* points."

He snorted and retreated a pace, her hand still firmly clutched in his and flattened against his armor. "Sure you do. And how would I know what you have to gain? Why would I care, come to that? You aren't getting between me and this quest, though. Even if—never mind that."

"Whatever." She tangled the fingers of her other hand in his hair; he swatted it aside. "So, if there's nothing I can do to keep you from this quest, and I have nothing to gain—" His eyes were wide, his look calculating; this time when she closed the distance between them, he stayed put. Xena wrapped her fingers in his hair, drew him close, and brushed her lips against his. Both his hands suddenly came up to rest against her jaw, and he drew a shuddering breath; his mouth was trembling. Before he could tighten his grasp, though, she eased her face just out of reach and murmured, "You got any wine?"

He laughed quietly. "You should know; you were trying to run off with it just now. But—what do you need wine for?"

"To get me in the mood, of course," she murmured huskily.

Draco eased away from her slightly, suspicious again. "In the *mood*? What are you talking about?" But as he reached for her, she eased out of his grasp entirely.

"C'mon, Draco. Indulge me, okay?" She waited while he crossed to the table, poured wine into two tall cups and handed her one. She took it, smiled at him over the rim, then headed for the balcony.

"Hey! Xena—what in Hades are you *doing*?"

She turned, one hand on the drape, and gave him a dazzling smile. "Gotta do it alone, sorry. Keep things warm for me. I'll be back." She slipped under the drape and crossed the balcony and hesitated briefly before cutting through the rose beds again. Behind her, she could hear Draco steadily, furiously cursing.

She was grinning broadly as she fetched up next to the prickly hedge and looked around it. Good; Gabrielle was standing close to the tree, and it was quiet out there. *Things are finally starting to go right.*

She undoubtedly would not have thought so if she had been back on the ledge overlooking the king's reception.

After downing a mug of warmed, spiced wine and listening to his serving man's latest tale, Menelaus had relaxed enough to decided he should deal with the last two would-be heroes before eating and had sent for Avicus. Draco had come, had been given a special story and a vision, had accepted the quest and the priest's little device, then left. But when Avicus would have sent for the last of them, Menelaus shook his head.

"Wait a moment; we have something to discuss."

"Yes, Highness?" The priest was gazing into his bowl, apparently amused by something he saw there.

"Xena is here. In Sparta."

Avicus was smiling as he looked up. "Yes. I know she is." A wave of his hand took in the bowl. "I have planned for that possibility all along, of course."

"Yes, priest," the king replied grimly. "So have I."

"Sst! Gabrielle!"

"Xena?" Gabrielle came to her feet, staff at the ready. "Well, that was fast—for once."

Xena gritted her teeth. "Gabri*elle*, don't start with me—"

"Why would I? They're over there."

The warrior held up the cup; a little liquid sloshed over her thumb and she sucked it off. "Good. I got it. Where are they?" Gabrielle was already moving. But when Xena would have dumped the contents over the three, the younger woman clamped on to her wrist.

"Don't—let me do it, OK? You just slosh it. They'll look like they were set up, not like they're drunk."

"Okay, good, fine. You do it." Xena glanced around and turned to leave, but Gabrielle still had hold of her.

"*Where* are you going?" she whispered sharply.

"Back in there. I gotta find out what Draco's up to, all right?"

"All right?" Gabrielle stared up at her. "No, it is *not* all right! You are gonna get caught!"

"No, I'm not."

"I—remember the plan, Xena? We get Joxer, we get *out* of here?" Silence. "Xena, you're the one who said being in Sparta is a dumb idea, remember?''

"Hey, hey, hey!" Xena set her fingers on her companion's lips, silencing her. "All right—look. You wait right here for Joxer—he's gotta come out those doors; they're the only ones open after dark. Okay? Okay. You know where I'm gonna be. If you get Joxer and have to leave to follow him—I know where he's going. He's headed southeast and there's only one road. So you can't lose him and I can't lose you, and . . ."

"Xena, I am *not* leaving Sparta without you, and I am *not* leaving Sparta to follow Joxer while you try to catch up to me! We did that! And I was not amused!" Silence. "I'm still not amused!"

"Okay. So, if he comes out, you grab him, keep him quiet and drag him over—"

"What, into Draco's bedroom? Oh, sure, I'm gonna go there, and with Joxer in tow. I get to strangle Joxer myself, remember? I'm sure not gonna let Draco have him, after all this!" She swallowed and added in a small voice, "Or—ah, have me, all right?"

The warrior sighed gustily. "Gabrielle, will you just let me finish? No, I am not offering you to Draco. Why would I? Think about it. What would I do? You drag Joxer onto that balcony, and you warn him first that Draco still wants his head for stealing your heart." She waited; Gabrielle's mouth opened, but no words came. "Fine. I'm not gonna be long. I just gotta find out what Draco thinks he's up to."

"What's Draco always up to. He's a warlord, remember? And why should you care?"

"Because he's been picked for this whatever-it-is . . . this quest. Like Joxer and all those others—"

"Others? No, wait, tell me about it later. When we're *out—of—Sparta!*"

"Fine. I'll do just that. But I really need to find out what Draco saw—no, tell you about that later, too, remind me. I need to know what he thinks he's after. And I have to know that he isn't going after Helen—I mean, what if he got a real vision from Avicus's little fountain thingie and actually found her for Menelaus?"

Gabrielle bit back a sigh. "Fountain—no, forget it. OK. Draco hunting Helen down would definitely be a bad thing."

"That's all I gotta do, I swear, Gabrielle. Then I'm outta there, and you and I are out of Sparta. If you and Joxer are waiting close to the balcony or in the roses, you'll see me come out; you signal and I'll see you. If you're not there, you'll be over here, still waiting for him to come out, right?"

Gabrielle considered this, reluctantly nodded and let go. "This better work," she warned.

Xena grinned. "What could go wrong?" And she was gone before Gabrielle could more than open her mouth to protest.

Draco hadn't moved, so far as she could tell, but as she slipped back under the drape, he smiled and came toward her. *Wow. That smile.* It warmed his whole face, transformed him into someone she could actually. . . . she shook her head to clear it and met him just short of the narrow bed. But when he would have wrapped his arms around her, she planted both hands on his chest and shoved, hard. He staggered back and sat. "All right, I'm back," she said flatly. "Let's talk."

His dark eyes were suddenly furious; she closed the distance between them with a bound and slapped a hand across his mouth as his jaw muscles bunched, and he drew a deep breath to bellow at her. "Don't—do—it.

This isn't your camp, remember? This is a place where you yell, and a lot of guards who are not loyal to you come looking to see what you're up to." She gazed down at him; his eyes were all pupil and his neck corded; he was far from happy. *Surprise, surprise.* Considering what he'd expected from her just now—and what he'd got instead—she wasn't too astonished. But after he glared at her for a long moment, he finally nodded; she withdrew the hand and took a step back, folded her arms. "Good. Okay, talk to me, Draco. Tell me what King Menelaus and his pet priest are sending you after."

Some distance away, Joxer tried to find a comfortable spot on the narrow, hard pallet that filled most of the small room where he'd been brought after his meeting with the king. There didn't seem to *be* a comfortable spot, and the room itself was depressingly plain: Other than the bed—such as it was—there was only a small table and a chest stowed under the bed. The chest turned out to be empty, the interior smelled faintly moldy, and one hinge was rusted through.

"Great," he mumbled. "They choose me to take on this really important quest for them—and then shove me in a lousy *servant's* room." He tossed his helmet onto the bed and tried to push the chest back where it had come from with one foot. It stuck on the rough, uneven floor; his foot slipped off the lid and slammed into the underside of the bed. He flailed wildly for balance; one arm caught the rickety little table, upending it. He rolled his eyes, hauled the table up and set it with down exaggerated care, making sure it was pushed up against the bed, so that it wouldn't go anywhere.

He settled on the edge of the bed, considered removing the rest of his armor, rejected the notion. There was nothing to see, nothing to do, and he was tired from so many long days of walking the unpleasantly steep roads of the past few days. But sleep was out of the question at the moment, and he couldn't sit still, even though the room wasn't made for pacing: five steps one way, eight the other. There was one narrow door, one window. The walls were unfinished, just plain dressed stone, two oil lamps mounted with leather straps to opposite walls, and a rough curtain over the window. He turned slowly in place, eying the chamber with rising dissatisfaction, then eased around the end of the bed to peer out the window. The sill was deep—the view nothing to brag up, at least at this hour. He could just make out a bare courtyard and beyond that, barracks or stables. The moon had set earlier—he thought it had—and it was dark enough that he couldn't be certain what he saw.

Things were very quiet, which meant it probably wasn't a barracks. And it didn't *smell* like stables.

The window itself wasn't barred, and it was big enough he could go out that way if he needed to. Or wanted to.

He looked both directions, along the palace wall. Not much to see here, either, except off to his right, two very young-looking men were doing the same thing, checking out their surroundings. When they saw him, one of the two pulled back out of sight at once; the other brought up a hand as if to wave, then seemed to think better (or worse) of it, shrugged, and vanished.

What's this? Joxer wondered, suddenly indignant. *I thought this was my quest! Unless those are new servants or something?* After all, this room couldn't be anything but a servant's quarters—a low-level servant at that. But it didn't make sense, combined with the rest of the evening. Something didn't feel right all at once.

"Yeah. Great. Story of my life, huh?" He edged back off the sill and went over to the door, listened intently for a moment, then gripped the handle; he yelped as it turned in his grasp, staggered back, and fell onto the bed. Someone rapped once sharply, then hauled the door open without waiting for an invitation. An elderly woman hobbled in, a tray clutched in wrinkled hands. She brushed past him and set the tray on the table, then turned and left without saying anything to him, though he could hear her talking to someone in the hall. Her voice was harsh and low, the words so accented, he couldn't understand a thing she said. The door closed as something with a squeaky wheel moved on up the hallway.

Joxer frowned at the door, then experimentally touched his left arm with his right forefinger, turned his hand back and forth before his eyes. "Okay. I'm here, all right. And, yeah, I'm visible. Well, I'm visible to me, anyway . . . ?"

Maybe she'd had a long day and feeding him hadn't been on her original agenda. Maybe she'd had orders not to talk to him. Maybe her feet hurt. Who knew? He dismissed the matter as unimportant—or at least unsolveable—and turned to check out what she'd brought.

The tray held peasant food: a thick red soup and several roughly torn hunks of dark bread. A leathery-looking apple was almost lost between a heavy mug of dark wine and a small jug of water. Joxer sniffed the cup cautiously, then sneezed: The stuff was unmixed, strong and sour and slightly off, as if the grapes had been moldy when harvested. That kind of wine, even mixed with all the water in that jug, would give him a foul headache. The soup didn't smell any better—possibly made the way his grandmother'd made soup, lib-

168

erally overdosed with garlic and wine to keep her family from tasting meat that was off and wrinkly vegetables past their prime. *Your grandmother made the soup because your mother was off playing tough guy with your dad and your brother Jett.* Joxer shook his head fiercely, clearing it of ancient family history (and the faint, distant, squirming memory of his two brothers singing: "Joxer the tidy, never goes out-sid-ey!").

Finally he shrugged, and a superior little smile curved his mouth. "Well, some of us have risen above the past, haven't we?" He cast a scornful glance at the bowl of soup, shoved the cup of wine aside. "And just as well I ate with the king, didn't I?"

The bread seemed all right and actually smelled good. He tossed a piece of it high, caught it deftly, and eased over to the door. Might as well see if he could figure out what was going *on* here.

The hallway was about as he'd remembered it: plain, dark, and all stone—no carpets, no paint, no hangings, no statues—nothing but barren, cheaply worked corridor. Torches in stone holders burned steadily every twenty paces or so; there were doors every ten paces, both sides of the hall—a regular hen coop of rooms eight paces by five paces, one window, one door.

To his left, there was nothing to see except torches and, well down there, the cross corridor he'd come up earlier, after his interview.

The other direction, an ugly one-wheeled hand truck stood midpassage, a large, bald man holding the back end up by its handles. At least ten trays like the one sitting on Joxer's table were stacked on it, a number of jugs and cups visible and one enormous wine keg. Joxer ducked back out of sight as the old woman emerged from the door two down and mumbled something as she edged around the cart. The wheel shrieked; Joxer gritted his teeth and clapped both hands over his ears. "I hate that noise, I really *hate* it!" he whimpered. It stopped; he cautiously removed his hands and listened to the faint clatter of a tray being loaded, the sound of a door unlatching. When he eased back to where he could see into the hall again, the cart was another torch-worth distant—and someone else, two doors up, was leaning into the hallway, gazing at the big servant. Joxer pulled back into his room at once and eased the door quietly shut. He leaned back against it, eyes fixed on the ceiling.

"This is stupid," he told himself aloud. "No! No, this is worse than stupid, this is—this is annoying!" Those men he'd seen at the windows and the boy in the hall just now—they couldn't be servants, new or otherwise, because why would a servant bring meals to them? Servants went to the kitchens or the barracks and ate there. They couldn't be soldiers; kings didn't house soldiers inside the palace; that was what barracks were for. And why would a servant bring food around to soldiers? Unless the soldiers in question were officers—and the fellow he'd just seen wasn't much more than a boy. Probably too young to grow a beard, from the look of the back of his head and that skinny neck.

"So." Joxer shifted his gaze from the ceiling to the tray and began enumerating on his fingers. "So, maybe the king decided he needed one hero and a lot of guys to help him on this quest—no, that doesn't make sense, because he'd've let me pick my own helpers, right? Or if I didn't get to pick them, he'd at least introduce them to me. So why all this secrecy?" Because, if there wasn't any secret involved, why weren't all of them eating together? Why individual little rooms, and individual

170

trays? He shook his head, eyed the bread in sudden disgust, and tossed it onto the tray.

"Great. So I got at least three guys for competition—probably a lot more, if all those trays mean anything." A *lot* more; there were plenty of doors between this one and that cross-corridor, if he recalled right. "Well, *this* is just great! Terrific!" He started pacing again, yelped as one too-long step took him into the wall. "Owwww!" He rubbed his scraped nose. "All right, that does it. Now I'm mad. Now I'm *really* mad. Think they can pull one on Joxer the Mighty, eh? Well—we'll just see about *that*!" He scooped up his helmet and set it firmly on his head, then strode to the door. But as his hand gripped the latch, he hesitated. Too well lit out there, and at least two witnesses, if he decided to slink down the hallway. Besides, he needed a better idea of what time it was and exactly *where* he was in relation to the city gates. After all, the important thing was to get past the city gates and get on the road, so that he could find the queen, warn her, take the relic from a (grateful) Helen, and return it here. All that would be a joke if he couldn't get past the gates before those—those— "Bah," Joxer hissed under his breath. "Buncha babies. No-beard babies. What chance they got—against me?"

He eased over to the window, ducked under the curtain, then hauled himself onto the ledge, shaking the curtain back into place. A little light still shone through it and onto the ground just beyond the wall, but not much. He cautiously poked his head beyond the sill and twisted around so that he could look at the sky.

The Water Cup—what Gabrielle claimed she saw as an enormous bear—was completely visible, the handle pointing up. Okay, that meant late, which would be almost middle night, this time of year. Which meant there probably wouldn't be too many guards on the streets and only the two at the gates. He leaned back against rough stone, thought hard.

Those two guards at the gates had seemed friendly enough; they'd talked to him about a lot of things, including that they had just come on at sundown and had guard duty until first light—which would be a full hour, maybe two, before the sun rose. And he still had the city gate pass that Dreno had given him, up in Thessalonika. *Trying to pull a fast one on me, are they? Well—sorry, King Menelaus and your Apollo priest, whatever your name is. Joxer the Mighty is in charge of this quest. So if anybody's gonna find Helen and make sure she isn't zapped by that family whatchamajoogie, it's yours truly. Joxer.* Joxer the Mighty. Not one of those green-looking boys.

He eased back into the room, checking his weapons, settling his armor. His fingers encountered the badge Avicus had attached to the mail, and he swallowed. But it didn't feel hot or anything. "That settles it," he told himself firmly. "If Apollo didn't want me to leave right now, that thing woulda—it woulda—anyway, it didn't *do* anything. So that must be a sign." He briefly clasped it, considered hauling it off and tossing it aside. "Naw," he muttered finally. "Think about it, Joxer. That priest-guy sends someone to help you when you—well, things are going bad and you could use someone to watch your back while you clean things up? Except the someone doesn't know you're the guy he's supposed to help, because you aren't wearing the badge-thingie. He gave it a fond smile and a pat, scooped up the bread and dumped it in his bag, then edged back onto the windowsill and slid quietly—for Joxer—to the ground.

One problem, he realized as he crouched low, back to

the palace, and gazed all around: From here, he didn't have a clue which way the city gates were. Obvious answer: Follow the palace wall around until he found somewhere familiar and go from there. "Let's see," he murmured. "There was that wide path and the big doors, and those fancy gates—yeah, and lots of light." Even just short of dusk, there'd been a couple guys by the doors, lighting torches, and there'd been other torches by the fancy gates.

Swell. Now, if he could mentally coordinate the sun's ups and downs and those of the stars. "Forget that, you can work it out later, all right? Bottom line is, you don't wanna be seen and have to stop and explain to anyone around *here* why you aren't back in that room, OK?" Just because there hadn't been any guards around when he'd come here from the main gates didn't mean there wouldn't be any at this hour. "Yeah. Or more guys to talk to the king and look in that bowl of water," he added sourly.

Well, it had been just light enough when he'd reached the fancy palace gates, so he'd taken his time. After all, how often did a man get the chance to just look around someplace like this? So—he thought hard. Yes. There had been a big hedge to his left as he cleared the palace gates, and beyond the hedge, some kind of garden.

He tried to figure how far and in which direction he might have to go, to get close enough to see the fancy gates and the double doors, and whether the garden would come first; he finally gave that up as a lost cause, mentally flipped a coin, and turned left.

Gabrielle watched as Xena ran, light-footed, around the hedge and across the rose gardens, until shadow covered her. She sighed, swore an oath that would have left her sister Lila red-faced and howling for their father to wash her elder sister's mouth out, then turned to glare down at the fallen guards. She crouched down next to Meritos, who was snoring softly, then eased past him to scowl at Thessalo, and across him at the massive Miklos. She smiled then and slowly, carefully dribbled wine across the corners of Miklos's mouth and onto the backs of his hands. A little extra on his trousered thighs, where a drunk guardsman might just wipe his hands.

She eased around to perform the same maneuver on Thessalo, then sat back on her heels, considering the moment as she swirled the cup. There was a *lot* of wine left. She sniffed it cautiously, shook her head. "Yuck. Nasty stuff. No way I am drinking any of that," she told herself flatly. Pouring it out here could be a mistake, too, though.

And the cup itself was probably part of a set that normally stayed in that room where Draco was housed— if she left it here, it would cause more trouble than it solved. She eyed the vessel with active dislike, finally shrugged and poured part of the contents into Meritos's thick, wavy black hair—he was drunk enough already, who could tell the difference?—and retreated, the still partly filled cup in hand.

Back at the tree, she eased the staff back into her right hand and considered her options. This really was *not* a good place to be: There was too much light and not enough decent shelter. She glanced around appraisingly: The tree where she'd hidden before wasn't bad, but anyone with a torch out on the main path could make out her shadow, even if she went flat to the ground under the weeping branches. Move behind the palace wall or the fancy gates, and she could conceivably miss Joxer.

The hedge? She slewed around to eye it. It was a

greater distance than she'd like to be from the main doors, but it was well beyond the torches, and it was very dark over there. Dark enough that she could stay in front of the hedge if she sat very still, and she could still see if the Mighty Warrior himself emerged any time soon.

That was another consideration. She glanced at the sky, and at the bear: Her paw was pointing straight up. That meant she had some hours to go before it started getting light in the east, but she knew from experience those hours could pass all too quickly—especially when she needed the cover of dark.

And who knew if there were more palace grounds guards, who'd come looking for Miklos and company when they didn't return to their barracks? "Okay, what would Xena do—never *mind* that! What are you gonna do to keep from getting caught by the king's guards?" Being rescued by Xena from the Spartan prison cells, after tonight, would be one of the more unpleasant experiences she could think of.

Ugly reality—and truly dreadful recent experience— thrust itself into her mind, the way it so suddenly and often did. Gabrielle gasped and fought it aside—and with it, the vision of Xena's son Solon, dead; young, red-haired, sweet-faced Hope dead and by her own hand. *Don't!* she ordered herself fiercely as she tugged at her hair. *Don't see it, don't think it! You can't change the past! And here and now, right now in Sparta, it won't help anything!*

It wouldn't help Xena, who was doing her best to keep Leda's beautiful but clueless daughter from being found by her hateful, brutal mate. Xena had to be right: Menelaus was one of those males who wouldn't let go. *Even Draco isn't that fixated: He wants me, sure; but*

175

he doesn't push his life aside to devote everything to me.

Fortunately. And Xena: *She is in there, in my place. Probably trying to suh—seduce him—and not just because she has the hots for Draco, but because she needs to know what's going on, just like she said. Men like Draco, men like Menelaus—Hades, even men like Joxer.* They could deny it. But for many women, there were events more important than just—well, that.

Xena did what was necessary. She still hurt, she had to. But she did what she had to.

Admit it, she told herself angrily: *You left Poteidaia to follow her to the ends of the earth as much for her inner strengths as for her weapons skills.* That kind of inner strength wasn't common; only certain heroes were able to keep going no matter how they felt. Like Prometheus, who had defied the gods despite the torture they placed on him and on mankind.

"But if I call her a hero, she laughs at me," Gabrielle whispered. "Not like she's making fun of me—well, no. Just—she laughs." Her own blue-green eyes were warm as she clasped the fighting staff in both hands, glanced over her shoulder to make certain no one was trying to sneak up behind her, and eased backward into the hedge.

It really was as prickly as it looked; she swore under her breath, then shifted cautiously onto her backside, ankles crossed, staff across her knees, so that she could wait. In this position, she could wait indefinitely. *As,* she gloomily thought, *I may well have to.*

10

She didn't actually have to wait very long for *something* to happen, however; moments after she reached shelter, the palace doors opened and two guards emerged, both armed with long pikes and swords. The shorter of the two also carried a bow. They turned back briefly; Gabrielle could just make out the shadow of another man inside—probably their captain, giving them final orders. The doors closed then, and the two squared their shoulders and marched down the path and out to the ornamental gates. Once in place, the shorter guard set his pike aside to string his bow and set that against the gate along with a quiver full of arrows. The two men conversed very briefly, so quietly she couldn't make out what they were saying—except for one, unmistakable word. "Xena." The taller man shushed his comrade vigorously; the two turned to face out into the night, pikes at the ready.

Behind, she clearly heard a heavy thud: Someone inside the palace had barred the entry.

Great, she thought. *What else can go wrong?* Apparently, someone in there knew Xena was in Sparta, though from the looks of things, they didn't seem aware she was actually in the palace. *And I'm gonna have to go find her—in Draco's rooms, is this my lucky day or what?—and tell her.*

One major problem and a minor dilemma had just been solved, though: Joxer wasn't going to be coming out *that* way anytime soon. Which meant she wasn't going to mess up at catching him here by going to warn Xena. And now she had a strong reason to persuade Xena it was time to get out of the city, like two sensible women who didn't want to spend time in the king's cells, and snag Joxer out on the road. After all, hadn't Xena just said she knew which way Joxer was heading when he left the city?

"Fine," she muttered. "So what exactly are we doing here? Still?"

With luck, they wouldn't be for much longer.

Besides, she'd already decided this part of the palace grounds was no place to be when day broke: too open. It hadn't been that good a location so far anyway. She slowly tipped her head back to study the sky—*remember what Xena taught you; no sharp or sudden moves when you're trying not to be seen.* The Hunter was farther down toward the west than she'd like; they'd spent entirely too much time playing games out here. "Xena has; I've had it with games. And with Sparta." She eyed the two guards for some moments, then cautiously went flat and began working her way around the hedge on her elbows.

It was a slow process, and by the time she'd melted into the deeper shadows on the far side of the hedge, she was hot and itched all over. Prickly things clung to her forearms and something had slithered down the back of her top; she sat up, briskly rubbed her arms, and shook the thing out—a long skinny leaf of some kind, she thought as she got to her feet. Better than something long and skinny with legs. She vigorously combed through her hair with her fingers; the ends were tangled and full of prickly bits.

The rose garden was once again ahead of her, the balconies and dark windows of the various royal apartments beyond them.

It was . . . she frowned, counted from the left and then from the right. Had to be the third from this side. *Or is it? Boy, would I feel like a complete idiot if I walked into the wrong one.* She considered this, cast up her eyes. *Almost as idiotic as I'd feel if I walked in and Draco and Xena were—well, no. Let's not go there.* Xena wouldn't. Even if the attraction Draco had once held for her was still there. Which—it wasn't.

Besides, the warrior might be in A Mood—but she'd never let her guard down that way, and certainly *not* in the middle of Sparta. She took one last quick look around, then crossed open ground and merged with the rosebushes.

Third balcony . . . If she squinted, she thought she could see light around the drape that puffed outward as a breath of air swirled across the grounds. All right; best route would be to get out of this pocket, move to the left and then—

And just then, two guards in full armor, heads hidden under horse-crested, slits-for-eyes-and-nose helmets, came around the corner of the building, moving stealthily down the line of balconies from her left. Both held drawn swords, and one swung what might be a whip or a bolos, it was too dark to tell. They halted on the balcony she'd decided was Draco's, one on each side of the opening; one held up a hand—possibly a warning to keep quiet. The other nodded, and both men settled into position. They looked ready to wait a long time; she assumed they were waiting for some kind of a signal.

They appeared to be totally intent on the room beyond the drape, Gabrielle decided as she tightened her grip on the staff and went crouching around the bushes. *Good,* she told herself in grim satisfaction. *They won't expect an attack from the rear. And would I ever like another crack at one of those stupid bad-hair-day hats and the snotty boys that wear 'em.*

The problem was when and how to do this. Unlike the drunken Meritos or his two companions, these men moved and acted like serious soldiers—certainly palace guards and possibly the king's own household men. Unlike Meritos or his two buddies, they would have no reason whatever to keep quiet once they saw her. *One of them—yeah, I could drop one of them without him yelling. Two, though . . .* She settled back on her heels, considering the problem, then finally shrugged. It didn't matter; those two were waiting for something, and the way her luck and Xena's had gone thus far, the something was going to be a whole company of soldiers.

Especially if they knew Xena was in that room. "Think about it," she muttered to herself, "they're not waiting around to take out Draco; he's *supposed* to be here." She tried to figure which way the rest of the company would come from—through the apartment doors or with these two—and decided it didn't matter.

Either way, there wasn't anything she could do but get close enough to deal with those two men, once the party started. She sighed, eased back down onto her elbows, and began a slow, cautious, and utterly silent slither through the garden—and as far away from the rosebushes as possible.

Not that distance really helped. By the time she'd reached the last bushes nearest that balcony, she'd had to stop half a dozen times to pull thorns out of her hands and forearms. And something else—something with legs this time—was crawling down between her shoulder blades as she crawled into her hiding place to wait for things to happen.

Back in the king's reception, Avicus signed for the last candidate to be brought in and walked up the long aisle with him. "Highness," he said when the two reached the dais and the guards had closed the doors, "this is Bellerophon of Corinth, who has heard of your need for heroes."

King Menelaus eyed the young man curiously: He had heard of Bellerophon, who was rumored to be the son of King Glaucus, but also, just possibly, the offspring of Poseidon. The boy was young, but already had a reputation for bravery—the kind that asked no reward and served those in greatest need. Not normally the Spartan ruler's kind of man, but Avicus had already warned there would be need for a journey over water, though he'd been unable to say more than just that—or unwilling to share his knowledge. With Avicus, it was impossible to ever be certain.

The boy certainly looked as if he might be half-immortal: he was tall, fine-boned, and golden: his skin bronzed by the sun, his eyes a deep, intense blue, his pale hair all crisp curls, and his mouth that double bow that seemed to smile and to hide secrets, even when there were no secrets and the owner wasn't smiling. He was clean-shaven and well-muscled, clad in muscled armor that was years out of date but well cared for: The bronze formed plates and connecting rings gleamed as if the owner polished his gear regularly, and the leather shone. The sword he wore at his right hip was of recent make, though, the scabbard beautifully crafted and the cross-piece of the hilt inlaid with pearl. Someone had rewarded the boy for a job well done—unless King Glaucus had given the boy his own outdated armor but seen to it that he was decently armed.

Menelaus rubbed his chin thoughtfully. Impossible to know the truth of the rumors—any more than he'd ever really known whether Helen was merely a beauteous mortal or really the daughter of Zeus. Women could have named any man—any god—as her child's father, and who would be able to say it wasn't true?

Still—unlike Sparta, Corinth was right at the sea, even though the water was a long inlet facing west. Still salt, and still the sea god's realm.

The son of Poseidon might just succeed where others failed, especially if the journey finished where Avicus had said he believed it might.

The priest cleared his throat gently; the boy was still on one knee, head bent respectfully. The king smiled and gestured for him to rise. "Bellerophon of Corinth. Your reputation precedes you, young man. But—are you a hero, Bellerophon?"

The youth smiled shyly as he got to his feet. "I—would like to be one, sire." His voice was low and resonant, and he spoke more like a noble than a peasant. "Or—well, sire, I want to accomplish deeds that men like Jason and Hercules and Theseus—and you, yourself, sire—have done. I—I am not entirely certain I would like to be *called* hero, as Hercules is, or Theseus."

"There are few heroes who would answer such a question other than you just answered it," Avicus told him. "Including Hercules." He led the young man over to the bowl, his face impassive but his mind still working furiously over how to manipulate this last would-be hero: What vision to show him, how best to play him?

Because there was something about this man, out of all those who had walked into this chamber over the past few hours, hoping to quest for the king: This one, Avicus thought warily, might actually be the real thing.

Which made it a chancy endeavor, showing someone like this a created vision in the mirror—the son of a god just might see past the falsehood. Though, if this Bellerophon *were* the son of Podseidon—well, the god had no quarrel with the Greeks, except perhaps Odysseus.

Still, it would be better if the boy knew nothing of the true quest: Someone like this would have nothing to do with returning a man's estranged wife, so that man could beat her senseless and then lock her in her apartments for the rest of her days. That wouldn't be—heroic. Avicus eyed the boy sidelong; a youth like this probably had foresworn all *that* kind of contact and quite likely looked upon females as a danger to his purity and as creatures to be worshipped and adored from a safe distance. He bit back a smile: That kind of thing—that, just perhaps, he could work with.

But if the boy could see through illusion, as a son of the sea god should be able to . . .

The priest gave a mental shrug. Keep things simple, he ordered himself. He would create a vision similar to that he showed Joxer and Draco; the woman's beauty might inspire him to worship from afar; the danger suggested would rouse a tiger in the boy's heart. And if he were one of *those* boringly pure types who saw all women as vipers, then another spin could be put on the vision, so that the boy would see the woman as enemy. Either way, he could well be the one to find Helen. *And keep my job here intact. I'd like that.*

The fact was, Avicus knew, living in the Spartan palace, in his own luxurious apartments, agreed with him. Delphi cell-like accommodations and the stone couches couldn't begin to compete with silken sheets, the nightly company of one of Menelaus's prettier laundresses, and decent food, a properly arranged gymnasium where he could work off what he ate.

Helen, he recalled himself sternly. Create the vision, let the boy interpret Helen however he would and make certain that, whatever else Bellerophon saw, the king would know to name it as heirloom and a danger to her; something to be retrieved in any event. Putting Bellerophon before him, he signaled the king of his intentions, then passed his hands over the liquid. "Look upon the water of the god, and tell me what you see," he demanded in a low voice.

Bellerophon eyed the surface for some moments, then glanced up, visibly perplexed. "I see nothing but my reflection."

"Try again," the priest urged, and passed his hands over the liquid again.

"But, I still see only—ah!" He stared intently at the surface, eyes moving rapidly, as if taking in a vista of wonders. "I—I see a woman—no, it is a statue! Of wood, I think, but the eyes are shell, and the whole so beautifully painted that it might almost be a woman— no, no human woman, a goddess, surely! Her hair is of palest gold, and she wears it in a simple plait across one milky shoulder. Her garments—" He drew a deep breath; his pale cheeks were very bright, all at once.

"She wears a simple toga of a deep green that bares one shoulder and her legs, though soft boots cover those to the knee. In one hand, she holds a longbow and in the other, green-fletched arrows . . ." His voice faded away as the surface of the liquid rippled. "She is gone," he whispered. "Arrows—a bow," Avicus repeated blankly. *Golden hair?* he thought dazedly. But Helen's hair was dark, a match for her eyes. Across the dais, the king stared at them, slack-jawed. The youth continued to gaze fixedly at the bowl, even though the priest knew there was nothing to see but his own reflection.

Somehow the priest kept his expression neutral; inside, he was seething. *I know what he saw! How—how dare he play with this?* He touched Bellerophon's arm to get his attention and murmured, "Wait here, watch the water, say nothing. I—" He glanced at the king, who was now frowning. "I need a—private consultation with the god." He strode quickly behind the dais, shoved past the curtain hanging there, and stepped into the servants' passage.

Joxer eased quietly (for Joxer, anyway) around a corner of the palace. The windows at his right were dark, the grounds even darker. Somewhere nearby, a cricket chirped once, loudly, and he jumped, banging his elbow on dressed stone. "Owwww!" He rubbed it vigorously. "I *hate* that, I really hate it!" Silence for some moments. The cricket began chirping again. "All right," he told himself. "Hey, piece of cake. I've made it all this way without any problems, so one more corner, that one right up there, and I should be—" He caught his breath sharply and melted back into shadow, then threw himself flat as four soldiers in those ridiculous horse-crested helmets hove into view, maybe forty paces away

and right where he was headed. To his chagrin, three of
them appeared to be set to stay there for some time. A
quick glance at the sky told him that he didn't have the
time to wait out a change of watch. "Great," he whispered. "I gotta go all the way *back* around this lousy
palace and I'm gonna wind up having to slink around
the gates, when I come up on the wrong side of them,
so I can get into that rose garden—oh, well. At least,
either way when I get there, I'll know where I am,
right?" He got cautiously to his hands and knees and
then to his feet, set his back against the palace wall, and
began working back the way he'd come.

Ten long steps down the passage brought Avicus to a
plain, narrow door behind another drape. He pushed his
way into the room, shoved the door closed behind him
with an audible click, and leaned against it, his jaw
working. "Deep breath," he told himself. "Another."
It was no use speaking to Apollo when he was angry.
Finally he shoved away from the door and stepped into
the chamber.

It was dimly lit by two lamps that flanked an altar.
The priest lit incense, shoved it into the prepared niche,
and let his head fall back, eyes closed.

The Voice came at once—dispassionate, deep, the
sound of it all around him. "I am here," it intoned.
"Why do you bespeak me at this hour?"

"Why," Avicus responded evenly, "have you given
the boy *that* vision? We had a bargain, you and I, an
enormous favor you have owed me ever since I spread
your plague among the Greek soldiers before Troy. Because of that, your Trojan priest got his daughter back—
and she was alive, wasn't she? There wasn't much I

could do about Achilles—or Agamemnon, who is at least as stubborn as his brother.''

"*Was* as stubborn. Where he is now, he learns patience and repentance. I recall the bargain, priest. It was to have been complete when Menelaus destroyed Troy and took back his woman.''

Your half-sister, Avicus thought, but wisely did not say. Apollo could be petty about things, and half-human siblings were high on the list. "We have agreed that Xena was *not* my fault! And we agree that the bargain between us should continue. Why else would I set up this fool's parade of supposed heroes?''

"I have told you, Avicus, that I cannot see Helen. She lives, but she is protected from me, possibly by one of my sisters who—well, for whatever reason any of them might have. I gave the boy his vision because you will only need his services a little while. Once you are done with him, I will then call upon him to retrieve my stolen image of Daphne.'' *Daphne*, the priest thought grimly. *I knew it, I simply knew it!* "She—the statue was stolen from me; I want it back, since the nymph herself is denied me.''

The priest shook his head. "We have a bargain, you and I. If the king of Sparta does not locate his wife through my intervention—and that soon—I will no longer be your priest in Sparta. There will *be* no priest of Apollo in Sparta—and I doubt very much there will be an Avicus. Is that your wish?''

The god's voice changed; no longer that of a supreme immortal above it all, he sounded angry, in a petty, spoiled-boy way. "How dare you question my judgment? Or my pain? The image is mine, carved for me by the dryad's brother. *He* knew I would not have harmed her; *he* was not like his father, Peneus—and who, after all is Peneus but a minor river god? And a pettifogging little god who thinks himself and his offspring too good for the likes of a son of Zeus? Do not argue with *me*, Avicus."

You can't win, not with Him, Avicus thought, and bit back a sigh. *If He can't thunder and scare you into going along with what He wants, He makes you feel guilty, or He whines until you'll do anything to make him stop.* "I do not argue with you. I'm tired, it's been a long day, the king is in a temper, and I simply would like to know how you want me to interpret your vision to the boy. *And* whether I can still count on your word, that the king's search is still . . ."

"Of course you can!" The Voice replied waspishly. "But once he has found the woman for you, I want him for my own quest. Since I cannot have the nymph herself, the image . . ."

There were tears in The Voice, Avicus realized in sudden horror. He hastily said, "I will have no use whatever for him, once Helen is found. But perhaps I should get back in there? You know how Menelaus can be, if he gets bored with waiting . . ." A breath later, Interpretation filled him, and Avicus bowed, very deeply. "Thank you, great Apollo." He backed away from the altar, eyes still closed, hands feeling behind him for the wall. Once there, he turned, fumbled the latch open, and eased back into the hallway, only then daring to open his eyes.

He did sigh then, heavily. "My feet *do* hurt, my liege is in a royal hissy fit, the god I serve has drunk enough mead that He is maudlin, and I am completely and totally *bored* with the demands of my job! I wonder if the theater in Athens could use a good effects man?" A corner of his mouth twitched; he chuckled briefly. Good humor restored—at least for the moment—he returned to the hall.

No one seemed to have moved much in his absence. Menelaus slumped on his throne, chin in one hand, eyes half-closed, and Bellerophon gazed, wide-eyed, at the bowl. Avicus quietly cleared his throat to alert the king, then crossed to the tripod. Bellerophon started as the priest touched him.

"Did you see anything else while I was away? No? Just as well. It is—you are certain the statue was of wood?"

"Ahhh? Ah—oh." He blinked and considered this briefly. "It appeared to me that it was."

"How large?"

"Ahhh—large? No longer than my forearm, I think."

"Good," Avicus said smoothly; he glanced sidelong at the king, who was beginning to look impatient again, and angry because of it. He'd want an explanation, and soon. But they didn't dare simply send the boy away: He needed information about which way to set out, where to find transportation, whom to trust, and who not. "You have been blessed, Bellerophon. What you saw was a statue of the goddess Artemis—not just any statue, but the image of her crafted especially for Apollo and dearly loved by him. But it vanished from his hall, ages ago. I believe your vision means that you will be the one to retrieve it for the god—one day. But that is not your quest, just now. Are you sure you saw nothing else? Anything at all, however small and humble?"

Bellerophon considered this, his brow creased. "There was—I saw an oil lamp," he said finally. "But—it was nothing, merely a plain-looking, brass oil lamp, except that—I think the handle was covered in braided leather."

Avicus was already nodding, the bland smile in place. Even better than a hunk of jewelry. "Good. That lamp is the thing King Menelaus urgently seeks. Lives hang in the balance, and it is vital someone retrieve the lamp and return it here as quickly as possible." He gestured sharply with the hand Bellerophon could not see, but the king wasn't responding.

A glance showed him why: Menelaus had already had enough tonight, long before his last two "guests" had come to be tested. Draco had been a sore point, of course; after all, the warlord and his army had taken full advantage of Menelaus's journey to Troy, to loot his lands. Bellerophon and all this unexpected nonsense about statues of Artemis—well. At the moment, the king was barely containing a formidable rage.

I wish he would learn to control that temper—after all, his brother did. Odysseus—well, he never had a temper to begin with. And if he won't give over these stupid fits, why can he simply not forget the wretched woman, and go attack the Hittites? Avicus sighed inwardly, mentally rehearsed the speech he'd taught the king and laid a friendly hand on Bellerophon's shoulder.

"You see," he explained, "the lamp is a family relic, passed from second son to second son in the king's family for generations. It is said—though," the smile widened slightly, "who can be certain?—that the lamp was forged by Hephaestus, because the king's family springs from the union of Zeus and the maiden Europa." The boy was actually following all this; Bellerophon apparently had received a proper education. "The lamp had only one purpose: to kindle the funeral pyre of a member of the immediate family—"

"—a *male* member, you mean?" the youth asked uncertainly, as the priest hesitated to choose his next words. Avicus bit back a smile; not just an education, but a proper classic one—the kind in which boys learned that men took women as mates, but other men were their only friends and close companions. *Now, if Menelaus had accepted that women, if seen, were to be properly covered, and not heard—if he'd kept her where she belonged, and not become besotted with her—well, we wouldn't be in this mess, would we?* They would have: until Helen, Menelaus had believed the same things.

Odd, how things worked: The vision of Helen that had so pleased Joxer would appall a young prig like this boy. Fortunately, after all, Apollo had overriden his own choice of vision.

"Male, of course," the priest replied smoothly, and began revising the tale as he went. "Now, the queen is a very beautiful woman, but she does suffer—as do they all—from the failings of their sex . . ." He paused; the boy nodded as if this were a given. "But her beauty was such that, at least for a time, it blinded the king to her willfulness, and lack of intelligence. And so, when she took a fancy to the lamp because of its age and lineage, he could not persuade her to leave it in the cupboard where the sacred oil and the ancient torches are kept. With my help, he was able to convince her that it must not be used to illuminate the table at such banquets where a woman could appear, nor could she have it set upon a table in her apartments, where she could see it."

"To—" Bellerophon glanced at the king, who was now slumped in his chair, one hand over his eyes; he prudently lowered his voice. "To allow a woman to do as she chooses—"

"Well, you might forgive a man under the circumstances," Avicus said with a shrug. "After all, they were not long married and she was—even I could appreciate her beauty, if I looked upon her as a work of art. But of course she was spoiled. Probably because she is rumored to be the daughter of Zeus . . .''

"I—had heard such a rumor,'' the boy replied, even more quietly. "Something to do with a swan—except it was really Zeus?'' He shrugged, suddenly looked shy. "I—of course, there are stories about many—ah—''

"I have heard those stories, Bellerophon. I judge men by their skills, rather than their lineage.''

He smiled. "Thank you, sir—''

"Call me . . . Avicus,'' the priest intoned.

"Avicus. Well, the woman will not affect me in any manner whatever; I have taken vows to—I mean, that I—'' The boy was blushing. Avicus laid fingers across his lips.

"I understand, do not distress yourself. Clearly, you are a youth who has avoided the snares of females and has pledged to live a life free of them?'' Not quite a question, but the boy nodded sharply; his color was still very high. "Good. No wonder you alone were given such a vision, Bellerophon. Because of all those who came here tonight, only you are pure in heart as well as—well, elsewhere. And such virtue is invaluable.''

"I see—I think I see,'' the boy replied doubtfully.

"It is true. Helen fled Sparta with the son of Priam of Troy, as you have surely heard.'' Bellerophon nodded. "What you will not know is that she took the lamp with her. The king did all he could to retrieve his befuddled wife and bring her home, without bloodshed.'' He paused; not surprisingly, the boy nodded again. *No doubt his tutors insisted he learn all the odes, the genealogy of the gods, the myths, and all of them completely ignored history as a pointless exercise. Good*, the priest thought.

"The king unfortunately failed," Avicus went on after a moment and another glance at the king, who was still slumped on his throne, one hand shielding his eyes. "The city of Troy fell to his army, but Paris was dead and Helen had vanished." He glanced at the boy, decided to risk it. "Rumor has it Helen was spirited away by a woman warrior named—Xena."

Bellerophon had clearly heard of *her*, the priest thought in satisfaction; his jaw dropped and his eyes bugged, most unherolike. "Xena? Do you—" He regained control of his face, but his hands were white-knuckled fists. "She is with Xena?"

"She may be; even the god has not been able to show her to me, and that is why we needed someone like you, Bellerophon. We do know that Xena was in Troy during the last days, fighting against her own people, the Greeks."

"Traitorous woman," the boy hissed. "Do you—can you tell me, is it possible that I—that I will be the man who slays Xena?"

Avicus smiled widely. "I cannot tell you that. But the man who finally frees us all of Xena will truly be a hero. At the least, you can find and return poor, foolish Helen to her husband. And the oil lamp."

"Oil—? Oh, yes; that lamp."

"Yes, Bellerophon; the lamp of the king's ancestors that Helen took with her, which we believe she took to Troy. You must find it and in the best instance, return her and it here. But if you cannot convince her to return, you must take the lamp and return it here. Apollo tells me that the god who created it says she will not be permitted to keep it for much longer. If it is not reconsecrated by my own hands and returned to its cupboard before the moon waxes and wanes again, Apollo will

193

cause it to ignite with at least the force of the volcano that sank fabled Atlantis. Helen, and all who serve her, hide her, protect her—or seek to save her—will die, along with every innocent human and beast whose only crime is to be anywhere near her.

Silence. Bellerophon gazed at him, wide-eyed. "We are truly desperate, young hero: The king has done all he can to ensure Helen's safety, and he—well, look upon him!" A sweep of the priest's hand indicated the still-furious Menelaus—furious to his own eyes only, it seemed. Avicus managed a sad smile and turned back to his young companion. "Behold a man torn by agony! To lose his beloved bride, before he can straighten out her confusion. Then, to be responsible for the deaths of so many innocents! Is it a wonder he can barely sleep or eat these days?"

"All of this," Bellerophon finally managed, "for a *woman*?"

Avicus shrugged. "For the lamp, more correctly. The king knows its value to his blood, and he fears the damage it will cause. Oh, about the woman herself—I am of your mind regarding the creatures, young hero. Such things distract one from the true goals of a pure life. Still, if all of us felt that way, how would you and I have come to live on this world?"

"Ah—well, yes, point taken," the hero conceded. "You wish me to—ah, I'm not sure what you want me to do?"

Avicus hesitated; he was still thinking furiously, trying to make sense of everything, and trying to make it *sound* sensible. *This is nearly as much fun as my first paying job, when I operated the machinery for the deus ex machina at the theater in Minos,* he thought sourly. *Good old Daedalus—master magician; lousy manager.*

Aloud, he said cheerfully, "Do? Why, it is simple. I serve Apollo. The god has blessed this enterprise and granted me the right to test those who would find the lamp and return it to king Menelaus before any harm can result.

"Some of those who came here tonight were told that the king seeks his queen's return only because of his love for her. And that Apollo blesses this. But the god does not involve himself in mere romantic entanglements as does his sister Aphrodite." Bellerophon's nose wrinkled in disgust; Avicus smiled and nodded. "Exactly my thought. An—untidy goddess at best. And yes, I dare say that, because I have her brother's divine protection. And the king's feelings for his wife are deep and true. But the gods played with him, through her. Remember that without Helen, there would have been no great war before Troy." The boy looked blankly at him. No history, Avicus reminded himself. Plenty of mythos, though. "Besides, if you recall, Aphrodite was responsible for Paris's attraction to Helen in the first place, and all so the foolish immortal could be crowned Miss Olympus—named the prettiest of all—some nonsense like that."

"So I have heard, sir."

"A foolish reason for men to leave their homes and die, I think. But—that is not our present problem, is it? And that problem is—?"

"The lamp," the youth replied at once.

"Good, you pay close attention. Listen some more, please. Apollo would not aid me in retrieving Helen for the king, not for a reason no more valid than love. But! He has agreed that no one should die for foolishness, and this of the lamp—well, judge for yourself. And so, the god granted my request that some hero be chosen to seek the lamp and return it here. You have already seen a true vision—but only the first of many. Others will come to you from time to time, and thanks to them, you will find the lamp.'' He pressed one of his badges onto the boy's shoulder and gave him the usual speech about its usefulness. A secretive smile touched the corners of his mouth; how amusing, if this incredibly innocent boy should be the one who led them to Helen, all unaware that Avicus watched his progress in this very bowl, via that badge—and another, possibly more, depending on how trustworthy his field agents were.

"And—Helen?'' Bellerophon asked uncertainly. "You—His Highness asks that I bring her back to Sparta?'' Avicus nodded firmly.

"Yes. And for one reason alone: Of all those who were tested before you, no one is less likely to be swayed by her beauty or her wiles.''

"Well—yes. But what if she will not come, or will not release the lamp . . . ?''

"The god tells me she *will* release the lamp, once you explain its dangers—not just to her, but also to those around her,'' Avicus glibly told him. A lie, of course. "He also tells me—as does the king—that if Helen will not willingly return to Sparta, you must not force her. Instead, you must give her this message from her husband.'' He paused to recall the exact words; they rang in his ears as Menelaus somehow got himself under control enough to speak them.

"Tell her that boys raised by warriors know only how to become warriors themselves—they sneer at gentleness, and love confuses them. But some such warriors can learn that war is a waste, while love: She will not believe. Still, tell her, from the man who married her, that he will do whatever he must to learn to be gentle and to love. That such a man is Menelaus, who has an undying love for his wife. But if she will not believe that, tell her that Menelaus has profited by the example of his brother, Agamemnon, who sacrificed every woman he ever loved, and because of that is now dead. Tell her that Menelaus does not fear death half so much as he fears the loss of his beloved Helen. But not just an object to love and keep safe: He also greatly misses his intelligent Helen, his clever Helen. Tell her that Menelaus now knows that beauty fades quickly, but that grace, intelligence, and the ability to converse and amuse will continue until two wary young lovers are white-haired and aged and still of infinite beauty, each to the eye of the other.''

Bellerophon gazed at the king, wide-eyed. "To love in such a manner!" he whispered. "But this is—surely this must be what my teachers spoke of when they named perfect love!" Menelaus would have spoken; Avicus gestured and faintly shook his head. The boy smiled; his eyes shone. "I envy you greatly, sire. For you are one man in thousands who might desire a pure love, and all those others will never attain it. I do not understand it, but I give it—and you—homage. Rest assured, I will convey your message to Helen, and do all I can to see that she understands the purity of your love for her.'' He knelt and bowed his head. "I cannot believe I am worthy of such a quest, but rest assured, sire, that I will carry it out—or die in the attempt.''

Avicus smiled and clapped him on the shoulder. "We do not ask your life, Bellerophon. Merely your best efforts. Go now, return to your chamber. Food will be brought to you, and further instructions. You will leave Sparta at sunrise.'' The boy went to one knee, then rose, turned, and strode from the chamber. Avicus waited until the doors closed behind him before muttering, "Sanctimonious young puppy."

"Young idiot," Menelaus growled behind him as he rose to his feet. "I hope there was some purpose in all of that, priest?"

"I think so," Avicus replied. He turned and smiled. "The god has another purpose for him—but it will not matter until Helen is found. And that—" he gestured toward the distant doors, "is the youth who will find her."

"Why not have brought him in first, then? And what were you saying about Xena?"

"I should have said," the priest broke in smoothly, "that I *believe* he is the one. Apollo does not speak in straight fashion to mere mortals, even his priests. And I still feel some—well, that doesn't matter. What matters is that Xena was involved back in Troy, and I believe she will be this time."

"You can't possibly think that green youth would actually kill her! *If* he got the chance."

"No. If it makes him happier about this quest to think he will kill Xena—well, why not let him believe it?"

Menelaus smiled unpleasantly. "Well, he will not have the opportunity, will he? Since she is here—"

"I know," Avicus said. "I saw her, in the water. With that, I should be able to see where she goes."

"Goes? She isn't going anywhere, except into one of my cells—after I question her. If she knows where Helen is, I'll learn it tonight. Well?" His mouth twisted as the priest stared at him.

"You sent men to take her? Are you mad?"

"Angry," the king said flatly; his eyes were opaque, all pupil. "Because of pointless delays, I remind you, priest."

198

"There won't be any delays if you let her leave! She knows you want Helen back. She'll go straight to the woman to warn her. And then we won't need any of these foolish would-be heroes. We'll be able to set the trap and take Helen, kill Xena . . ." The king smiled grimly and shook his head. "Highness, I can't believe you're doing this. You actually intend to capture Xena and force her to talk?" The king's smile widened, slightly. Avicus shuddered. "My king, she will absolutely not *tell* you anything, even if your men do manage to capture her!"

"I sent enough men; she won't stand a chance. And I owe that woman."

The priest shook his head. "I know you do. We both do. But you won't collect here and now. Call them off." But as he spoke, he head a distant clash of weapons, men yelling and above the roar, a woman's high-pitched battle cry.

Menelaus heard it, too. The smile widened. "Too late," he said.

11

Back in the royal apartments allotted to one particular warlord, Xena lounged against a pile of cushions as Draco paced, cursing steadily. He finally halted midstride and turned to glare down at her. "Damn you, Xena! Why do you always *do* this to me?"

She offered him a wry smile. "Because it's fun to watch you go nuts? Look, you're making my neck hurt. Siddown and listen to me for a minute, will you?"

"Why?" he snapped. "So you can pull another fast one on me? Xena, for your information, this is—ah, to Hades with it!" He snatched up a pear from the low table and snapped his teeth into it. She folded her hands and waited him out; he cast up his eyes, but finally came back over and dropped down cross-legged across the low table from her. "Look. Every time we've tripped over each other the past year or so, you've done this: Back on Ithaca, and then the last time, when I had the contract to sell all those Hestian virgins to that lousy slave trader—Hades, I can't even remember his name."

"I bet his mother can't, either," Xena drawled.

"Don't!" Draco warned sharply. "Doesn't matter. What matters is, you got cute with me, got me thinking you were maybe even in love with me—yeah, right. All the time, you were laughing at me. Playing your cute little game, making sure I didn't take those girls, keeping me from collecting one huge bounty—and just maybe making me look like a fool."

"Draco, I might do a lot of things, but I do not laugh at you. And it didn't have one damned thing to do with the dinars. But you should know by now, I'll do anything I have to, to stop you in a situation like that," she replied evenly. "And I didn't make you look like a fool—you did a pretty good job of that all by yourself."

His mouth quirked. "Thanks for nothing."

"Any time. Besides, I already told you—that wasn't the real thing, me falling for you: it was Cupid's arrows."

His mouth twisted. "Yeah, sure, Xena. Know what? I think that's about the crummiest lie you've ever come up with to justify toying with me. Besides, if that's true, then how come I still—?" He stopped abruptly, shook his head. "Forget it. What I want to know is, why are you here—now?"

"What do *you* think?"

"*I* think I'm too smart to second-guess you," he replied darkly. "I hope I am. Because the last time I tried, it nearly drove me over the edge: Is she acting like this to get my mind off the Hestian virgins? No—she's gotta know even I'd never fall for a dumb stunt like that. So, is the old flame still burning? Fat chance of that, more likely it's because she's jealous of Gabrielle . . ."

Xena chuckled throatily. "But you didn't fall for Gabrielle until after you and I first—ah—hooked up, remember?"

He bit into the pear, chewed savagely. She waited. "What is it with you?" he finally asked. "No, I really want to know! You keep pulling this same old stunt on me, and I am getting really tired of it! And I am getting even *more* tired of the fact that every single time you turn up anymore, everything gets stirred up like—" He struggled for a comparison, finally shrugged, and took another bite of fruit. "It gets crazy and strange. I don't want to do that again, if you don't mind," he said finally.

"Look, I'm sorry if it seems like everything goes to Hades in an eggbasket every time we see each other. These things happen."

"Oh, no," he informed her vigorously. "Not *this* time, they don't! Because, for one thing, I am *not* gonna trust you. Not—not even if you tell me the sky is up! And for another, you are gonna walk out of here right now, and you are gonna stay far, *far*, away from me! Because I got a good thing going for once, and I'm not gonna let you make a mess of it. I'm warning you, Xena—!"

She eased back into the cushions. "Give it a rest, Draco. Face it: You're pissed off because you think I led you on and then cut you off."

He leveled a finger at her nose. "No, that is *not* it!" He drew a steadying breath, expelled it in a rush. "Look, Xena—this isn't the Hestian virgins; it's nothing like that. I'm out to do something good for a change, so if you're planning on tripping me up—well, don't. That's all."

She crossed her legs. "That's what you think, huh?"

"No." He dropped the pear core and leaned forward to plant his elbows on the table. "That's what I *know*." Silence; he studied her face; she looked back at him,

203

impassively. "What's your angle this time? You want to be the one who brings her back? Or are you backing someone else to find her first and win the king's reward? Or maybe you just can't stand the thought of me doing something right for once!"

"You know me better than that, Draco," she growled. "I've never lied when I said I wanted you to fight for good. I still want that." His mouth twisted; she sat forward. "Look—this isn't about you and me, you and Gabrielle, not even about you and Helen, for that matter."

"Helen, huh?"

"Don't even bother. I know why Menelaus got you here. You and all those others."

His eyes narrowed. "So you say. What's it about, then?" But before she could say anything, he held up a hand. "No—don't bother. I don't want to know what kind of fancy lie you've got for me this time."

Xena sighed heavily and eyed the ceiling. "Will you just shut up and listen? I wouldn't be breaking into the Spartan palace if I didn't have a good reason. King Menelaus doesn't like me, in case you hadn't heard. And his pet priest Avicus likes me even less."

"Maybe, just maybe I heard something," Draco replied warily. "About you kidnapping Helen from the Trojans, just before King Menelaus could rescue her."

"I bet I know who told you that one—save it, will you? We don't have time for this. The Draco I know wouldn't make up his mind without hearing both sides of the story."

"Not when *you're* the one telling the other side of it," he said shortly. She waited. "Okay, lay it out. Just don't be too surprised if I don't go with it."

She shrugged. "Whatever. Troy wasn't about a

broken-hearted husband standing at the gates and begging his wife to come home.''

He cast up his eyes. ''So it was a war—so what? But if a man's wife's been kidnapped and they're holding her in an armed camp, what's he supposed to do, bang on the gates and whimper? Of course he went to war!''

''Fine so far,'' Xena said evenly. ''Except, what if the wife wasn't kidnapped? What if her husband was twice her age, and he married her because she was part of a package that included Sparta and a crown? What if he wanted that and also wanted to be known as the man married to the most beautiful woman alive?''

Draco shrugged. ''So? A lot of men would take a package like that. What's the problem?''

''No problem, Draco—unless the man in question got real jealous, didn't want the citizens of Sparta smiling at his beautiful wife, didn't want her smiling at anyone but him. Unless he kept boxing her into a smaller and smaller area until all she had was her apartments and whatever banquets the king *allowed* her to attend.''

He sighed heavily. ''Xena, you may not realize this, but not every woman wants to be you when she grows up. There's nothing wrong with the way a lot of royal women live. Some—most of them actually like it and some even prefer it. Most of them have a few rooms, a garden, a loom—a harp or something to play, and they really, truly *like* that. They don't have to chop wood, swing a sword, spill blood, or patch up the men who've had it spilled. They don't need upper arms like logs or shoulders that can carry a mule halfway across the village. You didn't hear Penelope whining because she couldn't swim naked in the bay and fight with the soldiers, did you?''

Xena scowled at him, narrow-eyed; Draco glared

back. "All right, you've made your point," she said finally. "Besides, I agree with you; everyone's got a right to live the life they want. That includes Helen."

Draco eyed her with patent disbelief. "What you're telling me—that's not what the king says."

"He wouldn't. Look, Draco, I was here once; I didn't meet Helen then, but I heard enough, just hanging around this palace. Menelaus pretty much kept her a prisoner in her own apartments—a set of rooms as big as this, all right? Finally, she got desperate enough to run away with another man. All right, he was younger and prettier than her husband, and he could recite poetry to her eyes and all that. And then, once she got snuggled down in his bed, she found out *he* wasn't any better, he just talked a better line." Silence. "That part I *do* know for a fact. She told me when I went to Troy at her request."

She paused; he waved her on. "Look, Draco, you gotta believe this much. Everything I have done for Helen, I did for a reason, and because she *asked* me to. When I was here last time, it wasn't that long since he'd married her. You could see it, even then—how he acted, the way his voice changed when he talked about her. He's not in love—if he ever was, he's obsessed. She's not his wife, she's a possession. I think he's reached the point where he's decided that if he can't have her, nobody can."

Draco was on his feet again, pacing the room. He stopped and gazed down at her. "That's crazy—it doesn't even make sense!"

"Don't give me that," she snarled. "You've seen men like that—men who get so jealous about someone—"

"Okay, I've seen them. Menelaus isn't one. Xena, I'm

206

smarter than that, I can tell when someone's lying to me, all right? He's genuinely unhappy without her. Sure, he wants her back. Why wouldn't he? He lives in Sparta. Why wouldn't he want *her* back in Sparta?'' He spread his hands in a broad shrug. ''That's all it is.''

''That's all, huh? And what if you find her and she says no?''

''Xena,'' he said with heavy patience. ''If I find her, all he asked that I do is pass on his message. Then, if she wants to come back, I escort her. And if she doesn't, I bring her message back here—and he lives with it.''

''That's what he *says*.''

''That *is* what he says,'' Draco agreed evenly. ''And whichever way it goes, I know that I did something good. Something that just might make some people happy. For once.'' He was pacing more; he suddenly turned on one heel, came back across the room, and loomed over her. ''You used to say you wanted that— all those times you tried to get me to turn my life around. Or was that another lie?''

Her eyes softened. ''That was never a lie; it still isn't.''

''Good. Then you can just walk back out of here, now, and let me get on with it.''

''Look, Draco—I want that, but you've got to believe me, this is *not* the time or the place! Menelaus will have you followed, Avicus has ways of seeing where you go—''

''Nice try, Xena. Nobody follows me if I don't want to be followed.'' Silence. Xena broke it.

''I am telling you. One way or another, if you find Helen, Menelaus will learn where she is. And he'll—at the least, he'll pack her back here and lock her in her rooms for the rest of her life. At the worst, he'll kill her.''

"You can't possibly know that, Xena. Anyway, I don't believe it." He was pacing again, divesting himself of his armor as he went. He now tugged at the neck strings of his dark blue shirt and hauled it over his head. Deep bronze shoulder muscle rippled as he quietly slammed his right fist into his left palm, left fist into right palm.

"What if you're wrong?" she asked quietly. "How good is *that* gonna make you feel?"

"I'm not wrong; you're lying to me." Silence again. He turned to face her, and there was doubt in his face, all at once. "You *are* lying; tell me you are. Don't do this to me, dammit!" She shook her head; he spun away, began pacing once more. "Thing is," he said after a long moment, "I've changed—I think I have. It's like— I didn't want to, but I didn't have any choice. Partly because of—of her. Gabrielle." He came back, settled on the edge of the low table. "Funny." A smile warmed his bow-shaped mouth. "When I first saw her, all I could think was, 'Dumb, nattering little blond. Why doesn't Xena shut her up?' And then, all of a sudden—" He seemed to search for words. Dark, intense eyes met hers. "You and me—oh, yeah, it was good. So good. But, this is—it's like nothing I ever felt. It's—I want to do things that would make her glad. Even if she never hears about them." He studied her face. "I know you understand that, because of Marcus." She stirred, her eyes suddenly cold. "Don't look at me like that. I knew him—"

"I know you did," she broke in harshly.

"Yeah, well—I heard about you and him. A—I don't

know, what the bards call a love you'd go to Tartarus and back for.''

"You don't know the half of it,'' Xena whispered under her breath, her eyes briefly bleak indeed. But when Draco eyed her sidelong, she shook her head impatiently. "None of your damned business, Draco. Go on.''

"So, I know you understand. Xena, I'm not good with words, but I'm just asking you, give me a chance with her. With G-Gabrielle. I won't—I'm not gonna try to carry her off this time, nothing like that. I'm not doing this so as to win her over, I know she has plenty of reason not to trust me. But . . .'' He swallowed, hard. "But I'd just—I'd feel better about things, if I knew she'd heard about—''

"Draco,'' Xena said quietly as he hesitated, "the best way you can do something about a mess like this, the one thing that would make Gabrielle happy, is *not* to go after Helen. If there's even a possibility I'm not lying to you, how can you take the chance?''

"I might've known you'd say that,'' he replied with a bitter smile, got to his feet, and turned away from her. "Story of my life. You have all the answers, every time, and I'm just the dumb warlord who's good enough to lead an army, not good enough for anything else.''

Xena closed the distance between them, stopping just short of where she could touch him; he eyed her over his shoulder, then turned away again. "Draco, it's not true! If it was, why would I have kept trying to change you?'' Silence. She laid a hand on his shoulder. He came around, met her eyes. "Draco, there is so much heart in you, so much intelligence. Anyone can maim and kill, burn villages, hurt people. You don't have to be like that.''

He picked the hand off his shoulder. "No one *has* to be like that. I chose it, same as you did. Just like I *tried* to be a good man, the way I promised Gabrielle after I gave up on taking those virgins." A corner of her mouth moved. "Laugh at me, go ahead. I really tried to follow through on that vow." He let go of her. "So it didn't work, big surprise. And this time, it cost me my army."

She shook her head in disbelief—but angry and sour as he looked just now, it had to be true. "Draco—I'm sorry. Believe me, I am."

"Yeah. Me, too," he replied bitterly. He turned away from her. "You know what it's like to build an army, man by man. Until it's a fighting force you can trust to back you, no matter what. And then, one afternoon, you come back to camp to find one of your chief officers is running things, and the only way out for you is through the gauntlet." He jabbed a forefinger at her. "Try *that*, and then you'll know just how good life can get."

Xena grabbed his shoulder. "You think I don't know?" she hissed in a low voice. "Well, guess what, Draco, we got more in common than you'd think! Remember Darfus?"

"Darfus—?" He nodded sharply. "Wait. Yeah. Pale hair, pale eyes, bad teeth, real lousy attitude?"

"You got it," she snarled. "Wanna compare scars? Because, I got 'em too. Lots of 'em, and not all the visible kind! So. Who stole *your* army?"

Draco looked down at her, clearly startled, then looked away. "Why do you care?"

"Maybe I don't; maybe I'm just curious. Indulge me."

He gazed past her; his mouth twitched. "Brisus," he finally admitted.

She stared at him. "Brisus! Aw, no, can't be! Short

little man, pale hair, pale eyes, neat little beard, mean little mouth?'' Draco nodded. "Yeah, I know Brisus. But, I left him in King Theseus's prison cells!''

"Yeah, well, he got out somehow and joined my army, late this last spring. *His* army, now. You know, I liked his attitude, especially the way he felt about profit. Funny how things change, isn't it?'' He wasn't smiling, though.

"No, it isn't funny,'' Xena said softly. Silence, which she finally broke. "Look, I gotta get out of here, especially if I can't do anything to convince you. Just—just *listen* to me for one last minute, will you?'' she added sharply as he would have interrupted her. He eyed her warily, finally gestured her to go on. "If you go through with this, and if you find Helen, pass on this message of the king's. And then—promise me you'll listen to what she has to tell you about Menelaus, about Paris. Ask her how she'd really feel about coming back here. Do that for Gabrielle, will you?''

He eyed her for a long moment, then nodded. "You're trying to play me—but all right. I promise. That's it?''

"No. Do *me* a favor, too. Watch your back. And watch your back trail.''

"I'd do that anyway,'' he said quietly.

"Good. I—what was that?'' Xena held up a hand and stole, light-footed, across the room, stopping at the double apartment doors, ear against the wood.

Draco snatched up his sword from the pile of armor and weaponry he'd just shed and caught up with her. He touched her shoulder. "In case you've forgotten, I'm *supposed* to be in here.'' She laid a finger against his lips and listened intently.

"I swear I just heard someone out there draw a sword," she whispered.

His eyes narrowed angrily. "Xena, I swear, if some-one saw you come in here and you've soured this deal for me—!"

She turned and gave him a dirty look. "Draco—do you *ever* think about anyone but yourself?"

He glared down at her, but before he could get a word out, someone slammed into the door, and a voice out in the hall shouted, "Get those doors open, and get the woman, by the king's order!"

"See?" Xena demanded sharply.

Before she could say anything else, another voice added, "Get the warlord, too: His Beneficence Avicus tells me they were once allies and I'm betting they still are!"

"You were saying?" Draco snarled, and thrust sharply to one side, sending the scabbard flying.

Xena laughed shortly. "So you gonna persuade 'em you're on their side—with that? C'mon, Draco, you wanna start pleasing Gabrielle, try *not* killing people for a change."

He stared at her, aghast. "Are you *nuts?* There must be half the Spartan army out there!"

"So when did you ever turn down a challenge?" She bared her teeth in a wild grin, took took two steps back from the double doors, and waited. From the sound of things, they wouldn't have long to wait. Draco gave her a wild-eyed look, then retrieved his scabbard, sheathed the blade, and tossed the whole thing into the linen store. The doors shuddered, the blow echoed. "All right," he said grimly. "You get out of here in one piece, you tell her I *tried* your way. And if we both don't—well, I'll see you in Tartarus.''

Don't bet on it, Draco.'' Xena flexed her hands and settled her shoulders.

Out in the rose garden, Gabrielle sat up sharply as six more men came trotting around the far side of the palace, weapons drawn, to join the two on the balcony. She swore and clawed at the palm of her left hand where a fallen thorn had just bitten in, tore it free, and edged to her knees, staff balanced neatly in an overhand/underhand grip.

The eight Spartan soldiers seemed oblivious to the presence of anyone behind them; no surprise there, since she could clearly hear someone inside the palace bellowing commands to break down the doors and take prisoners.

"I hate this," she muttered, and began easing forward. "I really, *really* hate this!" At least there wasn't much need for quiet. Still—Xena in her place would get as close as possible without being seen. *Element of surprise,* she reminded herself with a grim smile, rose slowly to her feet, and went crouching toward the balcony.

Joxer peered uncertainly around the corner of the building. The rose gardens should be on the *far* side of that lighted area where the hedge was, he'd already decided—but they seemed to be here, instead. Unfortunately, so were several of the king's men, all of them well armed and moving as if they had a purpose in mind. *Hope they aren't looking for me,* he thought in a sudden panic; he threw himself back out of sight; his mishmash of weaponry and armor clattered loudly, and he began patting at things, silencing the clangor, resettling strips of armor, making sure none of his daggers had come loose to poke him at the wrong moment. *That was loud enough to wake the—well, no it wasn't*, he assured himself quickly. It had been loud enough, though.

Still—a quick glance reassured him there was no one else along this wall, no one coming this way, headed wherever those guys had gone. No one apparently alerted to noise where none should be, at this hour. But another look down the way he wanted to go . . . He sighed in vexation and slammed his back into the wall again.

"Well, isn't this just *swell*!" he mumbled. "I could probably figure out where to go from over *there*, but no! There's all these guys with swords down there, and with my luck, they'd see me, and I would really rather they didn't." The gate guards—he was pretty certain he could charm or bluff them. Or both; they hadn't seemed that bright, and they'd appeared to be impressed by the credentials he'd presented. And they were both on guard until first sun—who knew what the king had on duty once the sun rose? Besides, the other "heroes" would be hot out the door by then—if he was going to get a head start on this quest, this was the only way he could think of to do it.

So—his best bet was to make it to the gates without drawing the attention of the closest guards. Because those guys down by the rose gardens already *had* their swords out, and it was his experience that men with drawn swords tended to look upon anything that moved as something to hack.

He swallowed hard and tried to dismiss the thought. Once he was certain he could move without his knees giving way, he stepped away from the wall and peered all around. No good: The wall surrounding the palace was high at this point, and it seemed to be in very good repair.

Nor had he seen anyplace better for a climber like himself further back—that left the main entry and that flower garden. He sighed heavily, dragged the helmet free and scratched his head, then eased over to look around the corner again. Someone down there was yelling. Maybe he had a chance after all. A grin twitched his mouth, and he chuckled softly. "Yeah, that's it. Just wait until those guys are busy, then, poof! Here one minute, then, ta daah! Gone in a flash, Joxer the Invisible—hey!" He mumbled tunelessly for a moment, then flapped a dismissive hand. "Naw, won't work. What could you rhyme with invisible? Joxer, the . . ." He leaned back against the wall, deep in thought.

Gabrielle had reached the last of the rosebushes. Time to go, she thought grimly: A man was yelling in there, but his voice was muffled by something and she couldn't understand what he was saying. Then Draco's voice—unmistakable—yelling, "Are you *nuts*?"

"Easy to figure out who he's talking to," she told herself sourly. Whatever else the warlord might have said was lost as the men on the balcony crowded forward, and those who hadn't already drawn swords drew theirs. The shrill sound of metal rubbing metal drowned out any noise her last steps might make.

But they weren't paying any attention to the grounds behind them—and thanks to whoever was yelling inside the palace, she had no further need for secrecy. She rose to full height, briefly stretched kinked shoulder and leg muscles, then strode forward. She cleared the low stone parapet with a bound and took up a wide-legged stance on the smooth stone floor. Somewhere inside, a door slammed into the wall; she could hear nothing for some moments but a wild clash of weapons, another echoing slam, men yelling—and over all, Xena's blood-curdling war cry.

Several of the men on the balcony would have surged forward at that, but the one who'd looked to be in charge earlier held up a hand. "You know the orders; we wait."

"Good," Gabrielle announced loudly and set the end of her staff down with a sharp click. Eight men turned as one. "That gives me someone to play with, while I'm waiting for Xena to come out."

Inside the apartments, the doors slammed open, and armed guards started forward, swords high. Xena waited until the two leaders made it in the left-hand side, then jumped high and lashed out with her legs: Her feet caught both under the chin and they staggered back, half-conscious, into the men behind them.

Draco stood his ground; the right-hand door hit the wall and rebounded, and he spun halfway around, slamming his foot into the moving panel. A man howled in pain as it rebounded off his nose. Draco snatched the door open, caught the fallen soldier in both hands, hauled him off his feet, and threw him into the men behind him.

"Hey, not bad!" Xena yelled at him. Three soldiers had dragged aside the two she'd dropped; they ran at her, swords out, but before anyone could connect, she was between two of them, backhanding both. One fell, the other staggered. Xena pushed off him, flipped, and came down behind the third, dropping him with a flashing, open-handed blow to the neck. She glanced across the room: More of the king's guard had forced their way into the apartment, which no longer looked spacious at all. She bit back a grin as Draco backed away from four attackers. He appeared to be trying to convince them he'd done nothing wrong, not to hit him—but it was only a ruse. Once he reached the low table, he leaped over it, snatched up the wooden tray that had held his fruit, and began using it to flatten swordsmen.

Hot breath on her neck; someone jeered, "Too bad, Xena! Thought you knew to watch your ba—*ack*!" He choked as her backfist caught him in the teeth.

"My back," she said flatly. "Yeah, I know. I'm watching."

The next minutes were a blur: Men charged in through the wide-flung double doors or picked themselves off the floor and threw themselves at her or at Draco, who at some point had broken his tray in half and was now pelting soldiers with pears and apples; he'd figured out how to hit exactly right on those helmets with the narrow eye and nose slits, so as to block the entire opening with splattered fruit pulp.

Xena was finding her own way to play with the ridiculous helms: All she had to do was get on a man's blind side, tap the far side of the bronze headpiece with her left hand, and when he turned that way, grab the base two-handed and give it a hard tweak. At last count, she decided gleefully, there were four men with broken noses, two with bad nosebleeds that rendered them generally useless—and another two who were still bumping blindly into the walls and trying to get their faces aligned with the front of the helmet once more.

A quick glance at the hallway—there didn't seem to be anyone else out there. Not that she was going to trust *that*. Menelaus had to have a larger in-house guard than these few. One of the earlier fallen rolled over, groaning, and tried to wrap his arms around her ankles. She kicked free and rapped the side of his head with her foot; he whimpered and went limp.

Somewhere nearer Draco than herself, she could hear the harsh voice from the hallway yelling: "Remove your helmets! I said *remove—your—helmets!* That is an order—!" Some of them were already trying, including two men whose hands slid on fruit pulp, and one of those she'd turned, who'd run into the wall twice, ringingly, and didn't seem able to figure out what he was doing.

There was a brief, sudden lull: She could all at once hear yelling outside, and the familiar *clack!* of a fighting staff, and Gabrielle's ringing, triumphant yell. "Gotcha! Thought you could sneak up on me, did you? Well, take *that!* And don't try that on me again!" A breath later, half a dozen men hastily retreated into the room, half-tangled in the balcony drape. A seventh, floundering for balance, stumbled in a half circle, wrapping himself in material as he went; he fell and brought the drape down in a flurry of fabric. Gabrielle, her teeth bared in a mirthless grin, leaped over him, her staff menacing the other six. Xena could see one other guard beyond her, just as he went down and stayed down.

"Gabrielle!" the warrior shouted. Draco came halfway around, completely dropping his guard, and three of the king's men leapt at him.

"Gabrielle?" He stared at Xena, then spun to gaze where the warrior's eyes went and he smiled, suddenly oblivious to everything but the pale-haired woman with the fighting staff. And her companion; he scowled, as suddenly, and spun halfway around again, his hands pale-knuckled fists. "Xena!" He bellowed. "You lied to me again, damn you!"

"Draco—look out!" Gabrielle shouted, but the war-lord brought up both fists and slammed them back into two unhelmeted men; one swayed, caught at another, and both went over together. Draco turned and brought both fists down on the third man's head. A dozen more men, heavily armed and helmeted, sprinted into the chamber from the hallway, all at once; and most of those Gabrielle had driven inside brought up whatever weapons they had left and turned on Xena.

"Gabrielle!" the warrior shouted. "Get—out—of—here! There isn't enough room for all of us!"

Gabrielle snapped her staff, roundhouse, at a soldier, and opened her mouth to protest. The hardened wood hit the nearest wall hard enough to make her shoulders ache, then slammed back, rebounding off the armored back of one of the king's men. "Gotcha!" she yelled back, and slammed the staff in a short overhand arc onto the nearest bare head before she began backing away. Four of the men she'd fought on the balcony earlier followed. *Easy pickings,* she thought cheerfully. She jumped lightly over the half-conscious man who was feebly trying to work his way out of the drape and set her feet and the staff just outside. "Hey, come on," she said as two of the soldiers eyed each other warily. "You gonna let Xena flatten all of you, or can the rest of us play, too?" With a roar of anger, six men followed her onto the balcony. It wasn't enough to noticeably clear the room, Gabrielle decided as she flattened two of them. But it did make for a halfway decent challenge, for a change.

The problem, Joxer decided, was that he could hear just fine but he couldn't *see* anything. All that noise—and that yell. "Sounds almost like Xena—except why would she be here, when she's supposed to be looking for Hercules up in Thessalonika?'' he asked himself. And why would she already be in the palace, when he'd just barely made it here himself? No, she and Gabrielle were days away, well up to the north. Probably doing something heroic and important, and he was willing to bet they'd either forgotten all about him—or Xena was congratulating Gabrielle on finally getting rid of their pesky companion, while Gabrielle sat there smiling, thinking how clever she'd been . . .

Cut it out, he ordered himself gloomily. *You know you aren't the most welcome companion either of them ever had.* Not something he'd ever admit aloud; not something he wanted to think about, either. ''So,'' he whispered angrily. ''So, go do something.'' He got down on hands and knees and eased around the corner. No one nearby, but he could smell roses. *Roses. Great. Like the ones you brought Mother the one time, for her birthday.* He couldn't smell roses without remembering how hard he'd worked to find the best wild bushes, to pick only the nicest flowers. She'd—no, he wasn't going to think about what she'd done to him for bringing her roses. He successfully fought a sneeze, pinched his nostrils with one hand, and crawled forward.

''Remember,'' he told himself softly as he edged into the garden. ''Remember, you're on a mission for the king of Sparta, you wear his badge—you're doing something important. Worthwhile. A lot better than just—just *hitting* people.'' He could hear a lot of fighting over there, on one well-lit balcony, but he couldn't make out anyone that he knew. All he could see, actually, he realized, were a bunch of those funny-looking helmets.

Great. With everyone busy in *there*, he should be safe to sneak away out *here*. He slewed around, and sure enough, whatever wall there was around the roses was either low to begin with or worn down to where even he could jump over it. He eyed the melee cautiously, got stiffly to his feet and after a delay to pick splinters and thorns from his shins and palms, he turned away from the palace, squared his shoulders and his helmet, and walked away.

Gabrielle, who had just downed the last of her opponents, turned at just that moment to see a tall man in an all-too-familiar hat, strutting in the direction of the city gates. "*Damn* him!" she snarled. Back in the room, Xena and Draco seemed to be winning, but there were a lot of men still standing. "Xena!" she shouted. "It's him! And he's—" Words failed her; she pointed as the warrior met her eyes.

"Got it!" Xena yelled. "Stay with him. I'll find you!"

"You'd better!" Gabrielle screamed back, then turned and ran.

12

It seemed much darker among the roses. Gabrielle paused to let her eyes adjust and listened intently. "There," she whispered to herself. She could make out the rubble of wall and clearly heard Joxer's muted yelp: From the sound of things, he'd tripped but hadn't fallen. *Too bad.* He *really* owed her for this one. She flipped the staff deftly back under one arm and set out to follow him.

Better to catch up with him soon, she decided as she scrambled over fallen stones and eased between two workers' platforms. Menelaus was having this section rebuilt. *Probably to keep Helen in, once he gets his hands on her,* she thought gloomily. "Maybe I should just let Joxer go after her," she mumbled. "I can't think of a better way to make sure she's safe."

It was tempting—so tempting, she half-turned to head back onto the palace grounds. But luck didn't always cut the way you wanted it to, and besides, there were still a few immortals who had a score to settle with anyone who'd been part of that whole ten-year mess at Troy.

Aphrodite was supposedly on Helen's side, but the volatile—and self-centered—goddess could turn on anyone, and over the tiniest imagined slight. And she'd used Joxer before.

With a sigh, Gabrielle took up the inept, would-be warrior's trail again.

Dark as it was out here in the city itself, she wasn't going to have any problem staying with him: Every few steps, he seemed to run into something, trip over something else, or get thoroughly turned around. In between, he sang—fortunately under his breath so she didn't get the full effect. He seemed to be trying out new rhymes for his favorite song. Mercifully, she couldn't catch many of the words, either.

Let him go—sure, fine, she thought, as angry with herself as she was with Joxer. *If you just wanted to turn Joxer loose on the unspecting world, you shoulda done that back in Thessalonika, and gone with Xena to look for Hercules.*

And just because no one had killed Joxer so far didn't mean it couldn't happen. *Yeah, sure; he's responsible for himself, just like I am for me. But I wouldn't like myself very much if I knew he'd gotten mangled because I treated him like the idiot he is, and he threw a hissy fit and stomped off.* That was just a little different from tossing him out on his ear. "Which just maybe I just will, once we get out of this mess," she gritted between her teeth, then clapped a hand over her mouth. Ahead, Joxer stopped humming and froze in place for a long moment. But he finally emitted a sour, wordless little verbal shrug, turned, and ambled off.

Street emptied into street, alley into square. He led—

probably lost—and she followed. *Every bit as lost*, she'd long since decided. Though technically, you couldn't get too lost in a small, walled city.

She skirted a fountain, prewarned by Joxer's yelp of pain and the splash a few moments earlier; her mind still gnawed on that last argument she'd had with him. Yes, he was an undoubted idiot—and an idiot with no equal—but he had helped them a few times, if only because he was so inept.

And once or twice because he'd done the right thing, even though it could have gotten him killed. Niggling in the back of her mind was the Amazon Ephiny's description of the day, not long after Solan's death, when a half-mad Xena had come in search of her once-friend—and Joxer, knowing the risk he took and how outclassed he was, still tried to keep himself between the two women.

Just as well I can't remember that very clearly. Well, she wasn't going to try, either. Not just now—not soon, and maybe not ever. She tried to shove it aside by returning to the quandary of the moment.

"Besides," she muttered, "if we turn him loose now, with his kind of luck, he really *would* find her, and then what?" She hesitated at a narrow cross-alley, listening for Joxer-noises and anybody else who might be abroad at the moment. Like city guards. The pause gave her direction and a relieved sense of where she was: She and Xena had passed this way some time earlier. The stable where they'd talked was to her left, the wall where she'd come over ahead, and a little to the right. Joxer was briefly visible in the light of a guttering torch, high above; he was drawing near the deserted stables and actually paused to peer inside.

She'd never get a better opportunity, Gabrielle decided grimly, and took off at a dead run. Joxer started as her hand clamped down on his shoulder; she transferred it to his mouth before he could yell, and hissed, "It's me, you idiot!" against his ear. He jumped again, eyes sliding sideways to meet hers. "Come here, you," she added between clenched teeth, indicating the shadowy stalls with a jerk of her head. "We gotta talk."

Joxer pried her hand from his mouth with what dignity he could manage and drew himself upright. "Gabrielle, I am deeply flattered that you followed me all the way from Thessalonika, but you know what? *I* have decided I don't need a sidekick after all. So, why don't you just—owwww!" He yelped as Gabrielle caught hold of his ear and yanked.

"Talk, I said, not bellow!" she hissed. "And not out here, d'you mind? Because I am *not* supposed to be in Sparta, unlike you. You want to bring the guards down on us and get me in big trouble?"

"Ahhhh—owww! Will you let go of me?" he complained, but his voice was prudently lower. "All—all *right*, fine! Let's talk! But, I swear, all bets are off unless you let *go*—!" She released his ear, caught hold of his shoulder and dragged him back onto his feet as he overbalanced, then hauled him into darkness with her—back to the stall she and Xena had used. It hadn't been completely dark then; it wasn't very dark now, either. She could just make out his face, if she stayed close enough to him. At the moment, that was a good thing; he wouldn't be able to lie to her without her knowing that he was.

"All the comforts of home," she said with a smile, and waved him in ahead of her. Joxer was rubbing his ear; his mouth twitched as he eased down onto his backside in a drift of straw and settled cross-legged. He wouldn't meet her eyes. She folded her arms, dropped down across from him with the staff across her knees, and waited him out.

"Huh," he said finally, and leveled a finger at her nose. "You know, Gabrielle, it is so maddening! You do this all the time! Have you ever thought about it? You can't just—just *pinch* a person's ear and then be surprised when they yell, you know!" He went on in this vein for some moments. Gabrielle finally jabbed her own finger against his nose, and he fell silent.

"Don't—start!" she said flatly.

"Oh, sure," he complained and eased away from her. "*You* can start, but I can't, just like always. Gabrielle, I am gonna tell you this, and it's for your own good: You are one *very* confused woman."

"Me?" she asked, her voice dangerously low and sweet. "I am confused?"

"Confused." He nodded; his helmet teetered wildly, then toppled. Gabrielle cast up her eyes and shoved it back onto his head. Hard. "Owww, do you *mind*? Yeah, confused. You can't make up your mind! One minute, you're giving me grief about there's no quest, and—and insulting me, and then all at once, here you are, right here in Sparta, following me around like you had a—" He stopped short, sat up, hauled the helmet into his lap, and scratched his head. "So—hey, wait just a minute. How'd you get here ahead of me, huh?"

"I wasn't ahead of you. I came into Sparta behind you."

"Oh yeah, sure you did," he scoffed. "Because I happen to know they were locking the gates for the night, right on my heels. So—just try again, okay?"

"I didn't *say* I came through the gates," she replied levelly.

"Oh, great," he told the ceiling. "I finally get a chance to do something that will make my reputation as one of the greatest heroes of all time—and what happens? I get someone breaking all the city's laws and rules and trying to get me tossed into prison, right next to her!" He clutched the helmet two-handed and glared at her. "Well! You and Xena had better not be up to something that I don't know about, here. *Or* just you. Or just Xena! Because, for your information, Gabrielle"—he squared his shoulders—"*I* have been chosen as King Menelaus's hero. Not more than a couple of hours ago, as a matter of fact."

"Yeah, right," she retorted. In the dim light, she could just make out that sappy, superior smile of his; the palm of her hand suddenly itched to smack his face and wipe out the smirk.

"Yeah," he replied loftily. "Right. Difficult as it may be for you to believe, it's absolutely true. So, why don't you just—go on back north and rejoin Xena? I mean," he added, spoiling the lofty effect, "I mean, if she isn't here already. Just—you two have got your chance to get rid of me finally, so . . ." He shrugged. "And anyway, I don't want either of you around this time, okay? Because just in case you *were* planning on ruining things for me—well, I am not gonna let you stop me from retrieving his family—his—the whatchima. That thing. Or let either of you get ahold of it before I can. Got it?"

She smiled; her eyes were stormy. "I have *no* clue what you're talking about, Joxer. Except, there is no— no whatsie. The king wants Helen to come home—and she doesn't want anything to do with him. End of story."

He shifted, shoving straw behind his back. The grin widened. "*I* know he wants her back; he told me so himself. And boy, who can blame him? That priest of his—Avicus? Well, he has this big bowl of water, except it's kind of like a vision-mirror or something? Anyway, I looked in it and that's when I got the vision.''

"Vision?" She couldn't help herself; she spluttered with laughter. "*You* saw a vision?"

He gave her an exasperated look. "As a matter of fact, yes, I did, Gabrielle. I saw her. Helen. And the—the whatever it is, the thing Menelaus needs to get back from her.''

"What—Pandora's box?" she demanded sarcastically. Joxer opened his mouth to say something, then clapped a hand over it.

"Nice try," he said finally. "Why should I tell *you* or anyone else? It's *my* quest, and I'm not sharing the glory or the reward.''

"Joxer, I am not interested in stealing your reward, I'm just—" Words momentarily failed her. Joxer sighed; he apparently had been following his own thoughts and hadn't heard her anyway.

"You shoulda seen her. Helen, I mean. She's a real— a really—well," he said finally. "You just *think* Aphrodite's a hot number, Helen's got it all over—!"

Whatever else he intended to say went unsaid, as Gabrielle leaped across the space between them to clap both hands over his mouth. She leaned close to his ear. "*Don't* even *think* what I think you were gonna say! Do *not* badmouth the goddess of love, you got me? Because we already got enough trouble here without putting Aphrodite in a bad mood by saying a human woman's prettier than she is! You know how Troy started, right?" She glared at him; he eyed her warily but finally nodded. "You want to wind up on Aphrodite's wrong side?" He shook his head. After a moment, she removed the hands and sat back. Joxer worked his jaw cautiously.

"Oh, come on, Gabrielle. I've seen Aphrodite, and she doesn't *have* any wrong sides." He smirked reminiscently. "And, c'mon, everyone knows about Troy: that Trojan guy—uh, Paris?" He leaned closer to her and lowered his voice. "Well, see, this Paris was here in Sparta, on the king's invitation, okay? And I guess he was wandering around where he shouldn't've been—and he caught a glimpse of Helen. So, he was hooked, right? But he wasn't just some ordinary Trojan, he was a prince, and you may have noticed people tend to believe princes."

"Yeah, whatever," Gabrielle said tiredly as he paused for some reaction.

"Well, they do, Gabrielle. Trust me. Anyway, he fed the king a line about some party down in Thebes or something, so the king believes it, and goes away to party with the guys, the other kings, and meanwhile, Paris sneaks back into the palace and kidnaps Helen." Brief silence: complacent on Joxer's part, stunned on Gabrielle's. "Well, I guess you know now why the king didn't want her just wandering around the streets where anyone could grab her. Just the vision I saw in that priest-guy's water-bowl—well, she's pretty amazing."

"Oh, yeah," Gabrielle said after a moment. "So are you, Joxer."

"Thank you—"

She waved him to silence. "Will you shut up? What I am trying to tell you is, I have never in all my *life* heard such a bunch of nonsense as you just—" Her voice was going up; Joxer did that to her. *Next, he'll accuse me of throwing a hissy fit, and I will murder him on the spot,* she told herself angrily; she drew a deep breath and counted on her fingers, mumbling as she turned digits down: "... eight harpies, nine harpies, ten—"

"I thought it was minotaurs?" Joxer asked earnestly, as if he really wanted to know. She waved that aside. "... ten harpies. Joxer, just—just listen to me! You—are—being—used. The king has an agenda that does *not* include Helen's future happiness. Trust me on this one! All he cares about is the part that looks pretty, and he wants it all for himself! And—and that priest: Well, Xena told me about him. And she says he is *not* a good man."

"Aw geez, Gabrielle, come on. He's a priest of Apollo," Joxer protested. Gabrielle got to her feet, paced a few steps, came back, and collapsed on the straw next to him.

"And Apollo is god of truth and healing, and visions, things like that, right?" she asked him.

"Well—sure." He scratched his head. "I guess."

"No. Not right! That's only the face he puts on when he's doing the vision thing with the oracle at Delphi," she told him. Joxer eyed her sullenly, patently unconvinced. "Look: he's a god. He can do or be whatever he wants, and it isn't always pure and good! Like—OK, you know Aphrodite, right?"

"Well—yeah," he allowed cautiously.

"Yeah." Gabrielle snorted. "Some goddess of love, isn't she?"

He looked alarmed. "Hey, I thought we weren't gonna badmouth her, Gabrielle!"

"I'm not—she knows what she is, and she knows I know it, and she knows I have a weapon she doesn't want to deal with. I only say that she's self-centered and vain. I," Gabrielle pointed out, "am not saying I'm pret-

231

tier than she is—I wouldn't even if I believed it," she added hastily.

Joxer sighed. "Gabrielle, is any of this important? Because, I mean, why do I care anyway? Look, I gotta go." He started getting to his feet.

All right, you do what you gotta, Gabrielle sighed inwardly, pasted a bright smile on her face, then dragged him back down, wrapped both arms around his arm, and turned adoring eyes on him. He could see her just fine, it appeared: He froze for one long moment, then cautiously smiled back, mouth twitching as he pulled the awkward helmet from his head. Without it, he was still a far cry from classically handsome like Theseus, but he wasn't that funny looking.

He was not, no way, her not-quite funny-looking man. Still: *There's one way I can always control him, and that's by keeping him off balance by letting him think I've gone nutty over him. And—Hades, you do what you gotta do,* Gabrielle told herself grimly. *And, boy, Xena really owes me this time.*

"Oh, Joxer," she murmured. He suddenly choked, pulled free of her grasp and staggered to his feet, backing away from her. The stable wall stopped him. Gabrielle patted his cheek and recaptured his arm. "All right—OK, look, I'm sorry, Joxer, I didn't want to—" She gave him a rueful shrug. "You—okay, you caught me."

"I—I did?" he asked blankly.

"Yeah, well, you know." She played with the staff, tugged at her skirt, did her best to look giddy. "I just—you know, if you hadn't tried so hard to make me mad, back up in Thessalonika, if you'd just said, 'Hey, Gabrielle, I could be in danger here if I try to do this alone, and I need your help, I could use a sidekick this time.

So, why don't you come with me—?' '' She let the words hang. He stared at her, jaw slack.

"You'd—I mean, you really would've—I mean—?" He fumbled the helmet; Gabrielle caught it before it could clatter away from him and leaned a little closer, letting him smell the lemony scent of clean skin and soft hair. He inhaled deeply, fought a sneeze. "Gee, Gabrielle. You—you really aren't kidding, are you?" She gravely shook her head. Joxer's eyes bulged. "But—I mean, you and Xena—I mean, well, you know," he babbled rapidly. "I don't mean *that*, but I mean—" He somehow managed to draw a deep breath and said, with as much dignity as he could: "You're Xena's sidekick. I can't compete with that. I—I mean, with her."

Great; he really was going for it. Now—what to do with him. But for the first time in days, it was simple: All she needed was to keep this idiot preoccupied long enough for Xena to break free of the king's guards— and that shouldn't take very long. Xena know that Gabrielle could only get back over the wall where they'd come in—that her companion would choose that way out so they'd meet up. She'd also know that if Gabrielle caught up to Joxer, she'd drag him someplace like this, somehow delaying him until the warrior arrived. If that didn't work, she'd know Gabrielle would find a way to drag him across the wall with her and somehow keep him outside the city with her. Either way, they'd be waiting somewhere they could see Xena coming—or someplace the warrior would know to look.

Simple. *Hah,* Gabrielle thought sourly. Still, the main thing for her was to keep Joxer in her grasp. Xena could straighten things out once she arrived. Wherever they all got back together. *And it's up to me to make sure good ol' Joxer's still here—wherever here is—when she does arrive,* she told herself flatly. So—what *would* Xena do in a similar circumstance?

Because this wasn't like fighting, strategy, or tactics, where she felt confident she could second-guess her companion. *Too bad I'm kinda foggy on that whole mess when Cupid's arrow made me fall for Joxer; I could use that about now.* She considered that and decided, *Maybe it's not.*

Still, she'd seen Xena keep Draco off balance, more than once. *It's acting,* she told herself. *If the theater actors can put on masks and pretend to be frogs—it should be pretty easy to pretend to be in love with—* Her mind boggled; she couldn't complete the thought. Besides, in this case, she had willing help. At least according to Xena, who claimed Joxer had a huge crush on— She shook her head, brought her attention back to the moment as Joxer swallowed noisily.

Go for it, Gabrielle, she thought dryly.

"Awwwww, c'mon, Joxer," she murmured throatily, doing the best imitation she could of Xena's seductive purr, even if her voice didn't comfortably go that low. "You didn't *really* think, back when we were rescuing those virgin priestesses from Draco—tell me you didn't believe that was Cupid's arrows, did you? You and me?" He stared at her blankly. She simpered. "Hey, what can I say? I was embarrassed, you know? All this time, I've been picking on you, calling you stupid and things like that? And then, to suddenly realize what a—" She reached out as if longing to touch him, gasped, and snatched the hand back. "Sorry, sweetie," she murmured. *That's bad; overacting,* she told herself angrily. *Xena'd never make it look that ridiculous—and she'd never use that word!* But Joxer was eyeing her in rising astonishment; the corners of his mouth quirked. He really was going for it.

She smiled contentedly. "What a really swell—heroic—guy you are. I hope you don't mind if I tell you that—I know what a—what a humble guy you are, too. You know, Joxer—Xena underestimates you."

Joxer tittered nervously. "I—ah—well, sure, I mean. She's the best at what she does. Of course, she's not—"

"Exactly," Gabrielle said as he paused to search for the right word; she had no clue what he meant to say, and probably he didn't have one, either. She wrapped one of the inevitable dangling strings at the throat of his armor around one index finger, leaned against him, and looked up to give him a radiant smile. "You know, I really, *really* love your song."

Just as she'd hoped, he got totally spooked when she turned seductive—she vaguely recalled that from the last time. *Except it wasn't me then,* she reminded herself firmly. It had been Cupid—actually, his baby son, Bliss. It had been excruciating to recall later, what little she did remember.

She clamped her teeth on the string and tugged, hard; he gulped loudly. "Ah—um. You do?"

"Awwwwww, Joxer! Come on! I mean, all the times we sang it together? You don't really think I'm *that* good an actor, do you?"

"Ah—well—ah—um. Well, uh—"

"Forget it," she ordered throatily and fought the need to cough. Women with her vocal range didn't drop that far down without paying for it; much more of this and she'd be hoarse for days. "Bad question. But—look, let's get out of here, out of Sparta. I'm not supposed to be in here, you know; the king or his guard finds out I followed you, and I'll probably get tossed into one of his dungeon cells, and he'll leave me to rot."

Joxer drew himself up. "No, he won't! Because, I'll tell him—" He stopped short and began babbling to himself, half under his breath. "No, wait, I can't do that, because if I have to go back, the others will get ahead of me, and—"

"Others? No, never mind." she waved that aside and clung to him, two-handed. "Look, Joxer, I'm in danger here, all right? And if king Menelaus knows I was in Troy with Xena—well, it won't matter what you tell him. He'll," she cleared her throat nervously. "He'll probably just break out the axe and the executioner."

Joxer stared at her, aghast. "He wouldn't do that! Ah—would he?" She nodded, bit her lip. "And you knew that, and you came here anyway?" Another nod. "For *me*?" His voice rose to a squeak; she clapped a hand over it, but gently this time. "Gabrielle, that's—I—gosh. We gotta get you *out* of here!" He took her hand between both of his, gave her a fatuous smile, then drew her down the stable walkway and over to the door, where he peered cautiously both directions. Gabrielle tightened her grip on the staff and forced herself to stay quiet, meek-looking, and nervous. She was fighting the urge to spit: That string had tasted like sweat, spilled stew, old wine—purely awful.

In truth, she *was* nervous. Just thinking about letting Joxer lead the way . . . She thought rapidly, tapped his shoulder. "Here," she whispered. "Let me go first. I know where I am, now, and I know of a way close by, where we can escape the city without anyone seeing us."

"OK," he said doubtfully, but gently eased her in front. He would have kept her hand, but she held up the

236

staff where he could see it, and he nodded and cautiously drew his sword. Gabrielle set her hands in fight-ready position, then set out down the narrow alleyway as quickly as she dared, Joxer right on her heels and—at least for the moment—planting his feet carefully. He didn't trip once, dark as it was.

They reached the low spot in the west wall several minutes later. There'd been three laughing guards a ways back, but the men were making enough noise that she'd been able to slip quietly past them; Joxer'd tripped but she managed to catch him before he fell, and a burst of laughter had covered the clatter of armor. At the wall, she laid a finger against his lips for silence and listened intently. No one nearby, it seemed. There was a little light high up and farther down the wall, where the gates were, but it was dark enough here. She felt along the rubble of stones for the place she and Xena had come down, took Joxer's hand and guided him to the right spot, then pointed up. "A little to your right, once you take the first four steps," she breathed against his ear. "Watch where I go." He nodded and stepped back to let her precede him.

She made the top without incident, Joxer a few paces behind her; he was breathing loudly but being careful, still. Once on top, she pulled him close to whisper, "Wait here a little, catch your breath. It's steeper on the front side." He nodded, settled between two large, squared stones that had been part of the parapet, and gasped for air. Once he was again quiet, she got to her feet and went crouching along the wall, searching for the way down—hard to tell, at first, since she was working in reverse. Joxer came behind her on his hands and knees. Gabrielle finally went to one knee and beckoned.

"It's right here. Maybe you'd better go down first, and I'll follow . . . ?"

He was gazing over the side. "Hmmm. What if I lower you first, and then you can move out of the way, in case I miss a step or something? I mean, now that we're almost out of here, I wouldn't want to do something clumsy and stupid and have you get hurt. Guh— Gabrielle." His whisper lingered on her name. She crossed her eyes. *Let's get down off this wall, and then I can deal with—with that.* If he didn't make her thoroughly sick first. Well, it wasn't as if she hadn't asked for it.

"Fine," she whispered hastily. A glance eastward warned her that day was close: She could make out the distant line of the far city wall and mountains against a still-black sky. It wouldn't stay black long. She turned around to feel for a foothold. The first step—a wide shelf of dressed stone—was right under her, but the next one down was harder to find. Both sets of toes clinging to the wall through soft boots, she held the staff away from the wall and let it drop, then gripped a pocked stone with her left fingers, extending the other arm upward. Joxer took it two-handed as he eased himself down flat and held on as she fumbled for toeholds.

It had been *much* easier going up, she decided. Finally, just as the link between them was stretched tight, she found the ledge. From here down, it wasn't that far to the ground, and the wall sloped out at a better angle.

"You can let go now," she hissed. Joxer released her hand at once; she rubbed pinched flesh and eased off to the side. "I'm out of the way now; you can come down," she whispered. Well above, she could just make out Joxer's outline as he got to his feet. Something about the way he was looking down at her didn't feel right, all at once. "Joxer?" she demanded.

His voice was low-pitched, noncarrying. "Gabrielle—I'm sorry, but I think it's best for everyone this way. You're outside Sparta, but you need to get out of sight before daybreak, and that's not far off now. And I—I have a job to do, a dangerous job. And I can't take you with me."

"Joxer? Are you *nuts?*" she whispered furiously. "You promised me—!"

"I know I did. But Gabrielle, it's just too dangerous for you, I can't let you . . . I mean, even knowing how you feel. Especially knowing how you feel. But if the king found you here, I'd never forgive myself. I'll—*if* I survive this, I'll come back to you." She stared up at him, stunned. Before she could move or say a word, he vanished, and she could hear him scrabbling his way back down to the street. With a furious oath, she started back up the wall, after him.

It took time: The three raucous guards were nearby; she could hear them, but they weren't making as much noise as they had been. Better, then, if she didn't make any more than she had to. Eventually, she found the street with her boots once again, caught her breath and set out for the main gates—he couldn't have gone anywhere else.

Keep in mind your staff's on the outside, she reminded herself angrily. A sensible woman wouldn't provoke a fight just now; however she felt, she couldn't really rip a man in half with her bare hands.

She eased quietly and quickly along the narrow alley-way that bordered the inner wall, checked cautiously at the base of the guard tower to make certain no guards were on their way in or out, then slid around to the gate side of the massive stone structure.

Sure enough, there he was. She gritted her teeth in frustration and pulled back into deep shadow, watching as Joxer kidded around with the two men on watch. Same ones as earlier, she was fairly certain—which effectively precluded her faking them into letting her go out after Joxer. He dug around under his ratty armor for some moments, finally produced a small badge; the guards laughed and one of them ran to unbolt the small side gate. Gabrielle's eyes narrowed as Joxer slapped the nearest man on the shoulder and went; she turned on her heel and headed back for the broken section of wall—and her fighting staff.

Maddeningly, the three guards who'd haunted her footsteps since the stable were way too close to where she needed to climb; she set her jaw and amused herself with images of what she'd do to Joxer once she caught up to him. The three slowly moved off, heading for the nearest tavern; she drew a deep breath, another, and then a third before daring to set herself to tackle the wall.

The sky was noticeably lighter when she reached the top, but still that dull blue-black that illuminated the horizon and nothing else. She worked her way down the outside as quickly as she dared, reaching the bottom with a skinned forearm and a banged knee—not bad, considering how fast she'd moved. The staff was still where she'd left it; her sore fingers closed gratefully around the thick, fire-hardened length of wood.

Now, which way to go. She sighed heavily. "Haven't we already *done* this?" she demanded of herself. "I can't stay here, obviously. Joxer's already out the gates and on his way. Xena's still inside Sparta, maybe still inside the palace.'' She considered this, swallowed. ''And she's got Draco with her, bet anything. The way our luck is going, of *course* she's got Draco with her.''

She scowled at the eastern horizon, then turned to glare at the road that went west, straight through fields and into the trees. Argo might well be that direction. Find her, wait with her—and here come Xena *and* Draco.

And there goes Joxer, she thought, scowling now along the wall, where she could just make out the pale line of road winding away to the south and east.

That finally decided her. Xena would find her, no matter what. She didn't really want to have to deal with Draco just now, on top of everything else. And Joxer—well, Joxer was really and truly gonna pay for the little stunt he'd just pulled on her. Oh, yes—was he *ever* going to pay.

13

The royal apartment was a total mess. Xena turned slowly on one heel, a loose helmet caught up in her hand, ready to throw, but there was no need: Except for herself and Draco, no one else in the room was standing—or, it seemed, even thinking about it.

The low table was in pieces: One of the bulkier guards had taken it down with him, scattering legs in all directions. Those had taken out two more men. A piece of the thick tabletop teetered where the warlord had let it fall, directly atop a whimpering, helmetless guard who clutched his bleeding nose with one hand and feebly shoved at the slab with his other.

Bedding had been flung everywhere, and pillows were reduced to shredded cloth and fill. Somewhere under a drift of feathers, someone sneezed weakly, then began swearing. Xena crossed the room, waded into ankle-deep fluff, and dropped the helmet. It clanged against metal, and the voice was abruptly stilled. The warrior murmured, "Thanks," and she went back to her check of the room.

The balcony guard caught up in the drape had picked up company since she'd last looked that way: Two men were now wound tightly in dark cloth, one of them glaring at the other, who appeared to still be out cold.

Draco dropped what was left of the splintered tray; it hit the floor and bounced; guards scrambled away from him and it except for one who simply huddled in on himself. Draco ignored the floor show. "Gotta admit, that was fun," he said. She raised an eyebrow, and he grinned. "Gets your creative spirit going."

"Something like that."

"So—" He looked around. Two men who'd started to crawl toward the balcony prudently went flat again. "What now?"

"What do *you* think?" she retorted. "We get out of here, now."

"*Out* of here?" The grin eclipsed. "Xena, in case you forget, I was invited to—"

"That was then, this is now," she drawled. "Think about it, you wanna spend the next month explaining to Menelaus how come you were busting heads in here? Smart man would get outa here, right now—then he could get on with whatever he had planned before those goons broke in here."

"Wait a second." He held out a hand. "You're telling me you won't interfere with me? Even if I still plan on going after Helen?"

"I'm saying you got a life and it isn't here. You want to get on with it, you leave with me, now. Once we're out of Sparta—well, that's up to you." He cast up his eyes. "Draco, c'mon, I can't keep you from looking for Helen. Not unless I kill you now or let you get tossed into the king's dungeons."

He gazed around in sudden distaste, then began gathering up his belongings. "You got that right," he muttered as he pulled the blue shirt over his head, shoved the laces inside the throat, and worked into his armor. When Xena came across to help him tug it down, he slapped at her hand. "I can *do* it, okay?"

"Hey, whatever!" She backed off to where she could keep an eye on the room. But as the warlord snugged his sword belt in place, she eased over to the hallway doors, listening intently.

"What?" he asked sharply as she unclipped the chakram.

"Nothing I can't handle." She stabbed a hand toward the balcony. "Keep an eye out there." He drew his sword for answer and moved light-footed through the destruction to settle his back against the far wall.

Xena grinned as she picked out more would-be stealthy footsteps, up and down hall. *Good thing Menelaus doesn't have a dryad to teach 'em the quiet approach. They're louder'n Joxer!* Grinning wickedly, she recalled the placement of certain decorative items in the mostly open hallway, then let loose with her war cry and she threw herself into the hall long enough to launch the chakram off the opposite wall, sending it on a careening course toward the barred outer doors. Hissing shrilly, it slammed edge-on from wall to wall, splintering plaster and sending stone chips everywhere—cutting torches in half as it ricocheted wildly in and out of niches.

Men yelped in terror, and an officer sprinted for the distant cross-hall while his men threw themselves flat. Sparks flew; the chakram hit the statue of Apollo with a ringing *ping!*, clanged against the opposite wall, and reversed direction, back the way it had gone with no noticeable loss of speed.

Xena ducked as it *whooshed* just over her head, then

watched with visible glee as it bounded between the walls, each hit propelling it even faster. It took out another torch and whipped around the necks of two men who'd foolishly stood up to stare as it receded toward the reception, then froze, slack-jawed, as it reversed. Both went down.

She snarled; she hadn't factored *them* in when she'd calculated the throw. But another of Menelaus's dreadful bits of sculpture was in the way; the chakram clanged flat on into a half-sized gilded swan, caught an edge on the pedestal, and cracked at just the right angle against the tiled floor to gain momentum.

Unfortunately, it was still going the wrong direction; but just then, one of the soldiers who'd dropped to his belly when she yelled jumped to his feet and turned to run. The chakram clanged into his helmet, leaving a dent the size of a fist; it angled off the ceiling, bounced off the floor, and headed back where it had come from. Xena ran out to snatch it from the air, ran up the opposite wall, flipped tightly back into the room, and slammed the doors, barring them from the inside.

Not, she thought smugly, that she had to; anyone still out there wasn't going start another round of excitement.

Draco was snugging down the last of his breastplate strings; as she checked the door bar, he hoisted his saddlebag and and blandly gestured her ahead of him, out the balcony opening.

A corner of her mouth quirked; she gave him a curtsy worthy of Princess Diana. He was spluttering with laughter as they eased into the night.

Gabrielle wasn't in the rose garden—of course. *She's gone after Joxer,* the warrior remembered gloomily. *Let's hope she caught him.* Any decent luck, and they'd both be waiting when she got to the wall. Because, unless she had clear proof Gabrielle was safely outside the city—with or without Joxer—she'd have no choice but to make certain her close companion hadn't been locked up. *I swear, I get her back after all this, I'm not letting her out of my sight ever again.*

She eyed her current companion sidelong and debated ditching him here and now. He had his own agenda, of course, but she didn't read him as well as she'd like to, these days. Maybe he'd leave her once they neared the gates. But for now, he was right on her heels, and he had that stubborn set to his mouth. *He wants to see Gabrielle. Of course he does, because you, bright warrior that you are, you're the woman who convinced Cupid not to break the spell on him!*

Gabrielle was gonna be one unhappy woman if she had to deal with Draco on top of everything else tonight.

Partway down the alley, she could hear men trying to sing: the same ones or three equally drunk and tone-deaf guards. She leaned against the nearest wall, listening intently, until Draco tapped her shoulder, hard. "We gotta get moving," he whispered urgently. "I can make out your face; a few streets back, I couldn't. It's getting light!"

"So?" Silence. "All right, okay. Gates are over there, you go down this road and—"

"Do I *look* stupid?" he demanded. "I'm leaving with you, the way you and Gabrielle snuck in. Because you owe me for tonight, Xena. I had a good thing going, and you—"

"You gonna bitch about it until the sun comes up?" she snarled softly. He shut his mouth with an audible snap of teeth, gestured for her to lead on. "Okay," she added, "you come out with me. But I'm warning you."

She leveled a finger at his nose. "Hands—off—Gabrielle! You got me?"

He swatted her hand aside. "I'm okay with that. You mind if I *talk* to her?"

"If we don't get caught between here and—yeah, you can talk to her. If she doesn't mind, but that is up to her, got it?"

"Got it," he growled. "Get moving."

They had to stop twice to let guards pass, but so far as Xena could tell, the men were on regular duty—and at this hour, half asleep. Finally she and Draco fetched up against the broken section of wall; she tapped his arm, beckoned him close, then indicated up with a jab of her thumb. Draco nodded—she thought. Shadow was still deep here. She felt along shattered stone until she located her toeholds and started up, going by feel the first few steps. She then reached back to grab the warlord's hand and set it where he'd have to start his climb. He waited until she was a body-length above him, then started up.

He'd barely cleared the cobbled street when three guards came clattering up, moving with purpose toward the gates. Xena waited only until they'd passed, then reached for the next handhold: she was making very little noise, and those men were making too much to hear anything but themselves.

She hauled herself over the top and moved back as Draco dragged himself up next to her. "Where's the main gates?" he whispered.

"That way, maybe a hundred fifty strides." She pointed, then turned his chin with her fingers. "See that pale line out there? That's the north road."

"So—all right, that's the road from the isthmus? And it goes on down past the walls to Phalamys—I mean, the road heads south from here to the sea, right?''

"I guess.'' She glanced overhead, where all but the brightest stars had faded. ''We better go. You ready?''

"Yeah,'' he replied shortly. ''Let's get it done.''

Gabrielle wasn't waiting for them at the base of the wall—but she'd left a torn bit of scroll wedged in the rocks at the last handhold down, where Xena's fingers would find it. The warrior tugged it free. It was still way too dark out here to read what Gabrielle might have written, but she got the idea: The bard had made it this far and was out of the city, because the scrap hadn't been there earlier.

Okay. Gabrielle won't be anywhere out in the open when the sun rises, so get Argo and ditch Draco. Xena stuffed the bit of scroll down next to her breast dagger and turned to the warlord. ''She's not here, but she was.''

"How do you know that?'' he demanded suspiciously.

"I know. OK?''

Silence. Draco broke it. He sounded oddly nervous. ''Ah—OK, that's fine. Tell her I said hello, will you? And—no, that's it.''

"I can do that.'' Another silence. ''Draco, look. About Helen—''

"Forget it, Xena, I'm not quitting, not just on your word. But—but for Gabrielle's sake, I'm gonna do what you asked. When I find Helen, I'll *ask* her what *she* wants. If she doesn't want to come back to Sparta, that's good enough for me. If she doesn't want to see the king, if she needs help getting away from him, like you say— *if* she decides to trust me—then, I'll help her. That good enough?''

"That's all I ask." She held out her hand. "Well, Draco, it's been fun, but—"

He brushed it aside. "Feeling's mutual. Let's *not* do this again." Before she could think of anything else to say, he was gone. She didn't wait to see him vanish around the nearest angle in the north wall; by the time he was up to speed, she was off across the fields, angling toward the line of trees where she'd left Argo.

With any luck at all, she could get Argo saddled and get them both around Sparta before sunrise.

Gabrielle better be on the south road. She leaped an irrigation ditch and wove her way through shoulder-high corn. The bit of scroll might tell her—if Gabrielle herself knew.

Back in the palace, King Menelaus turned slowly, eyes raking the destroyed apartments. His handpicked men were clearing the chambers, while Avicus prowled the room, seemingly without purpose. Menelaus snarled; the priest froze. "Stop that! You make me giddy!"

"As you please, highness."

"Appalling!" The king snapped a sleeve dagger free, leveling it at his priest's throat. "Do *not* tell me Xena did all this! Or—or her and that warlord!"

Avicus smiled faintly and pressed the dagger from his pulse with the back of one hand. "In that case, Highness, I have nothing to tell you." The two men eyed each other for a long moment. "Ask any of your guards, Highness, if you won't believe me."

Menelaus gritted his teeth. "Yes, of course! Any of them would of course *cheerfully* admit he and his mates were beaten by two fighters—one of them a woman!"

"One of them *Xena*," Avicus corrected him absently, and brushed chips of plaster from yellow silk sleeves.

The king closed the distance between them in a bound, but the priest fixed him with a pale-eyed glare. "With respect, sire, I did warn you," he said evenly. A nasty little silence, broken only by a groan from the hall, which someone else hurriedly shushed.

Menelaus finally sighed heavily and turned away. "Yes. You did warn me. It isn't important, anyway. Nothing is, except Helen. What next?"

Avicus straightened his sleeves. "Except for this—unfortunate incident, nothing's changed, Highness. The devices I put on the other men are intact, and they leave here within the next hour or so." *And Joxer is already gone, just as I had hoped—better, that little blond companion of Xena's was here and has gone after him. Just as the god showed me.* He smiled blandly. "The god has not revealed which of them is to find her, just that one of them will do so. When that occurs—" He paused. The king smiled grimly and nodded.

"Yes." The last of the injured and half-conscious men were gone; Menelaus followed his personal guard out after them. He paused in the doorway to say, "You've done well, priest," and was gone.

Avicus waited to be certain he was alone, then sent his eyes around the room until he found the battered device Draco had worn. *I wonder which of them destroyed it.* Xena, most likely. He'd known from the first time he saw her that she had a talent of her own. Still, what he'd sensed about her had been more Amazonian. Animistic. Someone with that kind of power shouldn't even be aware of his devices.

But it wouldn't do to underestimate Xena: He had too much riding on this quest.

He let the ruined spy-thing fall. The *rhodforch* in the rose garden was fortunately still working; otherwise he might not have known for some time that Joxer had come this way and that the girl had seen and gone after him.

Because of that, he'd been able to alert his priests at the various guard stations along the south road to the sea; the priests would in turn warn the king's guards to take the girl and bring her back here. Xena would quickly learn that Avicus had her friend . . .

He considered this, finally shook his head. That much the god had told him he must do; it didn't entirely make sense—unless Xena knew where Helen was hiding and would tell him in order to keep Gabrielle safe. Or, if Xena knew, maybe the girl did also. She'd been at Troy too, after all.

"Doesn't matter," he told himself gloomily. At some point, Apollo would decide he needed to know—and then he'd know. Too bad the king couldn't be made to understand that. "One day, dread god, he'll kill me in a rage because I tell him I don't know the answer once too often," he mumbled.

He will not. What I have told you will come to pass. Avicus felt the words shiver through him; he inclined his head, and the god's presence was as swiftly gone. The priest eyed the rubble around him and smiled, then strode into the hallway. A glance to his left—a guard stood outside the king's apartments. Good; Menelaus was in for the night, barring more excitement.

"There had better not *be* any more excitement," he growled softly. His smile went as if shuttered, and his eyes were pale blue fires. *Yes, Highness. You are a king, Highness, and I a lowly priest. But even men who were born royal can be toppled from thrones.*

Yes, Helen will return to Sparta—but not for you. She will be mine, the city will be mine, and before you die,

you will know who has taken them from you. And why.
He drew a steadying breath and went back down the hall
to the reception, where his scrying bowl waited. There
was precious little left of this night and much for him
to accomplish.

As the best and quickest way to the sea, Sparta's South
Road was broad and well cared for: for nearly two
leagues beyond the city, three of the king's two-horse
war chariots could take it at a gallop, side by side. It
was also well patrolled, with stations and heavy gates at
league or two-league intervals, all the way down the
passes.

Just past the first guard station, the road narrowed to
two-chariot width and narrowed again a league or so on,
leaving room enough for carts and wagons to go single
file. Once it wound down through the highlands and
dropped to sea level, it was again a wide thoroughfare,
cutting a straight line for the busy port of Phalamys.

Though it was the easiest and safest passage between
the sea and the city, there was little traffic of any kind;
Menelaus taxed all who used it.

The sky was a deep blue, the eastern horizon ruddy;
Xena glanced back at the last corner of the city walls
and urged Argo to a canter. Better to be past this broad
avenue before the sun rose. Two leagues or so to the
first guard station, she remembered, and tried to recall
the layout of the nearest: Menelaus probably hadn't
changed anything over the years. There had been seven
of them, last time she'd ridden this road—the least of
them nothing but a hut and a corral for horses, though
most consisted of a series of huts to provide shelter,
mess, and barracks for a dozen guards, stabling for as
many horses, and a paddock that could hold more.

Heavy gates blocked the road on either side of the stations; those who manned them were charged with collecting travel fees and arresting bandits. The stations also provided frequent changes of horse for messengers. Not that all messages went by horse-messenger; from her own experience Xena knew that Avicus used his own means of reaching the men along the road.

She neared the first station just as the sun cast ruddy light through the trees and slowed Argo to a walk. Trees and brush had been cleared along both sides of the road for maybe a tall man's length, but no further. *Better see what's up there,* she decided, drew the mare to a halt, slid from the saddle, and led her off the road.

The woods south of the road looked open, but after ten paces, she couldn't see the road at all. She went on until she could just make out a curl of smoke.

The warrior stroked Argo's muzzle for some moments, murmuring to her, then turned north and worked her way between saplings, to get as near the gates as possible. The mare moved a few paces away, pushing fallen leaves aside so she could crop pale green grass.

Xena moved quietly and quickly until she could just make out two men in full armor pacing up and down the road, then bent nearly double, and ran for an overhanging bush. Still only two men in the open, though she could see horses, saddled and ready to go. *Two I can see, it looks like seven—no, eight horses.* They could be riders who'd just come in, men on their way out— part of the regular company who kept this gate, or extras.

The two men on guard didn't look that awake; there would probably be a few sleepers, but in which of the buildings?

And she couldn't begin to guess if Gabrielle or Joxer

was here. "Great," she mumbled under her breath. "You gotta find out if Gabrielle came through here, or if she's here, if Joxer's here. You won't learn that by putting Argo over the gates or busting through them. And you do that or you pick a fight, they know *you're* here, and then the palace finds out—" She pantomimed a snap of the fingers. "That fast. Just like last time." A corner of her mouth quirked in annoyance. "I gotta be out of my mind, coming back to Sparta."

Best thing, she finally decided, would be to grab someone and get some answers—quietly.

The two guards had stopped pacing and were up by the north gate, staring toward the city and talking quietly. She'd never get a better chance. Xena glanced over her shoulder, south down the road, and sprinted across open ground to hug the outer wall of the nearest building.

The wall vibrated against her ear; someone in there had an incredibly loud snore. She glanced in the open doorway and decided against it; there were at least ten men in the little room. The cots were practically on top of each other, and two additional men slept on the floor in what might have been meant as a skinny aisle. She slipped around the building and crossed to the next one—a small shrine filled the tiny interior.

No priest, she told herself. Any priest around here might have a link to Avicus. Better to leave him out of it. The third building was longer and lower and turned out to be the mess: One long table ran down the back wall, and at the opposite end was an open-air kitchen, a gray-haired man in grubby looking pants chopping up vegetables to toss into a pot. Xena bit back a grin and came up behind him, then tapped him on the shoulder.

He came around with a gasp, knife forgotten in one hand, half a potato in the other; she slapped both aside and slammed two fingers into his throat, then eased around where she could make sure no one sneaked up on *her*. "I've just cut off the flow of blood to your brain," she murmured against his ear.

"Awwww, not again," he moaned. "It's you, ain't it? With the leather and the legs, you—just like last time, except they let me carry a spear back then, before you . . ."

"Will you *shut up*?" she hissed. "You wanna die? I'm looking for a warrior, funny-looking armor, and a girl, golden hair, fighting staff—?" He nodded, gurgled, and gestured frantically. She reversed the pinch, waited until he caught his breath. "You saw them?" she asked finally. He nodded again. "When?"

"Gimme a minute, okay?" he whined. "You can't just *do* things like this to people, you know what you cost me last time, that priest found out I spilled my guts to you? I was second in command here, and look at me now, cutting worms out of turnips and chopping—"

"Yeah, well, life's hard all over," she cut in sharply. "When were they here?" He eyed her sourly; she raised two fingers and he gulped, eased away from her a pace.

"Okay, that warrior-guy came through. It was still dark out, and they usually don't pass anyone until after sun's up, but he had the password and the priest already had word from the city to let him go through, whenever he came—"

"You sure about that?"

"Not 'cause anyone would tell *me*, oh, no!" he mumbled. "But I heard—"

"Never *mind*. He the only one?"

"Huh? Naw." He picked up the half-cut potato, tossed it aside in disgust. Xena leaned over and picked up the knife he'd dropped and began casually tossing it from hand to hand. He tried to smile; the effect was ghastly. "That girl—nice hair, real pretty, big fighting stick? She showed up a little later; priest said he had orders to hold her but the cap'n said no, who was king in Sparta after all—so she went on, too." He eyed the warrior resentfully. "I was out getting wood when she came through; no one ever thinks to get any for me, oh, no! I not only gotta feed 'em, I gotta—" She bared her teeth and he shut his mouth.

"And that's it?" she asked.

"Well, unless you count the other one," he said. "Big guy, real dark, riding one of our horses, went up to the city yesterday to get reshod and was supposed to come back today, but not like that! He jumped the gates and kept going—"

"When?"

"Eh . . . just a bit ago. Excitement just died down, and here *you* come," he added resentfully. Xena clomped him on the back.

"You never saw me," she said. His lips twisted. "You wanna explain to your captain how I was here and you never even raised the alarm?" He considered this very briefly, shook his head. "Good. And you aren't gonna raise the alarm, are you?" He met her eyes, looked away, and shook his head again. "Good," she murmured. "I think your luck's improving; you're gonna survive this." She handed him a rubbery potato and the knife and left.

She bypassed most of the other guard stations, leading Argo through uncleared forest on one or the other of the gates, once taking her along a high stone ledge above the road and back down below a twist in the road. Once, she found prints—Joxer's—crossing a low, muddy spot and overlaying this, a deep mark where Gabrielle'd slammed her staff into the soft ground. They'd made it this far, anyway, she knew, remounted and kept going.

It was late afternoon before she came down out of the high country. Before her lay a stretch of grasslands split by the road and in the distance, the sea. Well off to her right, she could see the masts of ships anchored in Phalamys's sheltered cove. There would be several merchant ships, and no doubt Joxer would be looking for passage on one of them.

"I hope he is," she muttered, and patted Argo's warm neck. But nothing else made sense: If Joxer had wanted to make for one of the other great cities, like Pylos or Thrace, he wouldn't have taken this route. Besides, something she'd overheard led her to believe that Avicus was directing the search overseas. Of course, by now, Menelaus and his priest must have made sure that Helen was nowhere on the mainland. "Now, if I had any idea about what the tides are . . ." Ships had to choose their hours carefully; Phalamys's cove was deep and large enough to hold a dozen merchanters and protected from storms by reefs and a jutting cliff. But the single entry to the cove was shallow and couldn't be run during low tides.

She glanced over her shoulder at the fast-sinking sun. Few merchant ships would be leaving a port this time of day anyway; the Spartan coastline was dangerous and most ship captains liked to have a man in the crow's nest, another on the bow, watching for rocks and reefs. You couldn't do that in the dark.

She urged Argo forward. She could reach the pier by sundown, if they hurried.

Movement to the north suddenly caught her eye: A long, sleek black sea raider's vessel had been drawn up on the sand, not that far away. And riding straight for it, unmistakable even at the distance, was Draco.

Epilog

Gabrielle leaned on her staff, one hand kneading her back muscles, and gazed up and down the long, curved pier. Her feet ached from the long walk—and on occasion, run; she was hot and tired and hungry, and despite catching sight of him often enough to be sure she was still going the right direction, she had yet to get close enough to Joxer for him to hear if she yelled. "I shoulda waited for Xena, I knew I shoulda waited . . ." Every time she'd considered stopping and waiting, though, she'd caught a glimpse of Joxer—a cocksure Joxer striding confidently down the road or through the king's various gates—and her fingers had curled around the staff hard enough to leave dents in the wood. The way her fingers ached, there should have been dents, she thought, and stretched her hands cautiously.

The air was still and muggy and reeked of long-dead fish. Boats rocked slightly; she swallowed hard and edged nearer the water to see if she could find Joxer. *At least boats don't sail at an hour like this,* she reminded herself. The idiot might find himself a boat, but he'd be stuck here for the time being, no one with half a brain sailed this close to nightfall. So she'd have time to grab him and hold him until Xena could get here, even if she didn't locate him just now.

She was ready to give up, go find a bakery, maybe find an inn—*some place where I could wash my hair would be good.* She wrinkled her nose and shoved the sticky mass away from her neck. The afternoon wind suddenly died away and beyond all doubt, she heard a familiar clatter, and a faint, whiny, "Owwww!" Not the nearest ship, she thought—it was rocking at the end of its thick rope and looked deserted, but the ramp was down from the tubby-shaped boat beyond it, and men on the pier were hauling on ropes, while others on deck dragged the bulging net into position over the hold. Gabrielle smiled grimly.

"Got ya now, Joxer," she said quietly.

There were at least a dozen men—mostly sailors, though one looked like a merchant—on the dock, another five or six aboard who were working the big net down into the hold. No one paid the least attention as Gabrielle walked up the ramp and onto the deck and stood near the rail, looking around.

The sun was low and cast long shadows everywhere, but finally she saw movement up near the bow—someone settling down under a mat of woven reeds, spreading out a blanket, and mumbling to himself. She stole along the deck quietly, pausing now and again to listen—but it was Joxer beyond any doubt, alternately grumbling about something in a voice too low for her to make out or singing under his breath. She closed the distance between them as he backed from under the low mat, caught hold of his ear, and dragged him back into shadow.

Joxer yelped; Gabrielle tightened her grip on his ear

and hissed against it, "Shut up! It's me!"

"It's—Gabrielle?" Joxer yanked free of her grasp. "What are you doing here?"

"Following you, remember?" she demanded sweetly.

He sighed. "Look, Gabrielle, I thought we worked this out up in Sparta; it's too dangerous—"

"Yeah, it is," she broke in. "For you, it is. Because if you ever pull a stunt like that again, I will kill you on the spot, you got me?"

He sat staring, absently rubbing his ear. Finally a grin quirked his mouth. "Gee, Gabrielle, I didn't know you cared."

"I didn't—I don't," she began, then jabbed a finger at him. "Do not start with me, you got it?"

The grin vanished. "Got it," he replied meekly.

"Good. Now, listen to me, Joxer. I know you think you know what you're doing, but trust me, you don't. There—is—no—quest."

He sighed in exasperation and turned his back on her. "You know, I can't believe you came all this way to tell me *that* again? I mean, if I didn't believe you way back up in Thessalonika, why would I believe you now? I mean, I've talked to the king and I've talked to his priest, Gabrielle. You know, it's just possible there are some things you don't know."

"Yeah. Maybe," she snapped. "This isn't one of them." Silence. He glanced over his shoulder at her, his eyes resentful, before he turned away again. "Look," she urged finally. "Will you just come with me, listen to Xena? Has she ever lied to you—"

"Maybe," he broke in. "In fact, yeah, I bet she—"

"Joxer, come on, that's not true."

"Look," he said evenly, his back still to her. "All I know is, I have a chance to do something important, be somebody. And ever since I got that chance, you and Xena have been trying to stop me." He glanced her way. "Some friends, huh?"

Gabrielle gritted her teeth. *Hades, why do I even try to argue with him?* "Look," she said finally. "Just— what difference is one day gonna make? Xena should be right behind me, just—just listen to her, why don't you?"

He slewed around to look at her. "Why should I?"

"Because you haven't yet. What's the matter, you afraid you're gonna hear something that makes you drop out of this quest because you learn it's not what you think?"

"No, that is *not* it—!" Joxer began angrily, but Gabrielle scrambled up next to him, her hand clamping his arm. "Owww!" he complained, and pried at her fingers. "D'you mind?"

Gabrielle didn't seem to notice. She was staring past him, at the bit of sky she could see between the rail and the edge of the overhead mat. It didn't look the way it had; dark, wet rocks cut off her view of the sky, and they seemed to be moving up and down, up and down, a little sideways, down, up . . . "Joxer—?" She swallowed. "Tell me we aren't moving. Tell me this stupid boat isn't leaving harbor until morning."

"Huh?" He blinked at her. "No, the captain said they were leaving port as soon as they loaded that big crate of hides, something about the tide and how they can only get in and out a couple hours a day, you know?" He eyed her with sudden alarm. "Ahhh—Gabrielle, are you all right?"

She gulped air and began backing away from him, out from under the sheltering mat. "Oh, yeah. Sure, I'm fine. I'm—just—" She staggered to her feet and stared around her. "—just fine," she managed weakly. To either side of the ship were rocks: a jumble of stone rising far overhead to her right, a low row of dressed stone like a narrow road on the left, and straight ahead, open sea. She clapped a hand over her stomach, turned cautiously. The sun dropped behind the Spartan peaks and torches burned along the pier—a pier now some distance away.

Joxer came from under the shelter to wrap an arm around her; she pulled free of him with an angry oath. "Gee, don't take it out on me," he complained. "It's not like I asked you to come along with me, did I? I seem to recall telling you this morning—gee, was that only this morning that I told you that—"

"Joxer," Gabrielle managed between tightly clenched teeth. "Shut up before I throw up on you!" He glanced at her doubtfully but said nothing else. Gabrielle drew a deep breath, let it out slowly and through her nose, then clamped one earlobe firmly between her thumb and forefinger. "Two things," she said. "Tell me where to find the captain, so he can turn around and put me back on shore."

"He won't—"

"Joxer!"

He pointed. "Over there, by the mast. Big guy, red shirt. What's the second thing?"

"Gods," she groaned. "*Don't* let me eat anything weird!"

The sun still touched the water far to sea as Xena rode back from Phalamys. If she'd bothered to look, she could have made out the mast of the *Euterpe,* which had just put out to sea. Two other vessels were right behind her, and of the ships still in port, three were loading cargo and the last listing heavily, its crew anxiously discussing the best way to get it down to the sand so they could haul it out of water before it sank.

No help for it; by the time she could have persuaded anyone to sail after the *Euterpe,* it would be full dark and the ship out of reach. Which left two possibilities: The fishing boat she'd seen putting in on sand, just outside the city—or that ship Draco had been riding for.

But the fishing boat was gone; she could see a single torch well out past the surf, and in its light, a man casting his nets.

Which left one possibility.

It seemed odd to her, all at once, that a raider's ship would put in so close to a port town—let alone one belonging to Sparta. *Of course, Menelaus could have a couple of pirates in his pay. If only to help him find Helen.* From the looks of things earlier, Draco had certainly known where to find transport off the mainland.

She drew Argo to a walk as they crested a grassy dune and stood in the stirrups to gazed north over the salt flats, then grinned widely. ''Think my luck's maybe changed.'' The ship was still well up on the sand, men swarming about her checking rigging, loading boxes and clay jars. From the size of the pile still on the shore, they'd be a while finishing loading. *They're in the king's pay, all right. How else would there just happen to be a load of supplies waiting for them in a place like this?*

She could see the horse Draco had been riding, but no Draco. He'd be with the captain, no doubt, on the other side of the ship and out of the wind or down in the captain's cabin. The floor'd be at an unwalkable angle, but ships like that always had a pile of pillows and bolsters that could be tossed against whatever wall was down while it was ashore.

She glanced west: The sky was still ruddy but darkening rapidly; out to sea, she could no longer make out the ships that had left harbor at high tide. It would be full dark in short order. She settled back in the saddle and leaned forward to stroke Argo's throat. "I'm sorry, sweetheart, we're gonna have to part company again." The mare whickered softly. "At least you've got some decent grazing here. And this time, I won't be gone long."

It took her a while to find a safe place to leave her gear; Argo nuzzled her for some moments; Xena whispered against the mare's ear and kissed the velvety skin of her nose. Argo rubbed against her shoulder, then sidestepped gracefully, turned, and trotted down the grassy dune. Xena watched her go, then blotted her eyes, turned and settled her pack and her weapons, and began a cautious, silent stalk that would bring her up against the raider ship.

Gabrielle smiled queasily, one hand clinging to her earlobe. The captain—a brute of a man in a sea of grubby shirt that might once have been red—scowled down at her. "Look, I think you don't appreciate the situation here," she began. The man cleared his throat ominously, and she fell silent.

"What I appre—uphu—what I *see* here, is a stowaway!" he bellowed.

She managed a laugh; her stomach swam. "Stowaway? You have got to be kidding! I can't think of a single place I would rather *not* be, than on this ship— or any ship. I don't do ships; they make me sick."

"Oh. Oho!" He was laughing, she realized bleakly. "So now this isn't a ship that you've stowed away on, eh?'' His black gaze moved beyond her and found Joxer, who tittered nervously until Gabrielle drove her foot down savagely on his instep. ''I hope you plan on paying for your wench,'' he said flatly. ''Or neither of you will be leaving the *Euterpe,* and that's a fact!'' Before either of them could say a word, the captain turned and was gone, bellowing orders as he strode down the deck.

Silence, which Joxer, predictably, broke. ''Well, maybe it's not so bad,'' he told her. ''You get to be my sidekick, just like you wanted, right? Listen, you hungry? Because I got a little bread. It's kinda green on one end, but the rest is all right, and this lady down at the end of the wharf had flounder salami. I don't know what it is, but she said it's really flavorful, and—''

''Yeah, I'll bet,'' Gabrielle said wanly as he paused for breath. ''Joxer, you feed me *any* of that, and I will die on the spot, and then I will haunt you for the rest of your life. Got it?''

''Ah—no?''

''Forget it. You even suggest I eat anything you have, and I'll kill you on the spot! Get me back to where your stuff is and let me lie down. And remember what you promised me—do not let me eat *any*thing.''

''Not anything,'' he chorused dutifully, but his usually clumsy hands were unexpectly warm and somehow comforting as he wrapped an arm around her and got her back to where she could go flat. *Sometimes,* Gabrielle thought, *he's almost okay.* Almost. Not that she was going to tell him so.

Full dark; the moon cast a feeble light on trees and crags high to the west, but the sand above the tide line was dark. Despite the stygian conditions, the pirates had only one small torch burning and that close to the few remaining bits of cargo; somewhere aboard ship, another, smaller light flickered—probably a lantern in the captain's cabin or one down in the hold, where Xena could hear two men mumbling curses or laughing as they shifted crates and baskets of supplies. Hard to see the pirates certainly were, but they weren't quiet; she'd easily evaded all of them, clambered over the ship's rail, and settled in shadow along the down rail, near the wheel, where she could watch moonlight edge down the western cliff face.

Before it had moved very far, men began swarming aboard, laughing and joking as the ship began moving down the sand in a series of awkward jerks. It tilted one way and then the other, wallowed as incoming waves struck the hull. Xena edged back out of the way as pirates clung to the rails on either side, waiting for the ship to move into deeper water.

As she'd expected, they'd picked a spot along shore where the sand dropped off rapidly; within moments, the men who'd remained below were frantically shifting ballast while two cat-footed boys ran barefoot into the rigging and began unlashing the mainsail.

By the time the ship had turned, everyone on deck was immersed in whatever task had been assigned to him, the men in the hold were oblivious to anything *but* the hold—and as Xena knew from her own days as a ship's captain, anyone else aboard had something vital to do. Except, possibly, the captain. Perhaps, the captain's guest. And who would notice the shadow that moved along the deck, avoiding those working the sails, the rigging, or clearing the decks and resettling things in the crew cabin that had been thrown to one side when the ship was ashore? She gained the captain's cabin in moments.

But just as she laid a cautious hand on the door handle, it moved under her fingers; she threw herself back and faded into shadow behind a pile of sacking as a huge, pale man with an enormous ruddy beard stalked from the cabin; Draco, who trailed in his wake, looked almost small in comparison. Xena watched them go; a grin creased her face.

Habbish. Who'd've thought the wily northerner would be this far south again? *Last I heard, he was spying on Caesar for the Britains.* Of course, Habbish had a good eye for profit. Could be he was taking coin at the same time from the Romans—and from the Spartans.

If this was Habbish's ship, it simplified things greatly. She stood still a long moment to feel how far out the ship might be. Not as far as she'd feared; they seemed to be wallowing in the outer waves. That definitely simplified things. She stole along behind the two men, caught up to Draco as he emerged from below, wrapped an arm around his throat, and touched the tip of his ear with her dagger. "Draco, funny meeting you here," she murmured. "You still remember how to swim?"

"I—damn you, Xena!" he yelled.

"Not what I asked," she said pointedly. "You still swim?" And, "Stay out of this, Habbish! You and your men, this is between me and Draco!"

"Ya, mons, leave be!" the northerner bellowed, his accent rendering his words nearly unintelligible. " 'Tis Xena, ya no' be messin' wi' her!"

"Xena, don't do this to me," Draco said flatly; one hand clutched at her arm, trying to ease the pressure on his throat while the free one felt for his dagger; she slapped at it with the blade of her dagger, returning it to just under his ear before he could react.

"Me? I'm not doing anything to you," she said. "Just

comandeering your ship for a few minutes. Don't worry, I'll send it back when I'm done.''

"Xena, you can't just—!" He yelped as she hooked the feet from under him and flipped him neatly over the rail; water spouted high as he hit. She held the dagger up where Habbish could see it, glanced over the side.

"Hey," she announced, pleased. "He can still swim. Armor and all." The amusement went out of her voice; the pirates who'd begun to creep toward her fell prudently back. "All right, Habbish, guess what. You're gonna get me out that way," she indicated open water to the southwest, "and we're gonna find a ship called the *Euterpe*."

"Fat little tub of a ship, has nae cargo worth taking," he said flatly.

"I don't care about the cargo, I want *on* it," she replied. "After that, feel free to come back here and pick Draco up. In fact, I suggest you do. He's gonna be mad, but he'll be even madder if you strand him, especially after he gave you enough coin to buy you a whole new set of plaids."

"I would nae leave him," Habbish told her with dignity. "He paid."

"Fine. Whatever," Xena snarled. "*Euterpe*. Go."

It took longer than she would have liked, but finally the sleek raider ship eased up behind the merchanter. Better yet, the merchant ship had been caught off guard—not expecting pirates in their home port, she thought. Just as well; Gabrielle wouldn't appreciate a zigzag chase across the sea. She probably wasn't appreciating much of anything, just now.

By the time someone on the merchanter realized they had company, the two ships were mere feet apart, and

Xena was balanced on the rail, one hand clinging to the ropes, the other cupped around her mouth. "Coming aboard," she yelled.

"Not aboard *my* ship, you're not, woman!" a deep voice bellowed back.

Another, familiar voice broke in, suddenly lifting a load from the warrior's heart. "Ahh—captain? You might want to know, before you get too rude, that's Xena."

"Xena?" Sudden silence. The warrior gestured for Habbish to pull nearer. "Xena, coming aboard my *Euterpe*? Oh, no, she's not, every sailor in this end of the world knows Poseidon hates her!"

"Gabrielle!" Xena yelled. The merchant ship was starting to swing away, she realized. She gritted her teeth and dug her toes in the rail, vaulted up and out, flipping twice before she landed firmly on the other ship's deck. Behind her, she could hear the pirates laughing as Habbish yelled orders for them to stand away, and the merchant captain was howling something in her right ear. She slammed an open palm across his mouth, silencing him. "Don't—start—with—me," she said flatly, her eyes searching the deck.

Joxer—there, halfway to the bow, hanging on to the rail with one hand, his arm wrapped around a swaying figure who eased away from him to stagger toward her. Xena closed the distance between them; Gabrielle wrapped strong arms around her and sighed happily as the warrior drew her close.

Behind her, the captain was still mumbling; without turning, Xena said, "I can pay you for passage—where are we going, anyway?"

"Rhodes, of course. But I won't—"

"You will," Xena said flatly. "Poseidon's not gonna

sink your ship and kill all of you, just to get back at me. Besides, I know your kind, you're not putting back in at Phalamys just to get rid of an unwanted passenger and lose half a day." He turned away, spluttering; she was vaguely aware of Joxer talking to the man, trying to jolly him along.

She tuned that out with ease of practice and rubbed her cheek against pale, soft hair. Odd; there'd been a time, not that long ago, when she'd been happiest—most comfortable, anyway—on her own.

Now it was almost impossible to imagine life without Gabrielle. *Best, dearest and truest friend,* she thought warmly. "Hey," she managed through a suddenly tight throat. "I missed you. You all right?"

Gabrielle leaned against her. "Yeah," she said happily. "I am now."

XENA
WARRIOR PRINCESS™

The top-rated television titans now have their own top-notch magazine

THE OFFICIAL XENA MAGAZINE
FEATURING HERCULES

XENA
WARRIOR PRINCESS
™

Everyone's favourite leather clad Amazon leaps off
the screen and into the pages of Titan Magazine's newest launch:

THE OFFICIAL *XENA* MAGAZINE
FEATURING *HERCULES*.

- Fresh and candid interviews with the stars of the shows, including **Xena's** Gabrielle, Renee O'Connor, in the launch issue.

- We speak to the writers, directors and producers to find out what really happens in the minds of the creators.

- Every issue features exclusive set reports covering the latest episodes to be filmed.

- In-depth features on the mythical and slightly madcap universe of **Xena and Hercules.**

- An exclusive column written by a member of the series' cast and crew.

- Plus page after page of features, reviews, interviews, previews and news covering every corner of the world of **Xena and Hercules!**

68 pages - FULL COLOUR THROUGHOUT
FIRST ISSUE ON SALE: SEPTEMBER 1999
COVER PRICE: $5.99 USA / $7.99 CANADA
FREQUENCY: MONTHLY
AVAILABLE IN BOOK & COMIC BOOK STORES

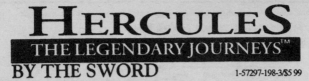

HERCULES
THE LEGENDARY JOURNEYS™

__ BY THE SWORD
1-57297-198-3/$5 99

A novel by Timothy Boggs based on the Universal television series created by Christian Williams

Someone has stolen the magical blade and it is up to Hercules to recover it—though he may be in for more than just a fight with ambitious thieves.

__ SERPENT'S SHADOW
1-57297-214-9/$5 99

A novel by Timothy Boggs based on the Universal television series created by Christian Williams

Hercules and Iolaus heed the desperate plea of a small village. A deadly sea monster has been terrorizing the townsfolk, and only the great strength of Hercules can save them.

__ THE EYE OF THE RAM
1-57297-224-6/$5 99

A novel by Timothy Boggs based on the Universal television series created by Christian Williams

It is called the Theater of Fun. Run by Hercules' friend Salmoneus, the traveling troupe has dancing girls, jugglers, comedians, and a first-rate magician named Dragar. But Hercules is about to discover that there is a fine line between magic...and sorcery.

__ THE FIRST CASUALTY
1-57297-239-4/$5.99

A novel by David L. Seidman based on the Universal television series created by Christian Williams

Someone is posing as Hercules. Someone with superhuman powers of trickery and deception. A certain cloven-hoofed god with a bad attitude...

Penguin Putnam Inc.
P.O. Box 12289, Dept. B
Newark, NJ 07101-5289
Please allow 4-6 weeks for delivery.
Foreign and Canadian delivery 6-8 weeks

Bill my: ☐ Visa ☐ MasterCard ☐ Amex _____ (expires)

Card#_____

Signature_____

Bill to:

Name_____

Address_____ City_____

State/ZIP_____

Daytime Phone #_____

Ship to:

Name_____ Book Total $_____

Address_____ Applicable Sales Tax $_____

City_____ Postage & Handling $_____

State/ZIP_____ Total Amount Due $_____

This offer subject to change without notice.